"No regrets?" Jamal whispered.

Reba's lips curved, and the pressure of her hand increased over his heart. "I'm still floating. You're a wizard, a dream maker, Jamal. I didn't know making love could be so beautiful. How could I regret it?"

Jamal tenderly traced her lips with his fingertips. Her answer should have pleased him. A few short hours ago it had been all he wanted to hear. Now he realized he wanted more. His arm closed around her tightly, his hand buried in the wild tangle of her damp hair.

As he looked out into the night with Reba's body curled against him, he wanted to dream like any other man. Of a future with Reba. Of Reba sharing his life. Of Reba having his children. Of their growing old together.

Dreams as fragile as the moonbeams that were dancing over them.

Dear Reader,

Happy New Year and welcome to another exciting month of romance from Silhouette Intimate Moments. We've got another irresistible lineup of books for you, as well as a future treat that I'll be mentioning in a moment. First, though, how about a new book from one of your favorite authors, Nora Roberts? *Night Shift* will enthrall you—and leave you eager to read *Night Shadow*, coming in March. Readers of historical romance may recognize the name Catherine Palmer. Whether you know her name or not, you will undoubtedly enjoy her debut for Silhouette Intimate Moments, *Land of Enchantment*. Round out the month with new books from Sibylle Garrett and Joyce McGill, two more of the authors who make this line so special.

Now for that future treat I mentioned. Next month we're presenting "February Frolics," an entire month made up of nothing but first novels written by authors whose futures look very bright indeed. Here at Silhouette Intimate Moments we're always trying to find fresh new voices in the romance field, and we think we've come up with four of the best. Next month you'll get a chance to see whether you agree with us—and I hope you do!

In coming months, look for new books from more of your favorites: Dallas Schulze, Heather Graham Pozzessere and Marilyn Pappano, to name just a few. And every month, enjoy some of the best books in romance today: Silhouette Intimate Moments.

Leslie J. Wainger
Senior Editor and Editorial Coordinator

SIBYLLE GARRETT

The Twilight Prince

SILHOUETTE·INTIMATE·MOMENTS®

Published by Silhouette Books New York

America's Publisher of Contemporary Romance

SILHOUETTE BOOKS
300 East 42nd St., New York, N.Y. 10017

THE TWILIGHT PRINCE

ISBN: 0-373-07366-6

First Silhouette Books printing January 1991

Printed in the U.S.A.

Books by Sibylle Garrett

Silhouette Intimate Moments

September Rainbow #184
Surrender to a Stranger #211
Rebel's Return #271
Sullivan's Challenge #301
The Twilight Prince #366

SIBYLLE GARRETT

is a world traveler who finally settled down on Long Island with her husband of twenty-two years and their two children. Her love of books, vivid imagination and desire to share her many personal adventures eventually propelled her toward a career in writing. Writing romances satisfies the dreamer as well as the realist in her.

To Bobby,
for all the Christmas Eves
spent together and
the great times in between

Chapter 1

The building was only a shell, and so were her dreams.

Reba Davis stood in the middle of the foundation slab, her head thrown back and her eyes narrowed against the sun's glare. With the late-afternoon sun burning on her head, she turned slowly within the space. The walls of concrete block rose only five feet tall, and the mortar between them was still dark and damp. Big gaps showed where the windows would be. But that was how dreams started, with a solid foundation, strong mortar and durable bricks. The dreams that became reality. The dreams that lasted.

Reba had wanted hers to last and grow.

She could imagine exactly what her department would be like in six months' time. She could imagine the high ceilings and big windows, the sunshine and space. The walls would be a sandy white, to make the rooms seem big and bright. She planned to divide the space into four areas, each large enough for wheelchairs to move easily around in. She needed an office and a waiting area, a gym and a place for treatment tables and whirlpools.

The building lot was large enough to allow for a small desert landscape, with palms, saguaros, cholla and bishop's hat to shield the office from the parking lot. It was just as she had planned it for years. Yes, she could see beyond the slab and the concrete blocks.

But was she ready to reach for her dream?

Already the floor was littered with planks, pipes and studs. Tomorrow the scaffolding would go up. Judging from the progress during the past few days, the outside walls would be finished within another week. If she wanted everything to her specifications she couldn't delay much longer. The whirlpools required special plumbing and wiring. She had to make a decision soon, before they started on the inside framing.

Before she lost her courage and before someone else beat her to the lease.

Suppressing her twinge of uneasiness, she turned with an anxious smile to the tall silent man at her side. Her brother was seven inches taller than her own five foot eight. "What do you think?"

Rafe Davis slowly smiled at the excitement lurking in Reba's eyes. "It's perfect for you. Just the right size. The location here in Scottsdale couldn't be better. And with five physicians also moving into this building, you'll have more referrals than you can handle."

"That's what I keep telling myself." Rafe had wanted her to strike out on her own for years. She could see her own vision reflected in his eyes. Like her, he also saw beyond the rough walls. The place had good potential as a physical therapy office. A hesitant grin spread over her face.

"Best of all, your apartment is only five minutes away, so I won't have to worry about you getting home safely at night," Rafe drawled.

Exasperation replaced Reba's anxious look. "Why don't you give me a beeper for Christmas?" she countered dryly, pushing a strand of midnight-black hair behind her ear. Her gaze flew back to the walls. Once she'd jumped horses over higher and wider oxers and ditches every day without hesitation. Once she hadn't had a timid bone in her body. "The engineer said the building would be finished by the end of February."

"Have you talked to the builder yet?"

Reba nodded. "I have an appointment with him on Tuesday." She felt another twinge of uneasiness. She had planned and saved for the office for years. Now that the moment to discuss the contract had arrived, the gamble involved scared her. What if she failed? She was risking her well-paid position at the famous Rana Clinic in Scottsdale and taking on a mountain of debts. Perhaps she should wait a little longer. Until . . .

Her hands clenched, her short nails biting into her palms. Until what? Until her savings had grown a little more? She grimaced. Whatever money she'd manage to save during the next year would then be offset by higher prices. She'd been through that before. Two years ago she had turned down an offer to buy a friend's office because her savings had seemed insufficient. Now she wished she'd taken the leap; today that same office cost at least one third more.

"Have you talked to Ronny yet?" Rafe asked.

Reba shook her head. Ronny was her lawyer, and lawyers were the next stepping-stone, a commitment from which it would be more difficult to draw back. Once she involved Ronny, Reba knew she would go ahead. "I thought I would do it later next week."

"Why don't you give him a call tonight. I'll mention it to him," Rafe suggested smoothly. "We're having a drink before I leave for Sedona."

"Not tonight." Reba refused to be pushed. "I have to take a wheelchair to a patient's house and he lives quite a way out of town. I don't know how long I'll be." She'd promised herself to make a decision after her meeting with the builder on Tuesday. She needed the Labor Day weekend to think it over, to look at her finances once again. Sometimes dreams crumbled and turned into nightmares, no matter how solid the foundation. Her last one had. This time there was no room for failure. She had to be sure.

"Then do it tomorrow," Rafe insisted firmly. "Ronny will tell you what to look out for. I don't trust builders."

"You don't trust *anyone*." Reba gave her brother an exasperated look. It was six years since he'd quit working for Army Intelligence, but the hard core of suspicion still remained. Then her face softened. These days, she could never stay angry with him for long.

Four months ago she had nearly lost him. Rafe had been on his way to Jordan to buy an Arabian mare when his plane was hijacked by terrorists. Even now the memory of those three long days and nights of waiting, hoping and praying for his safety seemed like a nightmare, sending a chill down her back.

Never a big talker, Rafe rarely mentioned those days and nights before the plane had finally landed in Omari. But they had changed him. He'd always loved the wide-open range, but now walls seemed to close in on him. He was restless, and he was pushing himself as never before. And now he was pushing her, too, as if there were no tomorrow. Perhaps he was right.

In a few months she would turn thirty. If she wanted to start her own office she would have to take the plunge now. She had a good reputation as a physical therapist and had more referrals for private patients than she could handle after work at the clinic. "I promise I'll give Ronny a call before I meet with Buckman," she said, casting a last glance around. "Don't mention it to Mother, though. I don't want her to start thinking up color schemes and designing murals for the walls just yet. There'll be more than enough time for that once I've signed the contract."

Their mother was an artist. After their father's death seven years ago, she'd left the ranch southeast of Phoenix, moved to Sedona and opened a small art gallery. Rafe was on his way to see her now. Originally, Reba had planned to follow him Friday evening after work, but there was something else she had to do before she saw the builder and struck out on her own.

Rafe's eyes narrowed. "Getting cold feet?" he asked.

"Rafe!" There was a note of warning in her voice. Then she saw the frustration and the flash of pain in his eyes. She swallowed her words. Rafe blamed himself for the accident that had ended her show jumping career, because he had brought the wild mustang to the ranch to break him to the saddle.

But he hadn't been anywhere near the stables the Saturday afternoon Reba dragged a stallion out of a thunderstorm into a stall to keep him from breaking free. A sudden gust of wind had slammed the stable gate shut, locking her in with a horse terrified of enclosed spaces. Even now, five years later, Reba remembered little of what had happened next....

She wound her arm through his. "I always tell my patients that the first step is the most difficult one. I've made the first move. Let me catch my breath and get my balance before I take the next. I don't want to fall flat on my face."

His squeeze was strong, reassuring, firm. "I'd be there to catch you."

"I know." With a grateful smile she released his arm, carefully stepped over a pile of rubble and skirted a stack of studs and pipes. "But you can't fight my battles for me any more than I can take the first steps for my patients. This I have to do alone."

As Reba drove into the hills, the sun lingered over the bare mountains surrounding Phoenix, painting their jagged crests a fiery red. Blue and purple shadows rose from the sprawling valley where the saguaro cacti raised their arms as if clinging to the fading light. In the distance, Camelback

Mountain had become a dark hump, and the Praying Monk merged with the night.

Reba turned off the air-conditioning of her red Jeep Cherokee and lowered the windows. She tilted her head into the rapidly cooling evening air to dispel the lingering scent of antiseptic clinging to her clothes. Hot, dry wind tugged at her blue-black hair and she removed the clasp to release the heavy shoulder-length coil. With the strands whipping around her head, she watched the sun sink deeper. Up ahead, a Harris hawk left the high perch of a cactus and spread its chocolate-brown wings. After working in a windowless basement all day, Reba felt like a caged bird suddenly set free.

From a practical point of view it made sense that the rehabilitation department with its heavy whirlpools had been placed in the basement of the Rana Clinic. There was never any worry about water damage caused by broken pipes or leaking tanks. And, even during the summer heat, when the climate control frequently switched to overload, the temperature rarely rose above seventy degrees. While her patients didn't seem to miss the sunshine and the bright blue sky, Reba did. Often the windowless place felt like a prison from which she needed to escape.

Noticing the speedometer hit sixty, she eased her foot off the gas pedal. She didn't need a speeding ticket on top of all her other expenses. She took a deep breath. She would take the plunge, but first she'd have to rid herself of her old fears.

The mere thought of mounting a horse—if one could call Ol' Ann that—for the first time in five years, made her break out in a cold sweat. Since the accident, she seemed to have become afraid even of her own shadow. It had to stop. Only, she couldn't ride with Rafe watching; she had to do this all on her own.

If she failed... She winced, deliberately imagining the slow smile on her brother's face when she greeted him this Saturday night, riding Ol' Ann.

She had three days to lay old ghosts to rest. She doubted that she would ever compete in any show-jumping events again, but that wasn't her goal. She was tired of being afraid to leave solid ground or take a step that was no more risky than jumping a three-foot wall, tired of freezing up every time a horse tossed its head.

At this time of day the narrow road that snaked through the mountains was deserted. Dusk softened the scars that drought, heat and wind had carved deep into the rocks. The hills in the distance seemed untouched and empty. In the twilight, boundaries faded and the lengthening shadows whispered with dreams. She could almost see herself riding, following the hawk's flight, unfettered. Free.

Suddenly, a white stallion crested a nearby hill. At the top the horse paused, tossing his magnificent head. His thick silvery mane rippled over the hands of his rider and his long tail flowed like finely spun silk. For breathless seconds both horse and rider were caught in the last rays of the setting sun. A moment later they plunged down a steep path weaving its way through yucca plants and ocotillo bushes, fading into the twilight only to emerge moments later from the shadows.

The beauty of the sight made Reba catch her breath. She pulled over, her fingers clenched around the steering wheel as if itching to hold the reins. Pebbles sprayed and dust stirred as horse and rider tore down the twisting path. The man did not use spurs or whip to urge the stallion on. Crouched low over the muscular neck, the rider seemed to control the horse with words alone. Two powerful bodies were moving as one.

Drawn by the magical sight, Reba got out of the car for a less restricted view. As horse and rider drew closer, she could feel the challenge, the abandon and the excitement both man and animal shared. Oh, to be able to ride like that again—with joy and without fear. To feel the freedom and the cooling evening air rush through her hair. Just watching them Reba could taste the power and the exhilaration that were unlike anything else in the world.

Yes, she'd once ridden like that.

Unconsciously, her body began to tense and relax with each jump. She was so entranced by the magical sight that somewhere, deep inside her, the unconscious fear eased its hold on her. She could almost smell the mixture of dust, sweat and horse; could hear the creaking of leather mingling with the rhythmic thunder of the hooves. For the first time in years she felt a yearning, a need beginning to burn. Maybe someday she would be able to feel the wind in her hair instead of the fear in her heart.

Maybe someday she'd be whole again.

The horse, Sultan, she knew by sight. A month ago Rafe had taken her on a tour of the famous Paradise Arabian Stud to see the fabled desert stallion. The rider's identity she could only guess at. But it had to be his owner, Prince Jamal of Omari, the valley's most illustrious resident. No one else would dare race the valuable stallion over rough ground with such confidence. As she watched him fly down a rock ledge with controlled ease, she had to admit he was a superb horseman.

Reba had admired his horses for years. Most of his breeding stock, including this stallion, came from the Nadj. The Nadj was a wild mountain plateau in the central part of the Arabian peninsula where Bedouins raised the Arabian horses whose bloodlines could be traced back directly to the time of Muhammad.

Until the hijacking, the son of the Emir of Omari, which was a small but oil-rich and politically important country on the Persian Gulf, had been just another one of the many celebrities with homes scattered among these hills. Since then, she'd read everything written about him, from the lurid details of his many affairs to his recent Formula One victories at Monte Carlo and the Nurburg Ring.

By birth he was part Arab and part American. His mother was Kitty Barron, one of Hollywood's great stars. Reba sighed. It was a pity that a man with so much potential preferred the life of a playboy, restlessly moving from one pleasure to the next.

What amazed her was that Rafe liked the man. True, her brother owed his freedom, if not his life, to him. Without the prince's decisive action, the hostages might have joined the many still being held somewhere in the Middle East. Rafe wasn't a man to forget a debt. But it wasn't mere gratitude that had forged an instant friendship between the two men. Rafe truly respected him.

Men seemed to judge each other by different standards, Reba thought, observing the prince handle the mettlesome stallion. Rafe had disliked Toby, the man to whom she'd once had been engaged, at first sight. She frowned. In the end her brother had been right in his assessment of him. Toby had been cruel, shallow and weak. She'd been too caught up in competition madness to see it at the time.

The slight breeze blew hair into her face. Reba pushed it back, watching the stallion's stride lengthen on a flat stretch of land. She sensed in the rider a certain recklessness, an arrogant disregard for personal safety, but there was also a steely control. And suddenly the word *decisive* didn't seem so much out of character. Spoiled playboy he might be, but he was certainly no fool.

The moment Jamal reached the top of the hill, he had spotted the bright red Jeep and frowned. "Damned paparazzi," he'd muttered as he saw the car slow down and park on the shoulder. Digging his heels into the stallion's flanks, he tore down the hill, deliberately seeking shadows that would play hell with the focus and exposure controls of even the most expensive cameras.

For a moment he wished he had allowed Hassir to ride with him. His bodyguard had a knack of dealing with nosy reporters. But he'd been in the mood for speed and there wasn't another horse in his stables fast enough to keep pace with Sultan.

Glaring at the red car still parked on the shoulder, he swore. The paparazzi were getting more brazen every day. Only last month he'd caught one of them astride the wall surrounding the villa in Cap d'Antibes with a telephoto lens aimed at his bedroom. He grimaced. God knows what the man had expected to find. Orgies weren't his style.

Perhaps he shouldn't have had the man arrested and instead allowed him a good look behind the trappings of glamour and wealth. Perhaps if the press realized that he often worked an eighteen-hour day they would look for different targets. His mouth twisted wryly. He doubted it.

The branch of a bush scraped against his boot. Swerving, he checked the stallion's stride and turned him determinedly toward the road. Damn it, a man had to be able to relax! Where else could he be himself if not on his own land?

He'd looked forward to a week of freedom from politics and palace intrigues. For nearly a year he'd been tied to the negotiation between the United States and Omari. Now the treaty was signed to the full satisfaction of both sides. The United States had gained a foothold close to the Iranian border and Omari had gained protection from her warring neighbor. Jamal had worked toward peace in the Persian Gulf for years. Now that the fighting had ceased, he should have been content; instead, he was restless and frustrated.

Both his father and his half brother, Muhrad, had been reluctant to give up neutrality and ally themselves with the West. The subject had caused severe friction between Jamal and the two men. Now, for the first time in years, the old desert fox was pleased with him. But Jamal's relationship with Muhrad was at an all-time low.

Not that they had ever been close, he thought grimly, jumping over a dry creek bed. They had too little in common. Different mothers, different faith, different ideologies. Still, they had shared a love for their father, Yussuf, and their country, Omari—or so he'd believed. Then he'd found out that his own brother had financed the hijacking.

Jamal's mouth twisted. His friends, Rafe Davis and Robert Sullivan had been on board that plane. Robert had almost been killed. Two good men were dead. He sighed. The treaty between the United States and Omari had already come dear.

And as yet, his father knew nothing about Muhrad's treasonous activities.

Only a handful of people did. They all wanted to avoid a direct confrontation between Yussuf and Muhrad, but no one more than Jamal himself. He was tired of lies and intrigues. A horse, he thought, leaning forward to stroke Sultan's damp arched neck, was definitely a man's best friend. Horses were true, loyal and without deceit.

As he drew closer to the electric fence, Jamal slowly pulled in the reins. Sultan tossed his head and snorted, objecting to the restraint. "This won't take long," Jamal promised soothingly. "I may not have Hassir's knack, but I'm no novice, either."

The slender young woman leaning against the Jeep was about five foot eight. Her hands were empty and he saw no camera hanging around her neck. He relaxed slightly. Thick, black hair framed her face and fell over her shoulders. The light blue pants she wore clung to incredibly long legs and nicely shaped hips. At this distance it was difficult to determine her age. But from the way she kept staring at him, he suspected that she was impressionably young and certainly without finesse.

He preferred older women, subtlety and a hint of mystery to the blatantly obvious. Unlike his brother, he wanted more in a partner than a sleek body and a pretty face. And always he was the hunter. Still, she was worth a closer look.

Her steady stare caused a mixture of uneasiness and curiosity to ripple down his back. Lightly, he urged Sultan forward, his eyes probing the dark glass of the Jeep and the lengthening shadows to his right and left.

When horse and rider changed direction, Reba shifted uncomfortably from one leg to the other. She hadn't expected him to make straight toward the fence. Why hadn't she left while she'd still had the chance? Now it was too late to drive off without making a fool of herself.

About fifty feet away from the fence Jamal stopped between a large prickly pear and a saguaro cactus behind which he could dive at the first sign of danger, but she still didn't move. "Do you need help?" His clipped voice cut through the soft silence like a whip.

Though he'd voiced an offer of help, it was also an order to leave if she didn't require help. Stung, Reba angled her chin. The county road was public property! If he'd wanted to remain unobserved, he should have ridden somewhere else. "No, thank you."

With the light in his face, Reba could see him quite clearly. He was tall and broad shouldered, his lean body shifting easily with each movement of the restless stallion. His thick, sun-streaked hair was ruffled from his wild ride and strands of it clung to his forehead, giving him a rakish air. His bronzed features were clean-cut and lean. She had expected signs of softness, self-indulgence and dissipation. Instead, she saw strength and a totally masculine beauty that made her catch her breath.

Straight dark brows, high sculpted cheekbones, a slim aristocratic nose and a stubborn square chin. This man was no pushover, no pampered weakling, she thought. He was arrogant, though. With his tawny head and white shirt silhouetted against the reddish sky, he sat his horse as if he owned the world instead of only one very small piece of it.

His shirt stuck in dark patches to his damp, bronzed skin, drawing her eyes to the well-developed muscles beneath. Despite her professional familiarity with splendid bodies, Reba's throat felt suddenly tight. "I was admiring your horse. He's one of the most beautiful creatures I've ever seen.''

Her approach was hardly original, Jamal thought cynically. Yet, despite her artless response, he felt a stirring of interest. Her voice was soft and her tone a little dry, as if she were taunting him. Perhaps she was older than she seemed. It was difficult to tell without clearly seeing her face. ''I know,'' he called back mockingly.

''Conceited jerk,'' Reba muttered under her breath, but unable to suppress a slight grin. She'd set herself up for that one, she admitted.

The slight evening breeze carried the words to Jamal and his eyes gleamed in response. He couldn't remember the last time someone had dared to call him a jerk. A *conceited* jerk. At least, not to his face. Lightly touching his heels to the stallion's flanks, he rode forward until he was within feet of the fence and could get a better look at her.

What he saw almost took his breath away. Her face was a classic oval, ageless, enduring, proud. The bones were delicately molded and perfectly shaped with a high smooth forehead and a firm, rounded chin. Dark sooty lashes framed her eyes. Her slim nose flared sensuously and her unpainted mouth was full and rich. He'd been pursued by beautiful and exotic women since he hit puberty, but rarely had he felt as if the breath had been knocked out of him.

But it was the absence of the usual come-on signals that intrigued him most. She didn't smile. She didn't laugh or move closer to the fence. Not that she needed to, he decided. She exuded a sensuality that was more potent than anything he'd ever felt. Shifting in the saddle, he watched the breeze lift her hair. There was something elusively familiar about its sheen, her proud carriage and her utter stillness. ''Have we met before?''

It was the perfect opening to introduce herself. Just why she hesitated, Reba couldn't explain. Possibly out of pride. Her looks were an accident of birth, something that was often more of a nuisance than a blessing. But she did have enough feminine vanity to resent being taken for someone else. Perhaps also, she sensed that he was a man who was intrigued by mystery. If he planned to stay in Arizona they would meet again. If he didn't, he might be puzzled long enough to remember her for more than a passing moment. "I would remember you if we had," she said, unable to keep the tartness out of her voice.

"Conceited jerks do have a tendency to stick in our minds," he agreed dryly, neatly tossing the ball back over the fence.

"You weren't supposed to hear that."

Her reaction vexed him. Other women would have squirmed or apologized profusely. He wondered what it would take to pierce her calm. "Wasn't I?" he countered with a slow smile, wishing he could see her eyes. What color were they? The need to find out made him move a little closer. "Would you like to make Sultan's acquaintance?"

"No, thank you," she declined swiftly. She had already made a fool of herself and once was definitely enough for one day. Besides, Ramon was waiting for his wheelchair and it was getting late.

Jamal had expected her to grasp the opportunity and make a play for him. Her sudden retreat deepened his interest. "Sultan doesn't bite," he said. "He is a perfect gentleman."

"I know." Reba accurately mimicked his mocking inflection, slid back into her seat and closed the door. Through the open window she added casually, "Another time, perhaps. I'm already late."

"Surely five minutes won't make a difference," Jamal insisted, refusing to take her retreat seriously, especially not after she'd sought him out and roused his interest. If she wanted to play games he was more than willing to oblige. He could use the distraction. Digging in his heels he rode straight toward the fence, intent on jumping it.

Reba reached for her keys, started the car and shifted into drive. With her foot poised on the gas pedal, she hesitated and looked back, just in time to see horse and rider soar over the fence. What a horse, she thought, licking her suddenly dry lips. For the return of her courage and one mad ride on Sultan's back, she'd barter with the devil.

She eased the car back on the road, and the memory of the rider remained with her for the rest of the night.

Chapter 2

That little witch! Jamal thought half an hour later, striding through the black-and-white-tiled foyer of his home, barely glancing at the giant Bedouin, Hassir, waiting anxiously for him. He couldn't get her out of his mind. She had teased and taunted him and then had left him standing in the middle of the road! He hadn't felt so alive in months. Or so intrigued.

It was almost a pity to unravel the mystery, Jamal thought, turning down the long hallway leading to his private apartments, with Hassir at his heels. If he'd had the time, he would have waited a few days to see if she came back. But he had only one week of freedom before he would have to join his father in Washington, D.C.

Passing his secretary's office, Jamal noticed a light and opened the door. "Still working, Alfred? Don't you ever take an evening off?" he asked with a mixture of irritation and amusement.

Alfred Briggs, a slim man of medium height with wavy brown hair, looked up from the blueprints spread out on his desk. Pushing his thick horn-rimmed glasses up his bony nose, he said calmly, "Occasionally. Your brother called while you were out."

Frowning, Jamal looked at his watch. What did Muhrad want? There was a ten-hour time difference between Arizona and Omari, which would make it almost 6:00 a.m. in Basjad. Since his brother rarely stirred before eight, it had to be urgent. His voice tight with urgency, he said, "Get me Muhrad, Alfred."

Fear shot through him. Lately, his father hadn't been well. The stubborn old fox refused to see a doctor, insisting that there was nothing wrong. At seventy it was normal to feel tired occasionally, he'd scoffed, when Jamal tried to convince him to delay his trip to Washington and check into a hospital for tests instead.

While Alfred pressed a button on the white phone that was reserved for palace business, Jamal quickly wrote down the license plate number of the red Jeep Cherokee before it slipped his mind.

"And your nephew called. He sounded quite anxious," Alfred said, while waiting for someone to answer the ring.

Hussein, Muhrad's fifteen-year-old son, was a never-ending source of delight and amusement. Sitting down at the edge of the desk, Jamal swung one booted foot and raised his brows. "If he called at four in the morning, he must be in trouble again." His nephew was at a boarding school in Montreux, Switzerland. "What is it this time? No, let me guess. He sneaked out of the school again to meet the baker's daughter and got caught."

Smiling, Alfred shook his head. "That was last week. Now he wants to buy a Maserati, but he's low on funds." Briefly, he spoke to the person at the other end of the line, then hung up. "Prince Muhrad is at his prayers, but they should be over soon. He's going to call back."

Startled, Jamal looked up. Muhrad praying? Now that was a change! His brother rarely prayed in the privacy of his apartments, although he visited the mosque regularly, especially since the hijacking.

Jamal wished it were his brother's guilty conscience driving him to prayer, but he knew better than that. Muhrad was one of the least impulsive men he knew. Since the signing of the treaty, Muhrad had lost support among those merchants who had traded with the Eastern bloc and he couldn't afford to offend the Imams also. Power was important to him.

His eyes fell on the blueprints of Basjad's new medical center. "Did you confirm the appointment at the Rana Clinic for tomorrow morning?"

"Yes. At eight." Alfred's brows rose above the dark horn frames. "I swear you've visited enough hospitals during the past three weeks to draw up your own plans."

Jamal shrugged. "Someone has to speed things up. With so many new firms opening up offices in Basjad we need more hospitals yesterday. And I want it done right. I want the best equipment, nurses and physicians."

"Are you going to buy Prince Hussein his Maserati?"

Looking down at Alfred, Jamal cocked one brow. "Do I look like a fool? He's going to wrap that car around a tree within a week. If he calls back while I'm on the phone, tell him I'll give him the money under the condition that he gets a chauffeur for the car. I'll even pay the man's wages."

Alfred's thin, serious face eased into a grin. "I don't think that's what he has in mind. He wants to become a racing driver like his uncle."

Jamal looked down at the blueprints. "That won't last any longer than his puppy love. It's his way of rebelling against restrictions. He knows he's going to rule one day. It's not an easy weight for a fifteen-year-old to carry."

"Is that why you race?" Alfred asked quietly.

Jamal met the shrewd brown eyes with a bland look. After ten years as his private secretary there was little Alfred didn't know about his personal as well as his business affairs. "No, Alfred. I've never wanted my brother's position. I race because I like the challenge and the speed. And the fact that for a few hours no one can ask me stupid questions."

The light on his private line started to blink. Tensing, Jamal rose and walked to his office. "I'll take it in here. And by the way—" Jamal said as he scribbled on a scrap of paper before handing it to Alfred, "—I want to know the name and address of the owner of this car."

Into the silence following his exit Hassir said quietly, "It is written in the stars that the fox will raise a lion cub and the cub will rule one day."

Alfred's mouth tightened. "An old wives' tale." He picked up the slip of paper, studied the license plate number and reached for the phone.

Inside his office, Jamal sat down in the gray leather chair behind his desk. He glanced at the wall of glass overlooking the rolling hills and the valley below where a shimmering sea of lights stretched to the horizon, reluctant to speak with Muhrad.

They always fought, and lately the fights seemed to get more vicious. Sometimes, it was difficult to remember that they were brothers, that the same blood ran in their veins. Their goals were the same—a prosperous, secure future for Omari and Omarians—but it was the methods they had fought over since way back.

Muhrad hated the desert and wanted to discard its traditions, to erase the image of roaming nomads from the minds of the rest of the world—perhaps because he did not want to be reminded of the fact that without the huge oil fields buried beneath the desert floor, he still would be little more than a nomadic sheikh.

Jamal wanted to preserve the Bedouin way of life for Hussein and the generations to follow. Someday soon the oil would be gone and the money spent, but the desert would still be there. Omari's strength did not come from beneath the desert, but from the endless sea of sand itself and the people who roamed it.

The light flashed persistently. With a sigh Jamal propped his boots on the glass top of the desk, picked up the receiver and steeled himself for another unpleasant conversation. "Salaam, Muhrad."

"And Allah be with you, Jamal," Muhrad returned the traditional greeting. Because he was nearly a hundred pounds overweight, his voice always sounded a little breathless. "I heard you were out riding. How's the stallion holding up?"

"Fine." Jamal's eyes sharpened at the seemingly casual question, wondering at its purpose. Sultan had been a present from Muhrad. No, a bribe. His brother had bought the stallion on one of his trips into the desert, a cover for his meetings with the major, the man who had organized the hijacking. Later he'd tried to buy Jamal's silence by giving him the horse. Jamal knew that if he'd refused the gift, Muhrad would have destroyed the animal and the evidence. His brother had as little appreciation for horses as he had for the men who raised them. "How is Father?"

"Always so impatient, so direct. So typically American," Muhrad taunted now. "We'll never make an Arab out of you. Our father is doing fine. At the moment he's once again looking for a suitable wife for you. If my mother is to be believed, some of his choices are quite beautiful."

"Great," Jamal muttered beneath his breath. Yussuf's last attempt to arrange a political marriage for him had ended in an argument that had shaken the palace walls. "You have room for two more wives, Muhrad."

This time there was amusement in his brother's voice. "My brotherly love for you isn't so great that I'd get you off the hook, Jamal." Then the laughter faded and his voice changed, becoming harder and more threatening. "It suits me very well to have Yussuf furious with you again."

Jamal leaned his head back, sighing wearily. Ever since they were boys, Muhrad had seen him as a threat to his position. The right of the firstborn to inherit didn't exist under Muslim and Omarian law. Theoretically Yussuf could choose his heir from among his legitimate sons. But Muhrad had been raised to rule; he was a Muslim. He thought like a Muslim. He belonged.

Jamal shifted in his chair. Perhaps because he'd been conscious of the differences between them, even as a child, he had never wanted his brother's position. But nothing he said or did had ever convinced Muhrad. Jamal's tolerance for his brother's spite suddenly reached a breaking point. "Perhaps you do not understand the ties between my father and myself," he said calmly.

"Is that a threat, Jamal?" When Muhrad's voice softened, he was at his most dangerous. "My mother always warned me that you'd show your true colors eventually. Have you finally decided to fight me for our father's affection?"

Jamal's fingers clenched around the receiver. Azadeh, his father's first wife, had poisoned Muhrad's mind against Jamal since childhood. Controlling his anger, Jamal managed to maintain his calm tone. "I don't have to fight for it. Yussuf is my father, too."

Muhrad hissed softly. "The treaty may have cost me some support among the wealthy, but I'm not without power yet. So, let me warn you, I'll fight you any way I can. What do you think would happen to your treaty, your hospital and your dreams of peace in the Middle East with our own country in turmoil?"

Hot, angry words rose in Jamal's throat, but he swallowed them just in time. Muhrad's threats were irrational—the ramblings of a driven, desperate man. As long as their father was alive, Yussuf's power was absolute.

Jamal's eyes narrowed. Muhrad wasn't given to irrational ramblings, which meant that something had happened to scare the hell out of him. And whatever threatened Muhrad, threatened him as well. Whether they liked it or not, their fates were intertwined. Now, Jamal thought, they were coming to the real reason for this call; he wished that for once in his life Muhrad would be direct. "Muhrad, you should know by now that threats don't work with me. If you want my help, ask for it. You might be surprised how well that works."

Before his brother could respond, Jamal guessed the answer. Muhrad must have received threats from the Holy Islamic Brigade, the terrorist organization that had hijacked the plane. Their leader, the major, was currently sitting behind bars in a federal prison in Washington, D.C., awaiting trial.

Jamal smiled grimly. The major's hopes that Muhrad would find a way to free him must be dwindling every day. Muhrad wouldn't lift his little finger to free the only man who could bring about his own downfall, and by now the major must have recognized that fact.

So now the terrorist was plotting his revenge. And the timing was perfect. In a week, Yussuf was coming to Washington! Jamal swore softly.

"I can hear the wheels clicking." Muhrad's voice had lost its heat. "You're not so stupid after all. For an American, that is."

Jamal's eyes softened at the familiar childhood taunt. "And for an Arab, you're amazingly dense," he repeated his own answer of long ago.

"I've been warned that there will be demonstrations. Or worse. The embassy and consular offices have been alerted. We can deal with those. Lately Yussuf has mentioned a desire to see the inside of an American prison. We'll have to make sure he doesn't visit a very specific one."

"Hell." Jamal sucked in his breath sharply. A direct confrontation between the major and Yussuf had to be avoided at all costs. Finding out about his heir's deceit might be too much for a man with a weak heart. "I'll see what I can do. It's getting late here and I have some calls to make. I'll talk to you later."

"I won't be here. I'm leaving for the Isht' Omari tribe right now. I know I can trust you with our father's health. Allah be with you, Jamal," he said, hanging up.

For a moment, Jamal stared blindly out of the window, the receiver still in his hand. The situation in Omari had to be worse than he'd been told. His brother was definitely feeling the noose of his deceit tightening around his neck. Not deceit. What Muhrad had done was treason.

And the penalty for treason was death.

Jamal doubted that his father would have his heir beheaded in the middle of the market square like the hijackers who had been caught. Exile was more likely.

"Damn!" Jumping to his feet, Jamal strode to the liquor cabinet and poured himself a stiff drink.

Princess Azadeh, beautiful, but ambitious and jealous, had a hell of a lot to answer for. She had destroyed his parents' marriage and had turned his own brother against him.

Tossing back his cognac, Jamal returned to his desk. As he reached for the phone, his hand stopped in midair. The position Muhrad was placing him in was intolerable. How could he ask Howard Barton, the secretary of state, for help—help for a man who had risked the lives of hundreds of Americans and who was responsible for the deaths of two.

But what choice did he have?

He picked up the phone. Compared to his father's life and Omari's peace, his pride was such a little thing. But he damned his brother anyway.

Twenty minutes later Jamal was breathing a little easier. Howard Barton had made no promises, but at least he had agreed to discuss the problem tomorrow. Leaving his office, Jamal paused at Alfred's desk and picked up the note leaning against the phone. "Prince Hussein said that if he wanted a chauffeur, he'd buy a Rolls.'' Jamal grinned and wondered what harebrained idea his nephew would come up with next.

He read on. As always, Alfred had been thorough in checking the license number, providing all the information requested and then some. The woman's name was Rebecca Davis, she was twenty-nine years old, lived in Scottsdale and worked at the Rana Clinic as a physical therapist.

She also happened to be Rafe Davis's sister.

His grin vanished. He'd always been careful not to become involved with the women of business associates and friends. Then he shrugged. He wasn't looking for an affair. This was hardly the time to become involved and distracted. But a mild flirtation, why not?

She was going to do it. Tonight she was going to saddle Ol' Ann. Reba entered the clinic lobby the following morning with butterflies in her stomach, but her mind firmly set. She was early. Rehab didn't open until eight, but she'd been too restless to sit on her small patio with a newspaper and a cup of coffee. She felt like a mountain climber suspended halfway between solid ground and the peak; she had come too far to scurry back to safety, but the climb ahead scared her to death.

Crossing the foyer, Reba felt suppressed excitement echoing from the brightly painted walls. Slowing down, she watched maintenance men cleaning the mauve-and-green-patterned carpet, polishing wood and glass. Security guards had been posted everywhere. Reba grimaced. All this busyness could only mean one thing: they were expecting another group of visitors.

The clinic was run by a private foundation and depended on grants and donations from government, industry and private patrons. Judging from the upgrade in security, today's guests included either politicians, foreign dignitaries or a movie star.

The tours were a necessity, but they played havoc with her schedule. It was just as well she'd come in early, she thought, her white shoes making little sound as she ran lightly down the stairs.

To her surprise, the department was already unlocked and the smell of fresh coffee greeted her. "Now that's what I call service," Reba muttered, following the scent to the small, crowded office she shared with her five therapists.

A slim, blond-haired woman in her mid-twenties was slumped over the big yellow desk dominating the room. Reba stopped, her mouth all but dropping open. "Katie, what are you doing here so early?" Her senior therapist usually rushed in at five after eight.

Katie ran her fingers through her short curls and struggled to suppress a yawn. "My car's in the shop. I had to hitch a ride with Mary from Pediatrics at the ungodly hour of six-thirty," she grumbled.

Chuckling, Reba circled the desk to get to the small table squeezed between two filing cabinets. She reached for Katie's mug. "What you need is a strong dose of caffeine," she said, pouring coffee. "How many new patients did we get?"

"Three. A burn, a hip fracture and an emphysema patient." Katie reached for the mug Reba offered before adding two of the new patients' names to the schedule on the wall. "This is going to be one hell of a day," she muttered. "Do you have time to treat the burn patient?"

After a glance at the treatment request, Reba studied her crowded schedule. Because of her administrative duties, she didn't carry a full patient load anymore. "Let me have a look at the patient before we bring her down. If we're lucky one of the outpatients will cancel."

I'll be here until seven, she thought. By then it would be too late to make the hour-long trip to the ranch and saddle Ol' Ann.

Reba felt a mixture of frustration and relief. It had taken her years to get to this point. Watching the magical ride last night had stirred within her a hunger that had lingered through till morning. But her fears were still deeply rooted. "I have a department head meeting at three. On top of it we're having visitors. Do you know who they are?"

"I put the memo on Louise's desk." Katie pushed back the chair and went into the secretary's office. "Reba, listen to this." All sleepiness was gone from her face when she returned with the pink memo clutched in her hand and announced dramatically, "Our visitor today is His Highness, Prince Jamal of Omari."

Reba caught her breath and her heart skipped a beat. Too soon, she thought, leaning against the desk. She hadn't had time yet to recover from their first meeting. Even now she could hear his deep voice, his laughter, and feel the magic.

She exhaled softly, thinking herself an idiot. She didn't even like the man. He'd probably dismissed her from his mind the moment she drove off leaving him standing in the middle of the road. Why couldn't she do the same? "When are they expected down here?"

"At noon. No lunch for you today." Katie's gray eyes narrowed. "Aren't you excited?"

Reba shrugged casually. "He's just a man." If she kept repeating those words often enough, she might even come to believe them herself. "If he stays here over Labor Day, Rafe will probably invite him to the barbecue. I'll meet him then."

"Just my luck. Why did I promise to visit my parents? Just think, I'll miss my one chance to dance with a prince." Katie sighed. "What is he like, Reba? Does your brother ever talk about him?"

"Rafe?" Reba smiled wryly, shaking her head. "Does he ever talk about anything but horses, cattle or feed?"

By midmorning the prince's visit had become the main topic of conversation in the department. Outpatients lingered long after their treatment was finished, hoping to get a glimpse of him. Even the five-year-old twins, Pete and Johnny, could talk about nothing else.

"He signed my cast." Pete pointed a stubby finger at the bold signature on the plaster of his right leg.

"He signed my book," Johnny, who was visiting his twin, told Reba. "And that's much better. Isn't it?"

"I think it was very nice of the prince to sign both the cast and the book," Reba said diplomatically. Prince Jamal's kindness surprised her. She had him pegged as another Toby—arrogant and spoiled. Children had irritated her former fiancé. At the time she'd blamed his impatience on his lack of experience. "Are you ready to walk, Pete?"

A grin brightened his pale thin face. Reaching for his crutches, he said tentatively, "Dr. Levine says I can go home if I can walk by myself."

"Only if you promise not to take a dip in the pool," Reba teased, attempting to divert the boy from his hesitancy. He'd been sheltered here for almost a month while his body healed from a car accident and he was a little scared to face the outside world again.

He giggled at the absurd notion. "I promise," he said, awkwardly getting to his feet. For a moment he stood there, testing his balance, holding the injured leg off the floor. Then he was off, hobbling down the hall, weaving his way past wheelchairs and stretchers.

"Slow down." Reba, holding her breath, walked close enough behind to grab him if he lost his balance. He was far from steady yet. Still, he managed to walk all the way to the gym and back to the wheelchair without stumbling once.

Sitting down, Pete laughed shakily, throwing his thin arms around Reba's neck. "I did it."

"You sure did," she said, hugging him and gently brushing the hair from his damp forehead. "That was great."

Suddenly Johnny cried, "There's the prince!" Before Reba could stop him he charged past the reception desk out into the hall. "Prince, did you see Peter walk all by himself? He's coming home tonight!"

Startled, Reba disengaged herself from Pete's arms and turned around. He was standing just outside the door with Tim Horner, the clinic administrator, at his side. For one instant their eyes locked over the heads of the twins; his face registered no surprise or recognition. Then he dismissed her with a slight nod and looked down at Johnny. "I did. Pete walked like a real pro. I'll bet you're going to celebrate tonight."

"With fireworks..."

So he'd decided to forget about their earlier meeting. That suited her fine, Reba told herself, turning her attention back to the glowing Pete. "We'll walk again right after lunch," she promised, placing his cast on the leg rest before unlocking the chair. With a gesture she motioned one of her aides, gaping from the doorway, to her side. "Take Peter upstairs," she said, handing him the patient chart. "And don't bring anyone else down until the prince has left."

Smoothing her lab coat, she followed the aide toward the visitors, a polite smile on her face. The prince was taller than she'd imagined, topping the administrator's six-foot frame by several inches. Dressed in a light gray business suit, he looked formidable, less approachable. And aloof.

She'd wondered about the color of his eyes. The press had called them green. Reba realized that they were hazel instead, a muddy brown with gold and green flecks. Cat's eyes, sharp and intense, yet curiously secretive, even when they smiled down at Pete.

"You're early," she said softly to Tim Horner while studying the rest of the group. There were only two more strangers waiting out in the hall. One of them, a giant with close-cropped dark curls and a prizefighter's build, she recognized from Rafe's description as the prince's bodyguard. The slim brown-haired man at his side, with thick horn-rimmed glasses and a clipboard in his hands, had to be some sort of secretary.

"They had an emergency in Pulmonary, so we came straight down here. How crowded are you?"

Reba shrugged. "No more than usual." Then, because this was too good an opportunity to miss, she added, "Now if I could have the two rooms across the hall . . . It would be less crowded in here and you wouldn't have to wait until lunchtime to show visitors around."

Smiling, Tim shook his blond head. "I'll think about it."

Jamal watched Reba as he stepped aside to allow Pete's wheelchair to pass. He had almost convinced himself that her beauty was an illusion, a trick of the twilight. He had been wrong.

Even in the stark, unflattering fluorescent light, he could find no flaws. With her hair pulled back into a French braid, her face was more stunning than he remembered. And the color of her eyes was extraordinary, a bewitching shade of gold. The shapeless lab coat could not hide the sleek elegant lines of her body or the natural, almost primitive sensuality that made him ache just looking at her. He shifted slightly from one leg to the other, wishing the formalities over with.

Unaware of the prince's impatience, Tim Horner turned to him with a polished smile. "Your Highness, may I introduce Rebecca Davis, the director of Physical Therapy."

Last night she'd called him a conceited jerk, teased and taunted him, then left him standing in the middle of the road. Now she tried to look through him as if he were a wall. But this time he wasn't going to let her get away with it, Jamal decided, holding out his hand. "It's a pleasure to see you again, Miss Davis."

She hadn't expected him to continue their little sparring match—not here, with Tim watching and her staff all eyes and ears. If she wasn't careful, she'd be badgered for the rest of the day about why she'd kept her previous meeting with the prince to herself. Her eyes narrowed fractionally as she slid her hand into his and said demurely, "It was a long time ago. I didn't expect you to remember."

Touché. Jamal acknowledged the hit with the faintest of smiles while his hand firmly closed over hers. He wanted to accept the challenge and continue their game. Not here, though, where the advantage was all his, he decided, staring at her long-fingered hand. Her nails were short and she wore no rings. The next round would be played without an audience, on equal ground.

"How's Rafe?" he asked, slowly relaxing his hold. Her palm felt smooth and soft. He had expected her to have a rider's callused hands. Because of her interest in Sultan and the fact that Rafe raised Arabians, Jamal had assumed that she also enjoyed riding.

His eyes were green after all—a wicked, mocking green. Reba almost snatched her hand away and hid it behind her back. Her skin still tingled and the tips of her fingers burned from his touch. "Rafe is fine, Your Highness. He's in Sedona visiting our mother. I know he'll be glad to see you when he returns."

"I was *wondering* where you two could've met." The puzzled look with which Tim had followed the exchange brightened to comprehension. "I forgot that your brother was on that hijacked plane, Reba." Turning to Jamal, he added, "The release of the hostages was quite a masterstroke, Your Highness."

As always when the topic came up, Jamal felt a surge of bitterness and guilt. But he maintained his public smile. "A great many people were involved in the rescue operation," he said, firmly closing the subject.

Perhaps because she was trained to look for signs of distress, Reba noticed the subtle change in the prince's demeanor. The devil's glint vanished abruptly, replaced by the suave, empty smile of the politician. Only the firm set of his jaw told her of the turbulence churning within. "Is there anything particular in this department that holds your interest?'' she asked quietly, deliberately drawing everyone's attention away from him.

He studied her a moment before answering, wondering if she had intervened deliberately, or if she was merely impatient for him to leave. The softness in her eyes touched him oddly and he felt his suspicion ease. ''We're building a new medical complex in Basjad. From what I've learned during the past few weeks, rehabilitation is a vital part of medical care. I'm interested in the basic setup of your department, what equipment you use and how much space is required,'' he explained. ''But first I'd like to introduce the rest of my staff. This—'' he waved forward the slight man with the thick horn-rimmed glasses ''—is my secretary, Alfred Briggs. And the big hulk here is my shadow, Hassir.''

Reba shook hands with both men. It surprised her that Jamal was involved personally in the planning of his complex, when he could easily have hired a team of experts. ''There's never enough space,'' she said, turning to point at the wheelchairs and stretchers. ''This is a three-hundred-and-fifty-bed hospital, and on an average day we treat between forty to sixty inpatients twice a day. I have five physical therapists, three assistants, four aides, part-time occupational and speech therapists, and three secretaries to keep up with the paperwork.''

Jamal stepped into the reception area and assessed the space. From what he could see every square inch seemed occupied. ''Where do you put them all?'' he asked, grimacing.

''We juggle things around.'' Reba shot Tim an amused look. The two rooms across the hall used for storage could easily be converted into offices for the speech and occupational therapists. ''We have a large pulmonary care unit on the third floor. Asthma and emphysema patients from all over the States come here because of our warm dry climate. One therapist is assigned to that unit on a monthly rotation basis. Another therapist is in charge of the coronary and intensive care units and the surgical floor, treating patients who cannot be moved.''

''How much area do you have here? About two thousand square feet?'' When Reba nodded, he asked, ''If you could plan the size of the department how much more footage would you ask for?''

She shot another look at Tim Horner. ''I would double it.''

''If I count in the space you've taken over upstairs, you already have,'' Tim pointed out wryly.

''I'm not complaining,'' Reba denied swiftly. ''The size of a rehab department is determined, though, by the type of patients. Rafe told me once that some hospitals in the Middle East primarily treat tuberculosis patients and eye diseases.''

Jamal nodded thoughtfully. He liked her clear, precise explanations and her quick understanding of some of the problems he faced. Most of all, though, he liked the way she moved; smoothly, unhurriedly, elegantly. ''Unfortunately, at least among the nomads, that's true. Bedouins prefer to die in the desert rather than in a hospital bed. But our cities are growing fast and so is the need for more sophisticated medical care.''

She had done him an injustice, Reba realized. He cared about the people his father ruled. It was in his voice and his eyes. ''What you say is also true of the old Indians on our reservations. My great-grandfather chose to die in the mountains.'' She moved past a curtain to stop in front of a small tank used for arm injuries. ''What about trained personnel?'' she asked. ''It takes more than space alone.''

He sighed. ''Basjad's university is only four years old. Like Saudi Arabia and Kuwait, we'll have to import some nurses, P.T.s and M.D.s until we can educate our own.'' He looked at her quizzically. ''Would you consider spending some time in Omari, say, twelve months from now?''

For a moment, just a moment, she felt a twinge of the old wanderlust. Once she had traveled all over the States and Europe to compete. Now she had different obligations, different goals, she reminded herself. Someday, though, she'd find the time and the money and hop on a plane that would take her from the North to the South Pole and anywhere in between. She smiled and shook her head firmly. "I have everything I want right here."

"I'm serious. Think about it," he said with the supreme confidence of a man used to getting his own way.

The arrogance of the man! Did he ever take no for an answer? she wondered angrily. "I don't have to," she said, a slight edge to her voice. "I have other plans."

"Your Highness didn't warn me that you planned to hire my staff away from me," Tim Horner protested lightly, following them.

"The hospital would have been compensated," Jamal said with an imperial shrug. "But since Miss Davis turned me down flat, you have nothing to worry about."

Looking back at Reba he caught a flash of anger in her eyes before she lowered her thick lashes. So she had a temper, he thought, smiling at the discovery. "How many whirlpools do you have?"

"Five." She had to raise her voice above the sound of the turbines. "As you can see, most of them are being used." She pointed at the curtains shielding the patients, her chin jutting out just a little bit. Damn it, he was making her nervous. And that smile! She couldn't remember the last time she had felt like floating just because someone had smiled at her. "Unfortunately, you'll find the rest of the department equally as crowded. This is one of our busiest times."

She desperately needed a breather and stepped sideways to slide past him back into the hall. "If you'd like to follow me, Your Highness, I'll show you around the rest of the place."

He moved at the same time. His hand shot out, stopping her. He felt a heated current running up his arm. She, too, must have felt the spark, because her eyes widened a little before they narrowed to slits. Jamal ignored the golden arrows she was shooting at him. "It is rather crowded," he agreed smoothly. "I have an appointment in an hour, otherwise I'd wait until lunch." Jamal turned back to Tim Horner. "Would you mind if I took another look around, say after five?"

"Not at all. I think that's an excellent suggestion." Tim looked at Reba questioningly. "If you have no objections?"

She did, Reba thought, but none she could voice. With an inward sigh she ditched her own plans and agreed smoothly, "Yes, that sounds fine."

Chapter 3

When Jamal walked back into the department shortly after five, silence greeted him. Motioning Hassir to stay behind, he crossed the reception area and turned down the deserted hall. In the secretaries' office the computers and lights had been turned off and the desks were clean. In the whirlpool room the curtains were pulled back, revealing gleaming stainless steel tanks and shiny tiles. The treatment tables were covered by clean sheets, and fresh laundry had been stacked on the shelves beneath.

He raked his fingers through his hair. Would the new hospital in Basjad ever run with such smooth efficiency? He could hire the best architects and engineers, buy the most modern equipment available and import a good staff. But all the money in the world could not bridge overnight the gap between centuries-old traditions and modern sterile techniques. If he wanted to preserve the Bedouin way of life, change would have to come gradually, an inch at a time.

Patience, he knew, had never been one of his strong points. There were times when he wished his father was an ordinary man, that he himself could've been born with a clean slate and allowed to choose his own direction and control his own fate. He wondered what road he would have taken. He shrugged. His life had been decided for him, and Jamal rarely wasted time thinking of what might have been.

His thoughts flew back to his discussion with Howard Barton and his frustration was eased. The secretary of state had agreed to have the major moved to another prison a few hours from D.C., albeit reluctantly. The move, they both had agreed, would probably result in protests or some other form of retaliation from the HIB, the Holy Islamic Brigade, either in the States or abroad, endangering more lives. Jamal clenched his hands. There were times when he wanted to strangle his brother.

He continued down the hall in search of Reba.

Her office was empty. For a moment, he wondered if she'd made a fool of him again, then shook his head; she was too much of a professional to allow personal feelings to interfere. Glancing at the crowded shelves, tall filing cabinets and huge desk, he wondered how she could work in this hole, day in, day out. He would go mad down here and so would Rafe. Was she so different from her brother? He thought of their meeting last night, out in the open hills. He could much more easily picture her racing through the brush, low to the ground, her beautiful hair tangling in the wind.

At that moment he heard the clink of metal, then a small thud followed by a heartfelt "Damn." Grinning, he followed the sounds down the hall. At the opening to the gym he found her sitting cross-legged on the floor, glaring at the stationary bicycle pedal she held in her hand. Scattered around her were wrenches, screws and washers. As he watched she fitted the pedal on the crank arm, added a nut and began to tighten it with a wrench.

He could have told her that it wouldn't work, that she'd forgotten to place a washer on either side. But for the moment he was content to simply watch her. Her hair curled damply around her face and the braid moved against her long slender neck like a lover's caress. She'd refreshed her makeup, but the tip of her tongue slid over her lips in concentration, licking the color off.

He tried to imagine what her lips would feel like beneath his. Would they be soft, a little moist and cool like the air after a desert rain, or hot, spicy and firm? Both, he decided, depending on her mood. And before this evening was over he intended to taste them both. He shifted impatiently.

His movement drew her attention. Startled, Reba raised her head and stared at him. How long had he been standing there, watching her?

He had changed into tan trousers and a fresh white shirt with the sleeves rolled halfway up his muscular arms. Informally dressed, he looked more powerful and larger than life. She blinked and caught her breath. "I didn't hear you come in." She wanted to jump up and wipe her hands clean. Instead she forced herself to move slowly to her knees and collect the tools before she faced him. "I didn't expect you so soon."

Leaning against the wall, he folded his arms across his broad chest. She looked a little flustered at his sudden appearance and a little annoyed. A slow smile curved his lips. "You did say shortly after five, didn't you?"

"Yes," Reba agreed dryly, placing the tools on a nearby chair. She hadn't expected him to be punctual, though.

His smile vanished. Annoyed, he slid his hands into his pockets and waited until she faced him again. Then he asked coolly, "I wonder what made you think that I'd keep you waiting?"

Experience, she wanted to say, but stopped herself. Thinking of him as another Toby made it easier to deny the attraction she felt for him. But the truth was that the only feature the two men had in common was the color of their hair. "You did mention that you had an appointment, Your Highness."

And all afternoon, she'd wondered with whom.

A few months ago the talk around town had been that he was having an affair with the sex symbol Leonie Walters, who owned the estate next to his. "Well, business lunches sometimes stretch into the night."

"Yes, they do." He didn't miss the faint emphasis on the word *business*. It didn't take a mind reader to guess what she was thinking. Usually it amused him that the image the press presented of him was so readily believed; now it irritated him. Somehow he'd thought her more perceptive. "If I'd been delayed I would have given you the courtesy and called. I realize that I made you stay late—"

"I don't work by the clock," Reba interrupted him firmly, just in case he thought that she had stayed for personal reasons. As department head she drew a straight management salary and no overtime. "I leave when all the patients have been treated and the paperwork is done."

She sounded so firm and convincing that Jamal wondered if he had imagined the signs of attraction. Then he remembered last night and the sparks this morning when he had touched her. She protested a little too much and a little too firmly. "I'm glad you didn't mind waiting," he said softly, smiling at her.

Reba watched his smile crease his lean cheeks, and the small lines around his eyes crinkled. Heat spread through her and her pulse rate increased. A smile like that should be forbidden, she thought angrily, trying to hide the effect it had on her. She failed miserably and grabbed at the only defense she could think of. "I would have waited longer, if necessary," she said firmly. "It's little enough in return for my brother's life."

Her words had the desired effect. Though his smile didn't vanish, it changed, becoming cool and distant. Instead of relief, Reba felt regret. She didn't like to inflict pain, and though he didn't show it, she sensed that somehow she had struck a festering sore.

Jamal slid his hands into his pockets and looked down for a moment. Would it be any easier ten years from now to smile, to shrug off the gratitude and hide his guilt? He doubted it. Grimly, he said, "You don't owe me anything, Miss Davis. As I mentioned before, many people joined the rescue effort."

Slowly, Reba shook her head. "But it was you who allowed the plane to land in Omari when every other airport from Beirut to Kuwait refused to become involved, despite the fact that the plane was running out of fuel. You also directed the rescue efforts personally. Rafe said that you refused to seek shelter during the sandstorm and stayed in a tent near the plane."

Jamal shrugged. "Since the reason for the hijacking was to sabotage the treaty between the States and Omari it was the least I could do. The passengers—especially your brother—were the true heroes." Without Rafe's help Jamal might never have discovered the connection between the major and Muhrad. During the days following the rescue, Jamal had come to appreciate the closemouthed rancher's discretion. "Let's get to the purpose of my visit and take a walk through your department."

The harshness in his voice startled her. Why, she asked herself, would the man be bitter about the rescue when he should have been pleased? It didn't make sense. Perhaps Rafe could shed some light on the mystery, though she doubted she would find out what she wanted to know. Rafe was persistently tight-lipped about the events that had taken place. She looked up at Jamal, her eyes troubled and her voice soft with regret. "I'm sorry if I recalled bad memories."

"They must be painful ones for you, too," Jamal said soberly.

Briefly, she recalled the nightmares that had lingered long after her brother's safe return. "I try not to dwell on the past," she said firmly. "If you work in a hospital you learn to accept the inevitable and try to focus on the bright side." She shook her head ruefully. It was always easier said than done. "It's either that or lose your sanity."

Jamal smiled, drawn to her warmth. He gently brushed his hand over her cheek. It was an impulsive gesture, not a calculated move, but the effect was the same.

Reba stiffened with surprise and shock. For a few minutes she had allowed her guard to drop. Now she pulled it firmly into place. Stepping back, she asked coolly, "Where do you want to start the tour, Your Highness. Here in the gym, perhaps?"

Her sudden withdrawal annoyed him, her formality frustrated him, and he wasn't going to stand for it! He looked at her grease-streaked hands, took her wrist and turned it palm up. "Perhaps you should get a cloth first."

At his touch her heart skipped a beat. Reba barely kept herself from snatching her hand away. His palm was hard, calluses scraping the back of her hand, and his skin was several shades darker than hers. "I will, the moment you let go of my wrist, Your Highness."

Frowning, he said sharply, "I've no patience with formality. Your brother calls me Jamal."

He was stripping away her defenses, one by one, she thought resentfully. And with every second she spent in his company her need to hold him at arm's length increased. Reba tugged at her hand and after a moment's hesitation he released it. "Is that an order?" she demanded, angling her chin.

Her challenge was irresistible. "More of a royal request, Miss Davis," he retorted softly, eyes glinting.

A mocking light came into her eyes. "I hate to disillusion you, Your Highness, but at the moment you're on the wrong continent."

"Then why, Miss Davis, do you insist on calling me by my title?" With his eyes on hers, he stepped closer.

Reba felt a tingle, a warning, and her eyes narrowed in response. He wasn't the first man to back her into a corner. Over the years she'd become very adept at avoiding potentially explosive situations. She didn't move. That would give him the wrong impression and present a challenge he'd feel obligated to pursue. Instead she forced herself to smile coolly and say calmly, "I only follow the instruction issued by our administration. This meeting, Your Highness, is strictly business."

Jamal noticed the small pulse beating at the base of her throat. She wasn't quite as detached as she pretended to be. "Do I make you nervous, Miss Davis?"

He did, but she'd be darned if she was going to let him see the effect he had on her. "Should I be?" She raised her brows and coolly stared down her slim nose.

He couldn't have done it better himself, Jamal thought, amused. "You're a very stubborn woman," he observed softly.

"So I've been told." He was so close his breath was fanning her heated skin. And he had the most absurdly thick long lashes she'd ever seen on a man, sable brown and tipped with gold. "The same can't be said about my patience. I don't like being stalked."

Her skin was flawless, the color of pure, clear honey with the flush of roses creeping into it. He wondered what it would taste like. His hand cupped her chin before she could retreat.

His kiss was firm—and mercifully brief. But it still left her shaken. Then she was free. "You've got some nerve—" She caught the glint in his eyes and bit her lip.

"Isn't this what you expected?" he asked blandly, fighting the need to reach for her again.

"No!" She walked past him with her head held high. Halfway down the hall, she turned to him with her face set.

"I wish you'd stop fencing," she snapped. "I didn't stay to keep you amused. If you want entertainment, find someone else."

In the bathroom she turned on the water full force, washing the grease from her hands. What was it about this man that got so swiftly under her skin? He was handsome, devastatingly so, but she knew a number of attractive men, and looks alone had never appealed to her. Since she couldn't come up with a logical explanation, it had to be body chemistry.

From the moment they'd faced each other across the fence the air had fairly sizzled with sparks. Frowning, she ran the scrub brush over the tips of her fingers. Only once before in her life had she felt that certain click, that instant electrical charge. The man had been Tobias Randall III, heir of one of New Mexico's oldest and wealthiest families. World-class rider. Gold medalist. And, as she'd found out after her accident, number-one louse.

If only a fraction of the stories printed about Jamal were true, Toby had been a fumbling amateur compared to him. Thus forewarned, she hadn't been as immune to his charms as she'd hoped. She was honest enough to admit that she had goaded him on. She had no one else to blame for the kiss but herself. She didn't know what devil had prompted her to bait him. But at least she'd learned one lesson she wasn't likely to forget: he was one man she couldn't handle.

In the gym Jamal gave the nut a final twist, turned the pedal around and watched it spin. He wished he could fix what had happened a few minutes ago just as easily. What was it about Reba Davis that made him behave like a...jerk?

Swearing, he jumped to his feet, gripping the wrench so tightly it bit into his palm. He had never before in his life pushed a woman. Pursued, persuaded, charmed, yes; but he'd never pounced on anyone before. Then again, there had never been any need to. He'd never before met with resistance. It was a lousy excuse, he thought, placing the wrench back on the chair.

But, damn it, he couldn't have misread the signs. The attraction *was* there, on both sides. He frowned. His reputation was catching up with him. But surely she didn't believe everything that had been written about him? Besides, she was almost thirty years old, worldly and unattached. He stopped short. Just because she didn't wear a ring didn't mean that she was free. In fact, with her looks and innate sensuality it was highly unlikely. Was smooth, pleasant Tim Horner the man? Surely she could do better than that. There was nothing wrong with him, but . . . He heard the soft pad of her steps on the vinyl floor and quickly collected himself.

When she entered the gym her eyes were veiled and her beautiful face was expressionless.

"Should I apologize?" he asked quietly.

The offer was so unexpected that her firm mouth softened against her will. "I'd rather you didn't," she said candidly. "Because then I'd have to apologize, too."

Her honesty made him smile. "I fixed your bicycle." He saw the surprise in her eyes, watched her lips open and warned softly, "Don't say it. Contrary to your expectation, I'm neither stupid nor helpless."

"I didn't—" Reba started to protest, eyed him suspiciously and stopped. She had never known anyone who could make her feel foolish and defensive quite so easily. If she examined his every word for hidden meanings, her pride would demand that she argue again. Tilting her head to one side, she asked, "Is a simple thank-you allowed?"

He answered softly, his face straight but with the devil's glint back in his eyes. "I'd rather you didn't. Because then I'd have to thank you, and we'd be right back where we started. Why don't you explain some of these contraptions to me instead?"

Reba jumped at the suggestion, grateful to be on familiar ground once again. He was the most exasperating man she'd ever met. During the next fifteen minutes she demonstrated and explained the uses of the various pieces of equipment, from the shoulder wheel and the parallel bars to the traction table. His pointed questions surprised her, showing her just how knowledgeable he was. Entering a small booth to show him the hot-pack machine, she stopped and asked, "Why is this medical center so important to you?"

He stared down at her. He realized that her head barely reached past his shoulder and her slender body seemed fragile compared to his. They were only a foot apart, yet she made no move to put more distance between them, as if she'd lost her wariness of him. Even her eyes had softened.

For a moment he wanted to explain why he was involving himself personally, why he was speeding up construction. Then he drew back. He'd learned, too early in life, not to trust on a whim. His glance settled on a small mural of cacti on the wall above the treatment table. "Most of Omari's hospitals are old, crowded and poorly staffed. With the new base being built, we need bigger and better facilities almost overnight. I want it done right, despite the haste."

She could understand that. She would never leave the planning of her office to someone else, but then it was only one small suite of rooms she would have to supervise, not a whole complex. "That's quite an undertaking. I remember when Rafe built our new stables. He had a terrible time getting the builder to do it his way."

Jamal shook his head. "You can't imagine what it is like. An American construction firm is building the center, but the Imams look over their shoulder, constantly arguing."

He couldn't hide his frustration over the delays the constant squabbles caused. It was in his voice and rippled through the strong muscles beneath his thin shirt, drawing

Reba's eyes. Her fingers itched to touch him on the shoulder, soothing— She caught herself just in time and took a small step back, until she leaned against the treatment table. "Tradition versus progress," she said thoughtfully. "A big project like that has to be planned for the future, not just for today."

"Yes." Her understanding surprised and pleased him. "Some things will never change. People will still sleep with their heads pointed toward Mecca many years from now. In time the strict separation of the sexes will be relaxed. In many places it's already beginning. But for right now the Imams insist that there will be two sets of departments."

"What a waste of manpower and equipment." Reba shook her head. "A central location and lots of folding doors would solve that problem."

Arrested, he stared down at her. "What do you mean?"

"Walls and doors instead of curtains. Scheduling would do the rest. If your Imams insist on a complete separation of the sexes, you'd need two entrances and two gym areas, but most of the equipment could be shared."

Interest sparked in his eyes and comprehension brought an appreciative smile to his face. "I'm no architect, but yes, I believe that could be done." His teeth were brilliant white against his bronzed tan. "Are you sure you won't change your mind about coming to Omari?"

When he smiled like that it was difficult to say no. The room suddenly seemed small and airless and her response sounded less firm than the last time she'd turned him down. "I'd love to visit Omari someday but for now, I have commitments here." She moved past him back into the hallway. "It's getting late. Do you want to see the rest of the department?"

"Another look at the whirlpools, if you have the time." He wanted to stay, just to sit and talk, about anything and everything. For the past hour he'd nearly forgotten about

the pressure and the dark clouds rising on the horizon.
"Would you have dinner with me?"

Her refusal was instant, a reflexive move of self-defense.
"I'm sorry, but I already have plans." The moment the
words were out, she wanted to call them back.

But by then his eyes had grown distant and his manner
was once again cool. "I understand. I have a mountain of
work waiting for me anyway."

When he left a few minutes later with Hassir, Reba stared
after him, feeling mean and small. He looked lonely, striding down the hall with his shoulders braced as if he carried
a heavy weight. Shrugging, she reached for her lab coat and
walked to the elevators. The notion was absurd.

Absurd or not, she couldn't dismiss her feeling of guilt.
It haunted her for the rest of the night. It followed her all the
way out to the Davis ranch the following morning and even
into the stables where she made straight for Ol' Ann's stall.
Preoccupied, she reached for the bridle.

Only when she slipped the bit between Annie's yellow
teeth did the fear return. For a moment her fingers stilled.
Taking a deep breath, she pushed her panic back into her
boots and finished the job.

Ol' Ann wasn't a horse in anything but looks, Reba told
herself sternly. The ten-year-old chestnut was as stubborn as
a mule, as placid as a cow and as lazy as Reba's mother's
overweight cat. There was no reason for her to break out in
cold sweat or for her stomach to churn. Before she could
change her mind, she reached for the currycomb and ran it
over the chestnut's flank.

As she groomed the mare, her thoughts strayed to Jamal
yet again. Angrily, she pushed a strand of hair behind her
ear. He was dogging her footsteps, invading her sleep and
driving her nuts.

She had spent a miserable evening cleaning up at the
clinic. Because of him. Her conscience had driven her out
of her apartment at five in the morning, again because of

him. Now that she thought of it, Ol' Ann had given her a look as if Reba were crazy when she'd entered the horse's stall just before six. When a thickheaded beast like Ol' Ann could sense something wrong, it was a sure sign of trouble. Reba groaned.

She straightened, wiped the sweat off her forehead with the back of her arm and moved to the other side of the horse. She didn't want to be attracted to Jamal. And she wasn't. Not really. It was her guilty conscience that had haunted her sleep. Never before had she judged a person on hearsay alone. She knew better than most what lies the rag sheets printed. She had been their target five years ago. She made a final sweep with the comb, then placed it on the shelf, her mouth setting determinedly. She was going to push him from her mind and from her life with the same speed he had catapulted into it.

She wasn't looking for romance. And she certainly didn't want to be a diversion for a playboy prince. She had a full-time job and so many private patients she rarely came home before nine. Like traveling, marriage and children were only distant plans. In the meantime she had her family, her friends and her dreams. Taking the reins she led the chestnut from the stall.

Over the past few years Rafe had renovated the old stables and added two modern buildings with plenty of windows and climate control. In this second one, most of the stalls were still empty. Apart from Annie there were only eight other occupants, all muscular cutting horses used for the cattle Rafe still raised. They whinnied softly as Reba walked past them to the big doors leading outside.

Bright, early-morning sunshine greeted her, making her squint. The yard was still deserted, but already Reba could hear voices from the bunkhouses and the old stalls. Slowly she crossed over to the corral fence, her boots stirring up dust.

As she tied Annie to the post, Matt, the ranch foreman, emerged from the old stables, coming toward her in the bowlegged rolling gait of a man who had spent a lifetime in the saddle. He stopped a few feet away with his dusty boots planted apart, tipped back his hat and stared at her from beneath steel-gray brows.

At sixty-three he had eyes that were still as blue as the Arizona sky and as piercing as a hawk's. Nothing escaped his attention, not the slightest limp of a horse, not the significance of the riding boots Reba had unearthed from the deepest recesses of her closet, not the mixture of fear and determination as she stared back at him.

"So you've finally decided to do it," he drawled, a slow grin cracking his leathery face. It was Matt who had pulled her from beneath the slashing hooves of the crazed stallion. "Always thought you'd come back to it eventually."

Reba watched several of the hands appear in the yard. She'd hoped to be in the saddle before she had too many witnesses. "Are you finished?" She raised her chin a notch. "If you've nothing better to do, perhaps you could get me a saddle."

Matt raised his straw Stetson, scratched the back of his head, then firmly set it back in place. "Your daddy always said, if you didn't know how to saddle a horse you had no business riding one. I sure admired the old man. He always knew what he was talking about."

Reba's brows shot up. "Funny, I don't remember that at all."

Matt nodded slowly. "Seems like it was just yesterday he said it, too. Besides it makes perfect good sense. If you don't have the strength to haul a saddle, you don't have enough strength to control even Ol' Annie here."

"Bull," Reba said succinctly and stalked away.

The tack room smelled of leather, polish and horse. The walls were covered with everything from hackamores to silver studded bridles. There were saddles in a variety of shapes and forms—from the small English saddle used in competitions to the heavy Western style.

Annie's saddle stood to one side, its leather scratched and scuffed. A blanket with a Navaho design lay neatly folded on top of it. Lifting the saddle, Reba almost staggered under its weight. The damn thing weighed a ton. She was a strong person—handling patients she had to be—but carrying a saddle called for muscles she hadn't used in years.

But old habits died hard. Within seconds she had mastered a hold on the saddle and even managed a triumphant grin as she walked up to Ol' Ann. The distraction was, of course, exactly what Matt had intended, Reba thought as she smoothed out the blanket before throwing the saddle on top of it.

Annie wasn't pleased to feel the weight of the saddle on her back and puffed up her already fat stomach to widen its girth. "Good try," Reba told her, gently kneeing her until the cinch was tight enough, fastening buckles and adjusting stirrups, trying to keep her mind blank. This time it didn't work. With each movement, the knot in her stomach grew bigger and her mouth felt as dry and gritty as desert sand.

"Want me to give you a hand up?" Matt took a few rolling steps and untied the reins.

Nausea welled up and Matt's face became fuzzy around the edges. *Don't push!* she wanted to scream. *I'm not ready yet. What am I trying to prove anyway? And to whom? I've groomed and saddled her, which is a heck of a lot more than I've done in the past five years. Isn't that enough?*

"No." She almost snatched the reins from his hands. If she waited, fear would root her to the ground. Blindly, she grasped the saddle horn, placed her foot into the stirrup and swung up.

Just for a moment she hung suspended. Just for a moment the pull of fear was so strong, she almost gave in. Then a gnarled, callused hand closed over hers and Matt said fiercely, "Don't you dare fall on top of me."

With a thud she slumped into the saddle, swaying dizzily. "Then get the hell out from under my feet," she muttered, grateful for his kindness.

"I won't stand for no cussing, not even from you, young lady," Matt said gruffly, struggling to hold back the smile splitting his face.

His voice was a little shaky and his eyes shimmered suspiciously. Concentrating on him, Reba felt the nausea recede and her dizziness fade. Drawing a deep breath, she unclenched one hand from the saddle horn and wiped the perspiration off her face. "Thanks, Matt," she said quietly and took her first look from a horse's back in five years.

All activities in the yard had stopped. The hands had given up all pretense of working and seemed to be holding their breath. Some of them had lived on the Davis ranch a long time. Skip, Matt's blond-haired grandson had grown up there and was already a junior at Saguaro High. José's gray hair had been black when he'd started working there. Now he and Maria, the housekeeper at the ranch house, were soon expecting their first grandchild. Slowly her eyes swept over the long whitewashed stables with bougainvillea creeping up the walls. Her eyes returned to their faces. "You look beautiful from up here."

Big grins and low laughter greeted her words.

"From my angle you look like a bunch of lazy good-for-nothings," Matt growled gruffly. "Get to work or I'll dock your pay."

Reba's lips twitched. Her plans had not gone beyond that first step—getting into the saddle—nor had she counted on an audience. Now, with ten pairs of eyes on her, pride wouldn't allow her to slip down from Annie's back.

She tightened her hands on the reins and tentatively pressed her heels into the flanks. Ol' Ann was stubborn and ignored the command with a swish of her tail. Reba remembered another lesson, one of the first rules she'd learned as a child: one never allowed a horse to refuse a command. Once lost, control wasn't easily regained.

She pulled a little more firmly and dug a little harder, until Annie moved a step forward, stopped, then took another few reluctant steps. When Reba maintained her hold on the reins, the horse consented to a small walk around the yard, circling back to the hitching post almost immediately.

"You lazy old nag," Reba muttered, forcing the horse to make another round. When Reba decided that persistence wouldn't get her anywhere, she took Annie back to the post.

Once she was on firm ground, Reba's knees felt like jelly, her clothes were damp from perspiration and her hands trembled. Reaction was setting in. "Don't unsaddle her," Reba told Matt, then made for the house on unsteady legs, before she made a fool of herself in front of this tough lot of men.

Chapter 4

By Saturday evening Reba's bottom was numb, her thighs were chafed and her palms had started to blister. But all her aches and pains could not dim the glow of satisfaction she felt as she swung into the saddle one last time.

Tonight she had no audience. Most of the hands had left right after their chores had been done and wouldn't return until late. Maria and José were visiting their daughter in Broken Promise and planned to stay overnight, and Skip had left to spend the Labor Day weekend with his mother. Only Matt was somewhere around the stables, probably watching her every move.

As she nudged Ol' Ann into a walk, her stomach still lurched and fear kept her back ramrod straight. What she needed was practice. She needed time and an opportunity to ride every day. She played with the idea of boarding Ol' Ann at a stable in Scottsdale, then discarded the thought. Her budget didn't allow any frills. For the price of stabling the chestnut, she could buy two office chairs.

This time she rode Ol' Ann past the stables toward the house. The sun was setting in the hills, purple shadows creeping up the slopes. When Rafe had called this morning he'd promised to be back by sundown. In another half hour it would be dusk. Impatiently, she searched the track leading to the highway. She wanted him to see her riding Ol' Ann, but as yet no dust plumes stirred in the distance.

Reba stopped in front of the old adobe house which had been in the Davis family for more than a century. A waterfall of pink bougainvillea spilled from the shaded porch onto beds of bright red geraniums and candy-striped petunias. Pale pink roses climbed up the pillars, buzzing with bees, and in the shade, the leaves of potted palms and ficus trees stirred lazily.

Over the years the three-room house her ancestor Jake Davis had started had mushroomed into an architect's nightmare as each generation had added rooms to suit its own needs. Reba loved each nook and cranny of this map of family history. Roots were important to her.

And then she wondered what Jamal's childhood had been like.

Rafe had once told her that Jamal had been shuffled between parents and countries every six months. How had he dealt with the religions, politics and values that changed with each trip? To a small child that lifestyle must have been very unsettling, confusing and lonely. Reba couldn't imagine what it must have been like to live half a year in a palace and the rest of the time in Hollywood or following his mother on location.

Last night she'd read an article in *Global Affairs* about his father's visit to Washington next week. The reporter had called Jamal "the twilight prince." A man trapped between the Orient and Occident. She sighed. Her image of him was changing, becoming less abstract, more human. Male. She didn't like it one bit.

Reba scanned the track again.

Suddenly, she spotted a dust plume in the distance. She dug in her heels and turned Ol' Ann to the side of the house. Thus hidden she waited until she heard the truck drive up and the engine stop. When she heard the truck door open, she urged the chestnut forward.

Climbing out of the cab, Rafe turned. He wasn't a man easily shocked, but he was completely unprepared for the sight that met his eyes. Reba watched him blink and his mouth almost drop open in stunned disbelief. "Cat got your tongue?" she quipped, grinning from ear to ear.

She heard another car door opening. It was then that she spotted the low-slung silver Porsche almost hidden behind Rafe's dusty pickup.

She hadn't expected to see him again this soon. She knew her brother had invited him to the barbecue on Monday, but it had never occurred to her that he might bring him tonight. In her mind she'd planned their next meeting down to the last detail. Her hair would be freshly washed and left loose. She would wear the soft white cotton dress with the nipped-in waist and long swirling skirt she'd bought for the party. And she would greet him with reserved friendliness, then leave him to Rafe while she returned to the safe circle of her friends.

Instead she was wearing dirty boots, a dusty work shirt, stained, frayed jeans and was clinging to her horse for dear life. "You might have warned me, brother dear," she muttered, pitching her voice low for Rafe's ears alone.

He grinned. "I could say the same. You just knocked me sideways."

But watching Jamal leave his car and join Rafe, her resentment fled. All she could think about was how good he looked. Faded denims rode low over his lean hips and the blue linen shirt was open at the neck, revealing his strong bronze throat. He was smiling, but his eyes remained secretive. It made her more curious than ever to find out what he was hiding from the rest of the world.

"It's nice to see you again," Reba said with all the composure she could manage clinging to Ol' Ann's back. She started to hold out her hand, but at that moment the mare shifted restlessly and she grasped the saddle horn instead.

"The pleasure is mine, Miss Davis." Jamal's glance took in the purity of her profile, her shining hair, the proud lift of her breasts and the long lovely line of her legs. Even dusty and sweaty, with her hair tied up in a ponytail, she managed to be beautiful. He had never known a woman who captivated him so completely as Reba did. Then he noticed how her hand came out and how swiftly she retracted it. As if she were afraid of him. Yes, now that he looked closer, he noticed her stiffness, too.

Annie chose that moment to take the bit between her teeth, turn sharply and break into a trot. Caught by surprise, Reba acted on instinct alone. A novice rider might have jerked on the reins and accidentally made the horse rear. Reba tightened them steadily, using her voice and her legs as well as her hands. But Annie apparently had suffered enough for one day and was determined to get to the stable, fighting her all the way back to the yard.

The moment the horse turned, Jamal started after her. One look at Reba's stiff back and he realized what was going on. She wasn't afraid of him. She was scared to death of horses! Anxiously he watched her struggle for control.

"Leave her, Jamal." Rafe's firm voice stopped him from breaking into a run. "Annie's not going to throw her."

Jamal looked over to his friend. "She's barely hanging—" He broke off abruptly. He noticed that the nag had indeed calmed down and was slowly coming to a stop. With a sigh of relief he said, "I guess you know your horses."

"That, too." Rafe rubbed the back of his neck. "In this case I was counting on Reba's skills. This is the first time she's sat a horse in five years. But she used to be one hell of a rider and some things are too deeply ingrained to forget."

Jamal fought the need to go after her, to snatch her off that nag's back. He had no right to interfere, he thought grimly, watching her take the old mare for another turn around the yard. The rider in him approved of her action and admired her courage. But the man wanted to hold her close, reassure her, kiss her—

The strength of his feelings startled him. For days he'd told himself that she was just another beautiful face. He'd almost convinced himself that the reason she'd been continuously on his mind had less to do with personal feelings than with the project they'd been discussing. And then the mare had taken the bit between her teeth. "Five years is a long time," he said quietly, turning back to Rafe.

"Yeah."

Usually Jamal appreciated Rafe's prudence; now it frustrated him. "I guess I'll have to ask your sister to find out what happened."

Shrugging, Rafe walked over to him. "That's no secret. It was all over the papers at the time. She had an accident five years ago. During a storm she was trapped in a stall with a wild mustang I was trying to break. No one missed her until the rain and the thunder had died down. Matt thought she'd gone back to the house and my mother believed she was with Matt at the stables. I don't know how she survived. She was in the hospital for six weeks. If she'd been able to get back with horses right away, she might have been all right. But by the time her ribs and her arm had healed, the memory of the fear and pain had set hard. The first time she tried to enter a stall, she fainted." Suddenly, he threw his head back and laughed out loud. "Damn, it feels good to see her up on a horse again."

Rafe's rare display of emotion cleared Jamal's nightmare vision of Reba trapped in a stall, of hooves slashing and tearing at her soft flesh. He swallowed. He had witnessed more than one accident and knew the damage a wild horse could do. It took a lot of courage to get back on a horse after what she'd been through. Clearing the tightness in his throat, he said softly, "She's quite a woman."

"You don't deserve a treat after the trick you just played on me," Reba told Ol' Ann sternly a little while later, closing the bottom gate. "How could you embarrass me in front of a prince, and one of the best riders I've ever met." Leaning against the gate, she reached into her pocket, withdrew a small apple and held it out to the horse. Annie gently lowered her mouth to Reba's outstretched palm, the mare's soft breath warming Reba's skin. Ears twitching, Annie began to chew noisily.

Reba watched dust dance on the weak sunbeams slanting through the high windows. She hadn't realized just how much she'd missed the feel of being in a stable. For five years she had felt like an outsider every time she forced herself to walk through this place. Now a sense of belonging stole over her, a feeling of peace. She felt weak, shaky and sore, yes, but also as if a great weight had been taken off her shoulders. She hadn't panicked. She hadn't fainted. She had been scared stiff, but she had made all the right moves. And with her feet back on solid ground, she could almost believe that someday she would be able to ride again without fear. She laughed shakily.

Then she heard boots on the concrete floor. Stiffening, she turned around and propped her elbows on the gate. She had guessed that the men would walk around the stables. But she hadn't expected Jamal to come alone.

He walked with such power and grace, covering the distance with long easy strides. As always when he was near, she felt heat well up in her and her senses sharpen. She didn't want him here. Not now, when she was too vulnerable and her feelings were too close to the surface. "Where's Rafe?" she asked.

"Talking to Matt about a bull named Nero." He stopped next to her, studying her upturned face. She looked tired

and wary. Of him, he realized, and controlled the swift stab
of impatience. He hadn't come to pounce on her. "Is Nero
as mean as his namesake?"

"He's got a nasty temper. But he'll do just about anything for a stalk of celery." He was so close she could see
tiny lines forming crescents around his eyes. She hadn't noticed the small, half-moon scar fading into the hairline at his
temple before. Every time she saw him she made new dis-
coveries, little, personal things that seemed to stick in her
mind. She took a deep breath. His nearness was making her
giddy, but her knees were too shaky to move away.

He leaned against the gate and ran his hand over the
mare's smooth neck. "And this one has a stubborn streak.
What's her name?"

"Annie, better known as Ol' Ann. There isn't a mean
bone in her body," she defended the mare, watching the thin
cotton shirt stretch over his broad shoulders and mold itself to his back. Muscles smoothly rippled beneath. Swiftly
she drew her eyes away. "She's used to getting her own way.
Dad bought her for my cousins. Whenever they came to
visit, they rode her two and three at a time, each of them
directing her a different way. Annie solved the problem by
doing exactly what she wanted to do."

She was rambling, watching his hand instead of his face.
She was afraid of what she would read there. She didn't
want him to know what a coward she was, that it had taken
her five years to find the courage to get back on a horse.
Strong men despised weaknesses, in themselves as well as in
others. And he was a strong and impatient man. She tried
to tell herself that it didn't matter what he thought of her.
But it did.

"You didn't let her get away with anything today." He
scratched Annie between the ears, making the chestnut snort
with pleasure.

"No." Clenching her fingers she braced herself for the
next probe, took a deep breath and decided to beat him to

the punch. "That was pure reflex, not conscious thought. Some things seem to stick in your mind even if you haven't ridden in years."

"Rafe told me what happened," he said quietly.

"He had no right." Her eyes flew to his face; she steeled herself against the pity she'd faced so many times in the past. Instead she saw a mixture of regret and admiration that almost brought tears to her eyes. She should have known he would be kind and understanding, she thought, remembering his patience with the twins. Why was she always expecting the worst of him? It was a question she was afraid to answer, so she pushed it aside.

Jamal shrugged. "I asked him. He said it was no secret anyway."

"That may be so," she muttered, wishing that Rafe was here so she could wring his neck. Since he wasn't and because it was easier to fight the effect of Jamal's crooked smile when she was angry, she snapped, "But I wish you'd keep your aristocratic nose out of my life."

His hand shot out, taking her chin in a punishing grip. No one, except for his immediate family, ever used such a tone with him. "I could have dug up old newspapers." His voice had cooled perceptibly. When she winced, he eased his hold, his thumb stroking her soft skin. "But I know just how twisted such reports can be."

The unspoken condemnation in his words made her bite her lip. She was guilty of *wanting* to believe the stories circulating about him. Yet with each meeting and each passing day it was becoming more difficult to believe any of them. Still, the apology seemed to stick in her throat. "I didn't mean to offend you," she said stiffly.

"I want to believe that." He stared down at her. "I'd hate to limit my visits here to the times when you're gone."

She shook her head, embarrassed and distressed. "I'm not usually rude to a guest," she whispered and impulsively placed her hand on his arm as if she could soothe the pain she'd inflicted. "I'm sorry if I gave you the impression that you aren't welcome here."

There was warmth in her touch and an offering of friendship, honest and generous as Reba herself. He stared down at her, drawn to her strength and at the same time resenting his own weakness. Trust never came easy to him, especially when it had to do with women; Azadeh had seen to that.

Yet how could he refuse what he wanted so desperately to accept and to give? His hand cupped her face, a rare tenderness washing over him. "The fault wasn't all yours," he said softly, his thumb circling her mouth. "I enjoy fencing with you."

His smile was irresistible, almost hypnotic, and so was his touch. She swayed a little closer, then caught herself, drawn between the need to stay and the need to run. Then his mouth covered hers and her desire for escape vanished.

There was a sweetness in his kiss, a giving of pleasure that demanded nothing in return. And for a few moments she took and absorbed. But with each touch of his lips strength flowed back into her tired limbs, her body began to stir and her mouth opened beneath his. Slowly, her arms went around his waist and her heart moved toward him. She wanted the kiss to be more than a merging of lips and a mingling of breaths. More than a kiss of friendship. So much more.

Jamal had no intention of drawing out the kiss. But there was a freshness to her lips, a slowly stirring eagerness that slipped beneath his control. After that first slow awakening she gave passionately with a kind of desperation that left him shaking and wanting more. His arms tightened, pulling her against him until there was nothing between them but heat.

She was so soft, so slender his hands could almost span her waist. Whenever they argued, he thought of her as strong and undaunted and well able to take care of herself.

But now, absorbing her weight, he realized that though her spirit seemed formidable, her body was not. He felt her tremors, sensed her weakness and took a deep steadying breath. Slowly he raised his head. But his hand stayed buried in her hair, reluctant to let her go, reluctant to admit that he had almost lost control.

Finally, as if recalled from a trance, she opened her eyes and willed her hands to fall to her side. It took her a moment to catch her breath and feel the floor steady beneath her feet. "You shouldn't have done that," she whispered and took a step back, out of his reach. So that was what it felt like to play with fire, to feel flames licking at your skin, to feel them burn deep inside—and to feel so cold once the contact was broken. She hugged her arms around her against the chill.

For a moment he watched her silently, wanting to pull her back into his arms. He couldn't allow himself that kind of madness, not now, when he already had more than enough trouble on his hands. "Passion is never rational, Reba," he said softly, the words directed as much at her as at himself.

His eyes weren't so secretive now, she thought. Small green flames flickered in their depths, a mixture of desire and need. She retreated another unsteady step. How could one kiss shake the ground beneath her feet when only minutes ago it had seemed so firm? She did what any sane person did when the earth began to rumble. She turned and fled.

Reba rinsed the lettuce, tore the crisp leaves into small pieces and tossed them into the salad bowl. It was quiet in the kitchen, the silence broken only by the purr of the microwave baking the potatoes and the occasional laughter drifting from the nearby den, where Rafe and Jamal were having a drink before dinner.

A long time ago, before her grandmother, Maureen, had married Jonathan Davis, the den had been the kitchen.

Maureen, who loved to cook, had insisted on a modern place with plenty of light, Mexican tiles and oak cabinets. Even now, when she came to visit, she considered this part of the house her kingdom and Maria her subject. The big covered patio beyond the kitchen had been added by Reba's mother, Naomi. She wondered what Rafe's wife would change—if he ever decided to get married.

"Reba, is the fire ready?" Rafe called.

Glancing through the large window above the sink she noticed that the flames in the grill had died down. Smoke curled up from the charcoal, filling the air with the pungent scent of mesquite. "Yes. Just about."

When she'd come into the kitchen after a quick shower and a change into a pair of white shorts and a crisp bright yellow blouse, she'd found Jamal trimming and seasoning the steaks, while Rafe had been setting the glass-topped table outside. She shook her head. Jamal might have grown up surrounded by servants, but he wasn't nearly as helpless as some of the M.D.s she knew, who were experts when it came to scalpels, but useless around the house.

With deft movements Reba sliced the tomatoes and cucumbers she'd picked off the vines only minutes ago. One of the things she missed in Scottsdale was fresh-picked fruit and vegetables. But then she rarely cooked for herself. Most of her meals she ate at the hospital cafeteria. Occasionally she had dinner with her friends Rachel Levine and Harry Mendoza, who both lived in the same complex she did. All three of them were so busy, they hadn't seen one another in a week. She was glad that both of them would be here for the party, she thought, tossing the salad. Like herself, they were practical, no-nonsense people who weren't given to flights of fancy. After cleaning up the counter, she carried the bowl outside.

The night air was soft, a balmy caress on her skin. Placing the bowl on the table, she checked Rafe's handiwork. He'd used the blue place mats and white stoneware, plastic salt and pepper shakers and bottles of steak sauce and ketchup. Simple and without frills. Not the gold plates Jamal was used to, she thought wryly, leaning against one of the columns supporting the roof. But she doubted that settings were important to him.

Behind her she could hear the men come through the kitchen, and she tensed. She'd tried to analyze the kiss in the stables logically, telling herself that she had been off balance before he entered. She wasn't a fool and she wasn't a person who lied to herself. She was attracted to him. But what woman wasn't?

During those moments in the stable, the attraction had become a little too intense. But a cool shower had taken care of that. Now, watching him step outside, she was once again in perfect control. Well, almost perfect control, she amended, feeling her pulse increase.

He carried two beer cans in one hand and a glass of wine in the other, handing it to her. Thanking him, Reba took it, carefully avoiding contact with him. If he noticed her awkward move, he didn't comment on it.

"I saw your trophies in the den. Rafe said you were one hell of a rider, but he didn't mention that you were a member of the Olympic team."

Reba thought she heard a slight wistfulness in his deep voice and wondered at it. "That was a long time ago."

Along with her boots, jodhpurs and hacking jackets, she'd put her trophies away in a closet more than once. But Maria had always dragged them out again. They were part of the family history and belonged on the mantel over the fireplace, she'd insisted. Seeing them displayed out in the open had, in time, dulled the pain. Now she could even smile when she added, "I had my heart set on a medal. Even my trainer thought that Sir Lance and I had a chance."

"Sir Lance?" he mocked her gently. She was always so practical, down-to-earth and direct. But the name she'd picked for her horse showed a different woman—young, soft and with dreams in her eyes, flying over a ditch, an oxer or a tall brick wall. He wished he had known her then, before her dreams were lost.

She laughed self-consciously, "He was a Hanoveranian, all black with a white star. He didn't have Lancelot's blue eyes, but he did have his big heart. He loved to jump. Lord, could he jump." She took a sip of her wine and looked into the flames, remembering the thick green grass that softened the sound of the hooves, feeling the stallion beneath her, his powerful muscles tensing, so eager to win. "With a horse like Sultan no one could have beaten me to the gold." Rousing herself back to the present, she asked, "Why did you never compete?"

He shrugged. There had been many reasons, security the most important one. "Until Seoul, Omari had no Olympic team and I could hardly ride for the United States."

The flat tone of his voice told her louder than words how much he had wanted to compete. "You could still do it," she urged him. "Most of the great riders like Winkler, Steinkraus and the D'Inzeo brothers were in their thirties when they won."

"So could you, Reba," he countered softly. "What happened to Sir Lance?"

Whenever she thought of the big black she felt a stab of pain. She had raised him from a foal and had trained him for years. Parting from him had not been easy. "I sold him to a friend. Rafe wanted to keep him as a stud, but he was a horse that needed to jump. Last year he won second place in the Pan American Games."

"Listening to her, you'd think that horse really was a knight in shining armor," Rafe drawled, coming out on the patio with plates of steaks balanced in one hand and the corn in the other. "The truth is, he had a nasty temper."

Reba grinned. "The only reason you say that is because he once tried to take a chunk out of your hide when you yelled at me."

Rafe placed the platters on the table and gave her an offended look. "I never yell at you. I wouldn't dare. Maria would stop cooking and Matt would probably quit." Turning to Jamal, he added dryly, "That day she came home with a coyote she'd found in the pasture. Both were bleeding like stuck pigs. It was hard to tell who was in worse shape, Reba or the wolf. The smell of blood had made the horse nervous. When I helped her from the saddle, he took a swipe at me."

"Oh, yeah?" Reba's chin went up. "That's not how I remember it." She turned to Jamal. "I distinctly recall Rafe yelling that I was a fool with more hair than brains before he hauled me out of the saddle."

"Is that all?" Jamal teased, tongue in cheek. "I'd expected something a bit more forceful, like...uh...jerk."

Reba tried to look annoyed and failed. "Men," she said with a toss of her head, "always stick together."

"Self-preservation," Rafe drawled, placing the corn on the rack, then adding the steaks. The coals sizzled and small flames licked at the juice.

Jamal watched the lights dance in her hair. He shouldn't look at her, but he couldn't take his eyes off her laughing face. He shouldn't think of her, yet ever since that kiss in the stable she'd been on his mind continuously. When she licked the wine off her lips with the small tip of her tongue, he almost groaned. "What happened to the coyote?"

"He's out there somewhere." Reba pointed into the night. "I took out the buckshot, then set him free."

"He didn't run very far." Rafe closed the lid and reached for his beer. "For a while he used to come for food every night. Then, a few months later, he disappeared and we never saw him again."

The phone rang, a shrill sound in the soft silence. "Watch the steaks for me," Rafe said as he crossed the patio and walked inside.

Reba checked her watch. Looking up, she saw that Jamal had done the same. "Five minutes?" she asked, smiling, marveling that she could feel so comfortable in his presence.

He nodded. For the past few minutes an idea had begun to form. "If I stabled Ol' Ann for you, you could practice every day."

Her eyes widened with surprise at his kindness. She shouldn't have been, she thought, because Rafe had often remarked that Jamal was one of the most generous people he knew. She swallowed. She wanted to ride so badly she could barely wait until tomorrow morning to saddle Ol' Ann again. And hadn't she already toyed with the thought of stabling the mare nearby? So why didn't she jump at the offer? Why was she hesitating?

It wasn't out of pride. Rafe had boarded horses for friends more than once. It was fear, she decided, fear and stupid fantasies. She could imagine herself riding with Jamal through the desert, with the sun burning their faces and the breeze in their hair. And she was afraid that the price she would have to pay would be much higher than two office chairs. "That's very kind of you. Unfortunately, I don't have time to ride during the week."

Her refusal didn't surprise him. After the way she backed away from him in the stables, Jamal had expected it. And perhaps, if he hadn't seen her eyes softening with dreams, he would have let it slide. "There's always time for the things one wants badly enough," he challenged her softly.

Reba watched Rafe through the window as he picked up the phone, hoping the call was for her. But he didn't wave to her. Not that running away would have been the answer, she thought. A reprieve, maybe, and a chance to get her feelings back under control. She took a deep breath and said, "I usually work a twelve-hour day. I sometimes treat two and three private patients after I leave the hospital. I really don't have the time."

His hand clenched around the can. Her stubbornness made him want to shake her. "I'm offering to stable your horse," he said coolly, "no strings attached. I'm only going to be here another six days. After next Friday you'll have the place to yourself."

Illogically, that wasn't what she wanted at all. Only six more days! He was a restless man, always moving across the globe. She wondered what he might be running away from. "No, that's not what I meant. I don't know whether Rafe mentioned anything to you, but I want to open my own office in six months."

"Another dream?" Jamal asked with a mixture of amusement and tenderness that made her heart start beating furiously again.

She grimaced. "A project. Compared to your medical center it's nothing."

He shook his head. "That isn't true. A dream is precious, no matter how big or small."

"I prefer big," Reba said firmly. "Enough room for wheelchairs to move around freely and lots of light." As always when she talked about the office, her eyes began to shine. "The location is perfect. No more than five minutes from my apartment. There are only six suites in the building, five already taken by physicians. There's light and space. My patients won't feel crowded at all. I have an appointment with the builder on Tuesday."

Jamal smiled. Her eyes were filled with the same excitement he sometimes saw on his mother's face when she spoke about a new role, a new production. "When I looked into your office at the clinic I wondered how you could stand working there. This place sounds more like you." Someday he would buy Reba yellow diamonds, though he doubted that they would ever shine as brightly as her eyes.

Suddenly the charcoals sizzled. Blinking, Jamal checked his watch and noticed that six minutes had passed. Time seemed to stand still when he was with Reba, he thought uneasily. "We almost burned the steaks."

And how could he plan beyond the next weekend when any day his world could go up in flames? Already there were protesters in front of their embassy in Washington, and that was only the beginning. Walking to the grill, he doused the flames, turned the meat over, tested it with his finger and rotated the corn. "Are you going to sign the lease on Tuesday?" he asked, wiping his hands on a paper napkin. Contracts were something he felt more comfortable with.

"No." Like Jamal, Reba had started toward the grill, but now she retreated against the column again. "I won't sign unless I see all the changes I want in writing."

Jamal chuckled. She was such a curious mixture of common sense and dreams. Perhaps this combination of softness and strength drew him to her more than her beauty. "A tough businesswoman, I see," he mocked her gently.

Annoyance flashed in her eyes. "Just because I have a few dreams doesn't mean I drift around in a cloud."

"No." His voice softened lazily as he leaned back against the wall with his hands in his pockets. "I like to see stars in your eyes. Though I'd prefer to put them there myself."

"I'll reach for my own stars, thank you." Then Reba realized that today he had learned all her secrets and had shared none of his. "What about your dreams?" As always, she refrained from addressing him by his name, as if by doing so she could keep him at a distance.

He sobered abruptly and said quietly, "Princes can't afford to dream. Too many lives depend on their decisions and often, no matter how careful the plans, lives are lost." A slight bitterness crept back into his voice. "The treaty is important to me. I've worked for it for years. Sometimes, though, I wonder if it was wise to urge my father to give up neutrality."

He'd always seen himself as an ambassador, a bridge between East and West, involving himself in Omari's internal politics only when his conscience demanded it. This division of duties had suited both himself and Muhrad. For years they had avoided major conflicts that way.

Until the first missile attack on Basjad's harbor.

Until his father had been forced to give up neutrality or watch all he had built go up in flames. The shift to the West had, at least in his brother's suspicious mind, upset the balance. Muhrad saw the U.S. military presence in Omari as a personal threat, a shift of power to the West. To him the West and Jamal were one and the same thing.

"The treaty did save lives. Without it, the war in the Persian Gulf might have gone on for years." Reba again wondered how she could have misjudged him so, how she could have believed that all he cared about was the next race and the next woman.

"Yes." Sometimes, though, Jamal asked himself if his desire to bring the two countries closer had been influenced by a personal desire to see his two worlds tied together. True, lives and property had been saved; but the swing to the West had turned Muhrad against his father. His brother would never meekly give up his right to the throne, and a civil war would destroy so much more than the treaty had saved. "Peace would have come eventually, though. Without the treaty there would have been no hijacking."

Reba's hand clenched around the glass, lest she give in to the need to touch and reassure him. "No one can hold that against you. Rafe doesn't. Princes are human, too." Beneath all his arrogance and charm Jamal was a caring man, she thought, sipping her wine. "You are not at all what I expected."

He looked at her, caught by the golden softness in her eyes, and shifted uneasily, suddenly recognizing just how much he had revealed of himself. Her sympathy and understanding made a person want to confide in her. Realizing the danger, he withdrew. His eyes moved from her beautiful face, lingered on her breasts, then slid down to her small waist, her gently curving hips and those incredibly long legs. "You're beautiful enough to make an iceberg feel human."

Irritated, Reba gave him a cool look. "What a waste. When the ice melts there is no substance. All you're left with is an annoying cold."

Grinning, Jamal pushed himself away from the wall and crossed the space between them. "Your sharp tongue could cut a man to shreds."

"But not you." She stiffened and angled her chin, standing her ground, but her heart was pounding. "You wear steel armor that's inches thick."

He stopped right in front of her and ran a finger down her nose. "Are you trying to provoke me, Reba?"

She shook her head. "It doesn't take much, does it?"

"Apparently not." He trailed his finger across her high cheekbone to her temple, feeling her pulse beat furiously. "You have a way of finding a man's weak spots and slipping through the armor. The trouble is I never know if you plan to stroke or to sting." She was softness and spice, strength and weakness, a practical modern woman one instant and a dreamer the next. No other woman had ever appealed to both the American and the Arab in him before. For the first time in his life he felt a need to look beneath the physical and uncover the mysteries hidden there. "We've drifted a little from our earlier subject. Since you're not afraid of me, there's no reason not to stable your horse." He ran his fingers through her silky mane, pushing it back from her face. "In time I'll teach you to ride Sultan."

"All in six days?" Reba scoffed huskily. Would she ever be that good again? Would she ever have the confidence and skill it took to handle the powerful stallion? With Jamal's warm breath fanning her skin and his touch making her pulse race, she could easily imagine things that were even more unrealistic and improbable. "I'm not certain I can do it."

He watched her carefully, but saw no fear. Apprehension and doubts, yes, but deep down he thought he also saw a small spark of eagerness. "Are you afraid to try?" he asked softly.

She tossed her head. No one else could sting her into temper with just a word or a look. "There was a time I'd have made you eat those words."

He almost laughed out loud at the fierceness in her voice. Another carrot and she would be caught. "That's easy to say, Reba, isn't it?" he taunted. "There's no way you can prove that statement."

"I know what you're doing," she snapped, pushing a strand of hair behind her ear. "But I won't let you seduce or goad me into this. I'll learn to ride again in my own time, in my own way."

"Fine. I won't push."

"That I have to see."

"I'll pick you up Tuesday at five."

"I have an appointment with the builder at five-thirty. And you're pushing already. How about early in the morning? Like six?"

He didn't flinch. He didn't blink. Angry as she was she had to give him credit for it. "Six," he agreed softly, sealing the bargain with a light kiss.

Reba closed the dishwasher, punched the buttons and threw a final glance over the clean counters before turning off the lights. Rubbing her aching back, she walked into the den where Rafe was sprawled in a big recliner watching the news on the satellite TV. With a disinterested glance at the television screen, she curled up on the couch and yawned.

It was a few minutes past midnight and Jamal had left an hour ago. The evening had been fun, filled with light-hearted banter and a game of poker. Reba still didn't know how deal with Jamal. He was such a contradictory man: an Arab prince who fixed bicycles and grilled steaks, a playboy who built hospitals and fought for peace, a maker of dreams with no dreams of his own.

And a man who made her feel weak and strong at the same time.

Suddenly her attention was drawn to the screen, where a newscaster stood among a crowd of young people, carrying signs of Yussuf Stay Home and No Extradition. "Today," the journalist said, "student groups gathered in front of the Omarian embassy in Washington, opposing the upcoming visit of Emir Yussuf. It is the first protest since the treaty was signed earlier this year. During the past few days rumors have been circulating here in Washington that Emir Yussuf will discuss with American officials the extradition of the leader of the terrorist group, the Holy Islamic Brigade, called only the major, who organized the hijacking of the airliner in April. Both the State Department and the Omarian ambassador have denied the rumors. Until a few days ago the major was awaiting trial in a prison here in Washington. Sources at the Justice Department confirmed today that he has been moved to another federal prison."

When the news changed to another topic, Rafe flicked off the TV.

Looking at her brother, Reba saw no surprise on his face. "You knew about the protests," she remarked. Rafe had once served in the Army Security Agency and had been stationed in Lebanon for a number of years. Reba guessed that his familiarity with the Middle East was another reason he and Jamal had become friends.

Rafe nodded, watching her from beneath lowered lashes. He had been aware of a subtle tension between Reba and Jamal all evening. "Jamal mentioned it. It wasn't totally unexpected. A number of Islamic countries still oppose the treaty—especially Iran."

Reba felt fear shiver down her back. "If he knew about the protests, why did he come without a bodyguard today?"

Rafe's eyes narrowed on Reba's face and issued a subtle warning. "There are times when he needs to get away, despite the risks. He's had to face threats all his life. They're part of his position."

"Sometimes it's easy to forget who he is."

Rafe picked up his beer and stared at the label, then said slowly, "He's been raised on American ideals. He builds universities, hospitals and has brought peace to Omari. But the same man watched the public execution of the three hijackers in the market square without a blink."

Reba swung her legs to the floor, realizing that her brother was warning her that she saw only one side of the man. "In his place, would you have been there?"

Rafe drank the last of his beer. When he looked at her, his eyes were cold with remembered hate. "Yes." Then he shook his head and added softly, "But I would have blinked."

Chapter 5

"I'm so glad that you and Rafe keep the tradition going," Maureen Davis said to her granddaughter, leaning back in her chair beneath a large red-and-white-striped umbrella. Her bright eyes darted everywhere, from the tables groaning under the weight of food to the big barbecue pit where two men turned and basted meat, to the big wooden dance floor placed in the center of the lawn and surrounded by tables and more umbrellas. Music filled the air, mingling with the laughter and shrieks of children playing nearby. "I always look forward to this day. It's the one time during the year when all of us get together. You young people are so busy we barely see one another during the rest of the year."

Reba leaned over and kissed her grandmother's wrinkled cheek. At eighty-three, Maureen still took care of her house and garden in Broken Promise and walked two miles a day. "I can't remember a Labor Day without a barbecue at the ranch." Even during the hard years following her father's death when Rafe had almost lost the land, they'd shared this day with family and friends. It had been self-service then, with everyone on the ranch pitching in. Today, her brother was using hired help to give his staff the chance to enjoy themselves.

Reba spied a look at Matt, all spruced up in new boots, dark blue slacks and a Western shirt with pearl snap buttons, and she smiled. He looked as if he was itching to take his turn at the spit. Maria, with a frilly apron tied around her ample waist, was adding last-minute decorating touches to the buffet she had pronounced perfect less than thirty minutes before. Maureen stared at a group of men talking in the shade of a pine tree. "The first party was your grandfather Jonathan's idea. No one would have guessed then that we'd actually have a prince among us one day."

Reba followed her grandmother's gaze. Since Jamal's arrival thirty minutes ago, she'd been conscious of his every move. He now stood next to Rafe with his hands in his pockets and his head thrown back. If she strained her ears, she could hear the sound of his laughter, deep and infectious, above the music. She smiled. "He seems to fit in so easily, as if he's lived among ranchers all his life."

"I read somewhere that his mother's parents owned a small ranch in East Texas. He probably spent some time with them," Maureen said thoughtfully, absently smoothing out a wrinkle in her pink linen dress. "Even without the bodyguard, no one with eyes in their heads would ever take him for an ordinary man, though. He conveys a sense of power that sets him apart."

"His position is more than a title to him, Gran," Reba agreed, noticing that even Tom Hardinger, their white-haired county judge, seemed to be impressed by Jamal. "He takes his duties seriously. I had expected him to be just another playboy, but he's much more than that."

Hearing the soft sound in Reba's voice, Maureen shot her a sharp, searching look. "You care for him."

"Of course," Reba said lightly. "It's difficult not to. We owe him a lot."

"Yes, we do," Maureen agreed quietly, her gray eyes resting on her grandson before sliding back to Jamal. "But that's not what I meant," she added dryly. "The prince has a charisma even your eighty-three-year-old grandmother isn't immune to. I don't want you to get hurt again."

"Don't worry." Reba squeezed her grandmother's gnarled hand reassuringly. Only a fool would take Jamal's kisses or his offer to teach her to ride again seriously. He was simply looking for a playmate while he was on vacation, and for some reason he had decided on her.

Maureen's eyes strayed back to Jamal. "He looks a lot like his father, except for his blond hair. That he definitely inherited from Kitty Barron. His mother's hair was almost a silvery blond when she was young."

"Gran, that was thirty-five years ago. How could you possibly remember it?" Reba teased gently, but very much intrigued, watching as Jamal took a tall, frosted glass of ice water from a waiter. She had noticed before that he didn't seem to drink much.

Maureen took a handkerchief from her white purse and dabbed her lined forehead, admitting sheepishly, "After the hijacking I went to the library and looked up some old newspaper accounts."

When Reba shot her a teasing look, she grinned. "Show me the woman who doesn't like to read about modern fairy tales," she demanded. "Grace Kelly's wedding happened about the same time. I can't remember whether it was before or after Kitty's marriage. Anyway, it was such an unlikely union. From the beginning the newspapers were speculating how long the marriage would last. Mind you, Kitty Barron wasn't as famous as Grace Kelly then, though she was definitely on her way up. I've often asked myself why a young woman would give up fame and fortune to become the second wife of some desert sheikh."

"She must have been very much in love," Reba said, reaching for her glass of iced tea and sipping it slowly.

Maureen shook her head. "When you're young, you believe that love is enough. But it takes more than spring fever to keep a marriage going. They were too different, if you ask me."

"Yet, she never married again. Perhaps, despite all their differences, she cared for him too much to live with someone else," Reba pointed out quietly, watching her petite Aunt Dolly and Judge Hardinger's elegant wife, Susan, join the group of men, both gazing at Jamal like star-struck teenagers. If his father had only a fraction of Jamal's charisma, to Kitty Barron every other man must've paled in comparison.

"You are an incurable romantic, Reba." Maureen shot her a worried look. "If she was so much in love with him why did she leave him less than a year later, and pregnant at that? Oh, Kitty said something about his first wife making her life hell and that she'd been afraid for the child she was carrying, but I really don't believe that."

"There's usually a grain of truth in those stories." Reba's fingers curled tightly around her glass, recalling that Jamal had spent six months each year in Omari. Had his stepmother made his life miserable? A jealous, spiteful woman could hurt a defenseless child deeply without leaving visible scars. Perhaps that explained Jamal's many affairs and why he didn't trust women enough to allow himself to fall in love, she thought, her eyes drawn back to him again.

Turning to place his empty glass on a passing waiter's tray, Jamal caught her watching him. As their eyes met, her shoulders tensed and a flush crept into her face. She looked much like a little girl caught with her hand in the cookie jar, he thought, raising one brow questioningly. Her eyes narrowed in response before she turned away.

Abruptly, Jamal left the group and made his way straight toward her table. He was tired of watching her from a distance, of having her smile at everyone but him.

Reba's heart skipped crazily. He was wearing gray pants that hugged his powerful legs and slim hips. The grayish-green shirt stretched across his broad shoulders and the slight breeze was ruffling his hair. Muttering something about having to circulate, she rose to escape.

She had waited too long, though, and he met her halfway. "Are you enjoying yourself?" she asked, as she tried to squeeze between him and an orange tree without smudging her white dress. Hassir seemed to close off her escape route with his massive bulk.

"Very much." Jamal smiled down at her. Most of his enjoyment had come from following her with his eyes, watching her as she greeted friends and relatives, directed waiters and paid attention to all the small details of the party with the same calm efficiency with which she ran her department. But what he'd found most satisfying of all was that there seemed to be no one special in her life. "You seem to be avoiding me."

She had been, of course, but she'd hoped that he wouldn't notice it because she didn't want to make him feel unwelcome. "I've been busy," she said lightly. "Some of my relatives I haven't seen in quite some time."

He raised one dark brow in disbelief, but merely said, "It's a pity that your mother isn't here. I'd looked forward to meeting her."

"This is one of her busiest weekends at the gallery," Reba explained, looking at him curiously. "Do you often spend your holidays alone?"

"I try to spend Christmas with my mother whenever possible. Since my grandparents died the rest of Kitty's family have drifted apart." Jamal gave a wry look over his shoulder at Hassir, who had retreated a few steps. "But I'm rarely alone."

Reba tried to imagine what it would be like to have virtually no privacy and asked softly, "Do you hate the constant need for guards?"

Jamal shrugged. "I rarely waste time on what can't be changed." The devil's glint came back into his eyes when he added, "And at times bodyguards come in handy."

"Like running interference for you?" Reba asked tartly. When he grinned unrepentantly she taunted, "I guess being used to servants all your life, you need some help." She watched his eyes narrow and felt a tingle run down her back. Ignoring the warning, she went on, "Now a real man—"

"Reba," Jamal warned blandly, his hand clamping around her wrist, staring down into her golden eyes. No one, not even Muhrad, would have dared to call him a pampered weakling. "If you keep sharpening your claws on me, you leave me no choice but to throw you over my shoulder caveman style."

"With Hassir's help?"

His narrowed glance slid from her face down her long neck, lingering on the swell of her breasts before sliding over her small waist and the slender curve of her hips. He noted she preferred clean lines to ruffles and lace. On another woman the soft white cotton dress with its sleeveless shirt-waist top and full skirt might have looked plain. On Reba it accentuated her stunning beauty. He felt his body tense, merely looking at her. "No, you little witch. Even this pampered weakling doesn't need assistance with someone your size."

At that moment the music started playing again, a slow country waltz. "Let's dance," he said, drawing her along the edge of the lawn, skirting the tables before she could protest.

After a few startled steps, Reba dug her heels into the grass. "I'd like to be asked."

He stopped and looked down at her. Beneath his finger-tips her pulse beat erratically. "While your eyes say one thing, your blood says something else," he taunted softly.

"I could give you any number of explanations why my pulse rate is up," Reba countered. He noticed too much, she thought, and turned her head away from him. Hassir had not followed them but was walking toward the bar instead. "Has Hassir been with you for a long time?"

"Yes. Since I was sixteen. Hassir's only six years older. You could say we grew up together."

"I'm not so sure you've grown up yet," Reba muttered.

Chuckling, he squeezed her hand punishingly. "Did no one ever warn you that you'll never find a husband if you don't learn to please a man?"

Reba tossed her head and said dryly, "I haven't found a man yet to please *me*."

She had stopped at a bushy avocado tree, her head framed by glossy green leaves. Feathery bangs clung to her damp forehead giving her laughing eyes a wicked gleam. Her thick loose hair was shimmering in the afternoon sun with blue-black lights and he remembered how soft and silky it had felt in his hands. His breath caught in his throat, desire pulsing through him. "And what does a man have to do to please you?"

There was both amusement and arrogance in his tone, but when she looked up she saw desire as well. She barely stopped herself from licking her suddenly dry lips and managed to say airily, "Respect my wishes. And *not* back me into corners."

A slow mocking smile creased his lean cheeks. "You may *think* you want dull, courteous and gentle. And perhaps such a man would have suited you a few months ago. But that woman would also have run at the mere thought of riding a horse like Sultan."

He brushed one finger over her mouth, then tugged sharply at her bottom lip. "You may still be a little afraid to jump. But when you finally decide to take the leap, I'll be there waiting for you."

Reba drew in a sharp breath. Did nothing escape those sharp hazel eyes? she wondered uneasily. The few men she'd dated since Toby's betrayal had been kind, dependable, safe—the type who looked beneath the skin, the type who wouldn't run screaming from a hospital room. "Courteous and gentle doesn't necessarily mean dull," she said coolly. "And if you're dangling Sultan in front of my nose with seduction in mind, let's cancel the deal. I don't go to bed with a man out of gratitude."

"It won't be gratitude, Reba," he said softly, drawing her toward the wooden platform where only a few couples swayed to the slow music.

No, it wouldn't be gratitude, she agreed. He had only to touch her lips with the tip of his finger and she began to burn. But she'd fight her weakness every step of the way. "It's still a little too hot to dance. Perhaps we should wait until the sun goes down."

He drew her against him, his hand firm in the small of her back, a sly look in his eyes. "I can think of nicer things to do in the darkness."

"I'm sure you can," she shot back. And so, dear Lord, could she, she thought. The muscles beneath her fingers felt smooth, subtle, strong. Their legs brushed against each other's as they slowly spun around, and with each step, with each breath, her need grew.

Abruptly, she pressed her hand against his shoulder to keep some distance between their bodies. When his arms tightened around her, she said firmly, "I don't want to be rude or cause a scene. But if you don't behave yourself I'll—" Her words faded as he raised his hand and gently brushed a strand of hair back from her heated face.

"You'll do what?" he taunted, his breath flowing over her skin like a soft caress. "Walk away? I keep telling myself that that's what I should do. When we first met I intended nothing more than a lighthearted flirtation. But no matter how hard I try, I can't get you out of my mind. You've bewitched me, Reba."

He wasn't smiling or flirting now. It wasn't casual attraction, either, that blazed in his eyes, but desire, man to woman. Basic, and so strong it made her head spin and her mouth go dry. She swallowed and said hoarsely, "I don't know what you want from me."

"I think you do." He spun her away from him until their hands barely touched. She followed his lead, light as a feather, with her full skirt swirling up from her ankles and her hair a dark cloud around her face. He knew he should break the contact now, while he still could, before emotions surfaced and were put into words. But his fingers seemed to have a will of their own. With a flick of his wrist, he pulled her back into his arms, holding her hips pressed tightly against him. "I want to make love with you."

What would it feel like to be held by him, not on the dance floor but in passion, to be desired, needed, loved? Glorious, while it lasted, she thought. And absolutely devastating when it was over. She placed a shaking hand against his chest to keep some distance between them and her voice was edged with panic when she said, "There are a lot of women who would jump at the chance to be wanted by a prince. Personally, I prefer a little less notoriety."

"Hell." Jamal swore succinctly, his hand biting into her waist. "I don't give a damn what you prefer. It's what you *feel* that I'm interested in."

Her heart pounded in her throat. Beneath her palm his heart beat as rapidly as hers. She couldn't deny what was happening inside her, but she couldn't accept it, either. Their steps were perfectly synchronized, their movements so coordinated they could have been dancing together forever. But off the dance floor they had nothing in common. "For how long?" she challenged him. "You'll forget me the moment you head back east."

Denial welled up in him. What he felt for her was too strong to be assuaged in a few nights. His relationships had always been straightforward, without pretenses, or promises, or regrets when he moved on. With Reba his emotions were different, stronger and so much more complex. He still remembered the fear that had rushed through him when Ol' Ann had taken the bit between her teeth and how he'd wanted to snatch Reba into his arms. Never before had he felt so protective toward a woman—or so challenged by one. He swallowed his anger and said calmly, "We'll discuss it when I get back from Washington."

For a moment his arrogance took her breath away and she glared at him with narrowed eyes. "There's nothing to discuss," she snapped when she finally found her voice. "When I want to make love with a man, there won't be any need for words."

He looked down at her thoughtfully. He wanted to tell her that he planned to come back to Arizona once his father had returned to Omari. But at this moment he couldn't promise her tomorrow. Hell, he couldn't even promise her tonight. Not with the Holy Islamic Brigade breathing down his neck. "Unfortunately, for me things are not quite that simple, especially not at the moment." As the music slowed down he spun her around a final time, then stopped, but his arms still held her loosely.

Reba glanced at him with sudden concern. "Are you worried about the protests outside your embassy?" she asked softly, her hands resting on his forearms. Yesterday's evening news had shown another demonstration in front of the Omarian embassy, not as peaceful as the one on Saturday night. At one point rocks had been thrown at the building, shattering windows. And new threats of violence had been made. She shivered slightly despite the heat. "I didn't watch the news today. Has the situation become even worse?"

"Not that I know of." Jamal stared down at her, touched by the warmth in her eyes. "Sometimes you remind me of the saguaro, prickly spines on the outside and all softness beneath."

Reba grimaced impatiently. "But you expect it to get worse," she guessed in a low voice. In a few days he was flying to Washington and the thought of him facing an angry mob made her fingers tighten with sudden fear. "How much worse?"

"Nothing security officers can't handle," Jamal said firmly, hoping that it was true.

Feeling snubbed, Reba snatched her hands away. "In other words, you don't want to talk about it."

He'd never been more tempted, Jamal thought, keeping his hands firmly on her waist. What would it feel like to be able to share his pleasures as well as his fears, to be able to discuss his problems openly without always having to guard his every word? Uneasily, he dismissed the idea. He couldn't afford to be weak and vulnerable, especially not now. "You are a dangerous woman, Reba," he said softly.

Reba barely heard the words, her senses occupied by something more stirring, infinitely more powerful than anything that had passed between them before. Panic welled up in her. She tore her eyes away and found several of her relatives and friends watching them curiously. "Jamal, let me go," she whispered urgently, color flooding her face.

He did, slowly, reluctantly. "All these days," he said with a quick rueful grin, walking with her from the dance floor, "I've waited for you to call me by my name. But I never imagined that the first time you did it would be a plea to release you."

She laughed a little shakily. "Perhaps it's symbolic." With an excuse that she needed to check progress in the kitchen she walked to the house to pour herself a cold glass of water.

Maria met her at the door, an anxious look on her round nut-brown face. "There's a phone call for Prince Jamal. It's his secretary."

Reba felt a chill feather down her spine. She doubted that the secretary would disturb Jamal unless it was urgent. "I'll tell him," she said to Maria and swiftly walked back outside.

Jamal noticed instantly that her skin was too pale and that her eyes had darkened with fear. With a few long strides he met her halfway. "What is it?"

"Your secretary is on the phone," Reba explained, laying a hand on his arm. "You can take it in the office. You'll have more privacy there."

For one instant Jamal didn't move. Yussuf, he thought with sudden fear. Then he regained a semblance of control. "Thanks. I know where it is." Glancing over his shoulder, he nodded sharply at Hassir to follow him, then walked into the house.

"Too bad, Pete couldn't make it," Reba said a few minutes later, joining her friend Rachel.

Rachel Levine shrugged. "That's the drawback when you date another pediatrician, especially someone working at the same hospital. One of us had to be on call." Hesitating briefly, she went on, "Have you come to a decision about that office space?"

Reba's eyes were drawn to the kitchen door. She couldn't forget the strained look on Jamal's face when she had called him to the phone. Hassir had followed him like a shadow, only to reappear seconds later to talk to Rafe. Since then the three men had been closed up in the house. Turning her attention back to her friend Rachel, she said, "Things should be fairly final by tomorrow evening."

A grin spread over Rachel's freckled pixie face, making her look more like one of her young patients than a doctor of thirty-three. "I knew you would go ahead with it. Harry," she called to a tall, lanky man with wavy dark hair, flirting with Reba's red-haired cousin Elaine nearby, "you owe me ten bucks."

With a few words and a smile that set every nurse's heart aflutter, Harry excused himself and crossed to Reba's side. "Not until she signs the contract," he teased.

"Your confidence in me is overwhelming," Reba said tartly. Sneaking another look at the house, she saw Rafe step outside and close the door. His face was deadpan, showing nothing—which was typically a sign that something was afoot. But when he stopped to talk to Matt, now supervising the carving of the meat, she relaxed a little, wondering if she had only imagined the sudden tension and the flash of fear in Jamal's eyes. Perhaps it had been a trick of the light.

Harry flicked Reba's cheek lightly to recall her attention. "Careful, *chiquita,* your heart's in your eyes," he warned gently. Then, because he'd been a little bit in love with her for years, he added, "After watching that dance a few minutes ago, maybe I should raise the bet to twenty."

"Take it, Rachel," Reba advised promptly, leaping at the challenge, but wondering how many others had noticed the pulsing need and the heady excitement that had rushed through her. It had meant nothing, she told herself. Hadn't she felt that same surge of power and weightlessness, that same rise of adrenaline every time she'd ridden over a six-foot wall? Arching her brows at Harry, she continued dryly, "I thought I saw a few sparks myself when you were flirting with Elaine."

"Jealous?" Harry asked casually, but with a gleam in his eye.

Reba reached up and patted his lean cheek. "Protective of Elaine. She's still young enough to take your flattery seriously."

He turned to Rachel. "Let's dance and see if we can't top Reba's performance."

"In this heat? Are you crazy?" Rachel protested as Harry began drawing her away.

For a moment Reba's gaze followed them. Why couldn't she have fallen in love with Harry? They shared so many things: their work, their ambitions, and even the same taste in Hitchcock classics. But when they met five years ago, she had needed a friend, not another relationship. They had been friends ever since. With a sigh she turned back to the house. Dinner was about to be served and she was needed in the kitchen.

From the window in Rafe's study, Jamal saw Harry's gesture and tensed. "Who's that dark-haired gigolo, Hassir?" he asked in Arabic.

Hassir moved away from the big Spanish oak desk and the telephone and peered over his master's shoulder. There were a number of dark-haired men, none of them gigolos, but even a one-eyed camel dung boy could have picked out the one his master meant, the one who was now smiling at Miss Reba. There was the hint of a smile on Hassir's lips. "He's a doctor at the hospital, but I don't remember his name."

At that moment a bell rang somewhere, its deep sound muted by the thick adobe walls. Outside, the guests stopped talking, put down their glasses and moved toward the food, obscuring Jamal's vision. "Go and eat, Hassir. This is going to be a long night."

Hassir hesitated. "What about you, master?"

Jamal shook his head and rubbed the back of his neck, willing the tension to flow out of him. The first sickening feeling, the fear that his father had collapsed, had disappeared. Alfred had assured him his father had been asleep when he called Basjad. The trouble was at their mission in New York.

Jamal began pacing again, needing the action to dispel some of his frustrations and his anger. "You better hurry. The helicopter will be here soon."

Reba heard the guttural flow of Arabic as she opened the door and the words "dinner is ready" froze on her lips. The air inside the room was thick with tension. Even before both men turned, she stiffened, an apology ready. "Am I disturbing you?"

Jamal stopped pacing near the phone. His control was such that he managed a smile. But Reba noticed that the softness didn't reach his eyes and that his body remained tense. "No. I was trying to convince Hassir to have something to eat."

Hassir frowned to himself as he walked toward her. It surprised Reba how the massive man could move so lightly, his soft leather boots barely making a sound on the oak-planked floor. "Why don't you stay here while I bring you a tray?" she offered.

Hassir stopped, hesitated, then shook his head. "That's kind of you." The prince would blister his ears if he allowed Miss Reba to serve him. "But perhaps you would be kind enough to bring a tray for my master. He—"

"Hassir!" This time the steel in Jamal's voice was unmistakable. Shrugging, the giant stepped into the hall.

"If you don't want to go outside," Reba called after him, "ask Maria to fix you a plate."

"Stop undermining my orders." Torn between amusement and irritation, Jamal sat down on one corner of the desk and crossed his arms over his chest. "I have enough trouble controlling him."

Reba closed the door, leaned against it and said tartly, "We abolished slavery more than a hundred years ago."

He didn't miss the faintly disapproving tone or the angled chin. His lips twitched and he felt his tension ease. She always seemed to have that effect on him. With a shake of his head he said, "Does Hassir behave like a slave? Sometimes I wonder which of us is master and which is servant. You just tipped the scales a little bit more in his favor."

"I didn't mean to interfere," Reba said swiftly. Encouraged by his smile, she stepped a little farther into the room. Hesitantly, expecting another rebuff, she went on, "I couldn't help but feel the tension when I burst in. Is something wrong?"

"Yes." For a moment he felt an overwhelming need to explain, to share his troubles. Then he turned away from his temptation and strode to the window, sliding his hands into his pockets and balling them into fists. He had enjoyed the past few days. He'd been tempted to forget about his duties and obligations and the clouds gathering. For a while he had felt just an ordinary man.

The bomb this afternoon had put an end to the illusion.

Glancing over his shoulder, he found her watching him with a hurt look in her eyes. He hesitated briefly, then relented. By tonight it would be in the news reports anyway. "A bomb went off in our mission in New York," he said grimly, his anger once again building.

Reba caught her breath. At that moment her only thought was, Thank God he's here. Then the shock passed and her mind began to function again. "Was anyone hurt?"

"One guard." He turned and walked back to the desk again. He hated the inactivity, the waiting. Patience had never been one of his strong points. He wasn't a man to sit back and allow the HIB to destroy what was his. He wanted those who had planted the bomb caught and punished.

He looked like a caged lion, angrily pacing, impatient for the gates to open so he could seek revenge. Her mouth went dry and she clenched her hands, wondering why he was still here, and glad he hadn't left and charged into danger.

"Do you know who is responsible?" His unruly hair had fallen onto his forehead again. When he stopped in front of her, she raised her hand and gently pushed it back.

"The HIB has claimed responsibility." That, too, would be on the news. For a moment he stared down at her, then he started pacing again.

Reba's hands curled into her skirt, twisting the soft cotton. "Again?" she asked, her voice rough with angry pain. "Don't they ever give up? How many more people are they going to kill? How many more families are they going to destroy? Can't anyone stop them?"

Her outburst froze Jamal in place, each of her angry words cutting into him like the blade of a knife. Her golden eyes were blazing with such glittering fire he wondered grimly what her reaction would be if she ever found out about his brother's role in the hijacking. "They will be caught and punished," Jamal promised harshly. Everyone but Muhrad, a voice inside him taunted.

He said it with such suppressed violence Reba shivered abruptly. "There are rumors about the major being extradited to Omari. Is that why they planted the bomb?"

Jamal shook his head. "Those rumors are false." Extradition would put the major right into his father's hands, the one thing he had been trying to prevent for months. "We feel the bomb was a warning directly related to my father's visit." A warning to Muhrad and to him himself, trying to cover up his brother's involvement with the HIB.

Fear settled like ice in Reba's stomach. Despite the heat, goose bumps formed on her skin at the thought of what might happen next week. "Surely your father is going to delay his trip."

Jamal walked to the window, searching the bright blue sky for a sign of the helicopter. "And let the HIB win? Of course not," he said harshly, turning back to Reba.

"But that's suicide," Reba argued hoarsely. She had almost lost her brother. She couldn't bear it if something happened to Jamal. "Can't you convince him to put off his trip until all the hijackers are caught?"

Jamal made a sharp negative movement with his head. "I'm not going to tell him to hide in Basjad until the threats have stopped! Even if he asked my advice, I would tell him to come."

Reba could understand why he wouldn't give in to terrorist threats. She even agreed with the principle. But Jamal said it without blinking, without any show of emotion, the way he must have watched the executions. She took a step backward at the steely, implacable look on his face. "You are a hard man, Jamal. Don't you care that your father would place himself in danger? Don't you care about your own life?"

"If we allowed this threat to intimidate us where would it end?" Jamal's eyes grew opaque and his mouth hardened into a thin straight line. "My father is the Emir of Omari."

And this man, standing so proudly before her, was Jamal ibn Yussuf, Prince of Omari. She had been warned by her brother and grandmother, had even said herself that to Jamal the title was not an empty one. But until now she had not truly accepted the complete truth. For all his ties to the West, his life belonged to Omari.

The small fantasies she had indulged in so briefly shriveled and died beneath Jamal's hard stare. "If you don't need anything, I have to get back to the other guests," she said quietly and turned to leave.

He should have let her go then. He should have sent her away with a swift nod and never looked back. Why he didn't do so, he didn't know. Perhaps because he was already on edge and his control was low. And also because he'd never denied himself, or been denied, the things he truly wanted. And he wanted Reba Davis. "Let them wait," he ordered arrogantly, striding toward her.

Opening the door, Reba hesitated briefly. "Do you want me to send Hassir back to you?"

"No!" Reaching past her, he closed the door with a bang, imprisoning her between his outstretched arms. He was so close he could see tiny flecks of pale gold flaming in her amber eyes. "I don't want Hassir. I want you."

Reba forgot to breathe. Blazing desire transformed his face into hard unyielding lines. Instinctively, she raised her arms to hold him off. "Don't touch me, Jamal," she protested, her eyes as turbulent as the sky during a storm. She tried to fade into the door, afraid that if he touched her, she would be lost.

Her movement snapped the last of his control. With his hands clamped around her wrists, he drew her against him. "Don't shrink from me. I'm the same man you wanted less than an hour ago."

"Your outsize ego won't let you see the difference between a flirtation and an invitation," she snapped, her breath quick and erratic now. "And I don't shrink."

He shifted his hold, one arm snaking around her waist; the other buried itself in her hair, tilting her head back. "Let's find out if I imagined it all."

She wasn't going to give an inch, Reba thought as his mouth came down on hers. She wasn't going to lose control and become another casualty of his fatal charm. She compressed her lips and her hands pushed against his chest, bracing herself for the assault. Silent resistance would be much more effective than an undignified struggle.

Jamal felt the need to conquer and to tame. He kissed her hot and hard, a swift, full-blown attack on her defenses, followed by retreat. The next charge was a taunting softness and lingering withdrawal, a sweetness that he knew weakened her. The third try was a full charge of touch and taste and scent, breaching the walls.

By then it was too late to resist, too late for control, too late to stem the tide of feelings swamping her. When his mouth came down again she tried one more evasion and turned her head away, only to find that the move gave him access to places far more sensitive than her lips, moist heat sliding up her throat. She caught her breath, then exhaled in a soft moan.

He was too skillful a lover to use force. His tongue parted her lips to coax and to tease. But the moment her lips opened he forgot about everything, losing himself in the taste and touch of her.

The kiss was everything she'd ever dreamed of. Not merely sparks, but fireworks. There were flashes of heat, frissons of excitement, thunder and lightning and a burst of glorious color that blinded her. For a moment she just stood within his arms, fascinated, stunned. Then her mouth opened, becoming eager, demanding, hot. The hands holding him off slid to his back, pulling him closer until their bodies were molded together.

Jamal's arm tightened around her. Her response was like Reba herself: honest, aggressive, giving. His tongue plunged deeper as if he couldn't get enough of her. And with each taste he slipped closer to the edge of sanity, wanting, needing more.

A knock on the door made them spring apart.

Dazed, Reba stumbled to the desk, steadying herself and keeping her back to the door.

Jamal ran a shaky hand through his hair and took a deep steadying breath before saying, "Come in."

Rafe opened the door, his eyes darting from Jamal to Reba. "The helicopter is here." Then, with a slight tightening of his mouth, he turned and walked down the hall, calling over his shoulder. "I'll direct him where to land."

Jamal stared after Rafe and cursed silently, his blood still thundering in his veins. How could he have lost himself in her so completely that he hadn't even heard the chopper arrive? Turning back into the room, he found Reba watching him with eyes that were too big for her face.

"You're flying to New York," she said, her voice tight with fear. Her fingers curled around the edge of the desk to keep herself from reaching for him. "Is it wise to take such a risk? Can't you send someone else?"

He shrugged impatiently. "Whom? Our ambassador in Washington has his hands full at the moment. Besides, I'll be so well protected I won't be able to breathe. You can be sure that quite a few cops and agents in New York are cursing me right now for keeping them from their beds tonight." The helicopter was almost overhead, filling the room with deafening noise and making the windowpanes ring like crystal bells.

Reba wrapped her arms around herself, waiting for the noise to die down while struggling against fear. Then she looked at Jamal, forcing a weak smile.

Jamal wasn't deceived. Despite her valiant effort, her bottom lip trembled and the smile didn't quite reach her eyes. Tenderness filled him, making him ache to take her back into his arms. "Little witch," he said softly, his deep voice caressing her. Because the need to touch her again was still barely controlled, he kept his distance. "I won't be able to ride with you tomorrow morning, but I made all the arrangements for you. Saiid, my head groom, is expecting you. When Rafe brought Ol' Ann yesterday, she wasn't too happy, but this morning she seemed to have settled down."

Then, without waiting for Reba's response, he turned away and left the room. There were so many other things he wanted to talk about. But perhaps, he thought walking down the tiled hall, it was just as well to leave them unsaid. For now.

Outside, the party had shifted to the front of the house. A lifetime of training allowed Jamal to move through the crowd with a smile here and a quick goodbye there without explaining himself. Hassir, he noticed, was out on the road waving the chopper down.

Rafe stood well back, beyond the stirring dust and the air turbulence. When Jamal joined him, he turned his head. "Be careful. If I can do anything, let me know."

Jamal nodded, hesitated briefly, then asked with a hint of humor in his deep voice, "Aren't you going to ask me what my intentions are, Rafe?"

Rafe hesitated briefly, then his hard mouth twisted ruefully, "Frankly, I'm not particularly thrilled, but that's beside the point," he said in his slow drawl. "Reba does as she pleases and she wouldn't thank me for meddling in her affairs. Besides, I have the feeling that it's too late to interfere."

Jamal slid his hands into his pockets and balled them into fists. To speak of Reba and "affairs" in the same breath was distasteful to him. "What makes you think I only want an affair with her?"

"At the moment you're hardly in a position to offer her anything else," Rafe replied dryly, raking his fingers through black hair. "You have more than enough problems on your hands without complicating your life even further."

Jamal touched Rafe's shoulder in a gesture of friendship he rarely showed, then walked to the helicopter without looking back.

Chapter 6

There were days when everything went wrong, Reba thought the following evening as she zipped into the builder's parking lot. Today had been one of them. First she'd overslept and been an hour late for work. At the hospital she'd found that Housekeeping had waxed and polished the floor to a high gloss, turning the hall and gym into a skating rink. Stripping the floor had played havoc with the schedule and everyone had missed lunch. Just when she'd thought they had caught up, one of the hot-pack machines had given up the ghost. And now a fender-bender on Pima Road had made her ten minutes late for her appointment.

Reba pulled into an empty parking spot, jumped from the car and ran toward the building as fast as her high heels allowed. Stopping in front of the tinted glass door, she nervously smoothed a few strands of hair back into her chignon, checked her reflection and opened the door.

The brown Mexican marble of the entryway floor also lined its walls. Cream-colored studded leather chairs and dark mahogany tables filled the space. Expensive and at the same time very conservative, Reba thought. Ronny, her lawyer, had informed her that while Mr. Buckman had a reputation for being rather inflexible, as a builder he was excellent.

Looking around, Reba didn't doubt it. The signs of success and quality were everywhere. The ambience of old wealth always made her uneasy, though, she thought, clutching her brown leather purse with damp hands. The foyer reminded her too much of the one at Toby's parents' house. The older Randalls had looked down their patrician noses at the small rancher's daughter—and one of mixed blood at that.

Trying to shrug off her uneasiness, Reba turned the corner sharply, then stopped in front of a glossy, dark-stained door. This was hardly the time to think of past humiliations, not when she was about to take one of the most important steps of her life.

She took a deep breath. There was no reason to be nervous, she told herself sternly. She was no pushover when it came to business. She had never found it easy to ask for payment from a patient who couldn't afford treatment, but insurance companies were another matter. Dealing with them had taught her to be tough and to persist no matter how many different forms she had to fill out. And today she was the buyer. That should give her an extra edge. Thus armed, she breezed into the suite.

The reception area resembled the foyer, except that here a thick cream carpet covered the floor and gold-framed landscapes hung on the walls. Turning to the sleek brunette at the reception desk, she said, "I'm Reba Davis. I have an appointment with Mr. Buckman."

The woman's scarlet mouth slackened a bit, then tightened into a thin red line. "You're late, Ms. Davis," she pointed out, staring at Reba down her long elegant nose.

Reba was tempted to check her slim brown linen dress. Was she missing one of the shiny brass buttons? Had she torn her pocket on the car door? But she knew that it wasn't a lost button or a torn pocket that had prompted the woman's rudeness. More likely it was the color of her skin and hair. Reba's back straightened a little. She'd dealt with prejudice before, though she hadn't expected it here. "Has Mr. Buckman already left?" she asked calmly.

"No. But he is a busy man."

"Then perhaps you shouldn't keep him waiting any longer," Reba suggested firmly and had the satisfaction of seeing Miss Edith Reeves, as her name tag stated, get to her feet and disappear into the inner office without further delay. Frowning, Reba wondered if Miss Reeves's attitude reflected that of her boss.

There was, however, no sign of resentment in the smooth businesslike manner with which the builder greeted her. But her suspicions didn't die. Perhaps it was because of his slight resemblance to Toby's father—the smooth tanned face and expertly cut, graying blond hair. Whatever it was, it made her brace her shoulders as she sat in the maroon leather chair.

Dan Buckman sat down behind the mahogany desk and rolled out the blueprints in front of him. "I've looked over the changes you want done." His pale blue eyes met hers briefly, then gazed lower, following the long line of her legs.

Reba stiffened imperceptibly. Had she done Miss Reeves an injustice? Had the receptionist seen her as a rival instead? "Will the changes cause problems?" she asked coolly.

"Yes. But I'm certain we can come to some agreement." He placed a smooth manicured finger on the blueprint. "My architect pointed out that an exit door here would spoil the appearance of the rear of the building. I tend to agree with him."

"I won't get Medicare or Medicaid approval without it," Reba reminded him firmly.

"I realize that." Again his eyes slid over her, more direct now. "We came up with an alternative solution, though." He pointed at a window overlooking the parking lot. "If we put the exit here, it would hardly be noticeable. The disadvantage is that we'd have to build a ramp. There will be a significant drop between the first floor and the parking lot. Built in a straight line, the ramp would be too steep to meet the building codes. In order to comply with regulations, it would have to run alongside the building and end at the rear."

Looking at the blueprints, Reba estimated the length of the ramp at about twenty-five feet. It would cost a small fortune to build. Was that the subtle game Dan Buckman was playing? Pricing the office so high it would be out of her reach? Steeling herself for the next hurdle, she asked, "Is that the only possible solution?"

"I'm afraid so." He leaned back in his chair, a small smile on his face. "The other changes are fairly simple, if expensive. The special floor, the plumbing in the whirlpool area and the extra wiring you require won't come cheap. I don't have all the cost estimates at hand, so I can't quote you an exact price, but it's safe to say that all these changes will nearly double the original price." He smiled fully this time, revealing sharp, slightly yellowish teeth. "Perhaps if we sit down together, we can cut corners some place."

The emphasis was definitely on "together" and "corners," Reba thought angrily, wondering how much he would be willing to lower the price. To hell with it, she thought, rising unhurriedly to her feet. "I'd appreciate it if you'd send the new cost estimates to my lawyer. I will give you my decision then." Later, when she was alone, she would kick something, cry her heart out or both. But for now, she was determined to keep smiling even if it killed her.

"If you insist." His pale brows drew together in a slight frown, as if he hadn't expected her persistence.

That made her forced smile seem a little more natural, though it didn't diminish her anger or lessen the pain. "I do." With her head held high, she walked out of the office, stopped briefly at the reception desk to hand Miss Reeves her lawyer's card, then made for her car.

Sliding into the seat, she sat with her hands clenched around the wheel and her shoulders slumped in defeat. Was she always reaching too high? she wondered, tears pricking her eyes. Was that why her dreams never became reality? With slow mechanical movements she slid the key into the ignition, started the engine and headed back home, for once not sparing a single glance at the many building sites littering Scottsdale.

"Thanks for a smooth flight, Jerry." Jamal shook hands with his pilot, walked down the steps of the plane and crossed the tarmac to the black stretch limousine waiting a few feet away. A wave of heat, noise and diesel fumes engulfed him, making his eyes burn and the dull pain at the back of his head throb with renewed intensity. With a grateful nod and a muttered "Salaam" for Rashid, his chauffeur, he sank into the haven of the limousine's soft gray velour and closed his scratchy eyes. The door was closed and he was finally alone.

Silence. Blessed, cool, tinted silence.

For a moment he sat, trying to keep his mind blank and allow quietness to seep in, but frustration kept gnawing at him. This whole damn affair was rapidly getting out of control, involving him more deeply with each passing day. Restless, he opened the bar, poured himself a glass of water and drank it while he watched Hassir and Rashid handle the luggage.

"What are you going to do about Abdul Assam, Jamal?" Alfred asked a few minutes later, joining him.

Frowning, Jamal watched Alfred place his black leather briefcase at his feet and buckle his seat belt. "Nothing. At least not until after my father's visit." Under different circumstances he would have fired the mission chief on the spot for posting only one security guard, and an inexperienced one at that, while the rest of the staff had left to watch the Labor Day parade. Unfortunately, Assam was Muhrad's first cousin and, Jamal suspected, deeply involved in his brother's affairs. It was the only plausible explanation of why Assam had ignored the security alert. The fool had believed that he had nothing to fear from the HIB.

Taking off his glasses, Alfred shot Jamal a searching look. "The man is getting senile. He must have asked me at least five times to mention to you that his appointment is running out in three months."

Jamal smiled grimly. "He knows well enough that the renewal rests with Muhrad and not with me."

Cleaning his lenses, Alfred muttered something about rats leaving a sinking ship.

Beneath his half-lowered lids, Jamal's eyes became sharp and wary. How much did Alfred guess? "You never miss a beat, do you?"

"Not often," Alfred agreed calmly, replacing his glasses. "That's why you hired me."

"Then perhaps you can tell me if my father knows anything. Sometimes I find it hard to believe that he suspects nothing."

Alfred shrugged. "He's been different lately, more quiet, not his usual irascible self, but then he hasn't been well."

"He gave me free rein to deal with Assam." Jamal frowned. Never before had his father placed him in direct confrontation with Muhrad.

"Perhaps he left the decision up to you because Muhrad is still with the Al Assam tribe." Alfred shook his head. "Sometimes I don't understand you. Why don't you want to rule? The bedouins have been grumbling for years about Muhrad's lack of interest in their affairs. Over the past few months several council members have approached you. You even have the Imams eating out of your hand."

"That would change the moment I took control." Jamal dismissed the words quietly. "Have you ever known a country where all parties are content? Besides, except for this sordid affair, Muhrad has not been negligent. His ideas simply differ from mine. And he is my brother, for God's sake. And then there's Hussein." Jamal took a sip of water. "After this weekend, the position may be forced on me anyway. So let's enjoy the last two days of our vacation, Alfred," he advised.

"Some vacation!" Alfred reached for the phone and punched in a set of numbers to call Mellie, Jamal's housekeeper, adding lightly, "Your crazy life-style leaves little time for pleasure. Now, if you had a wife and some kids and settled down perhaps the rest of us would have time for dates and such." Then he spoke into the phone. "Mellie, we're leaving the airport now."

As if on cue the trunk lid closed, Rashid and Hassir slid into the front seats and closed their doors, and the limousine slowly moved forward.

Marriage had never really entered Jamal's mind. For him, falling in love would never be simple. He wanted, needed, more than his father had. Yussuf had married Azadeh, the daughter of the powerful sheikh of the Al Assam, to secure his position; he had married Kitty for love. Both matches had failed.

Love alone, as he had learned from his parents' example, simply wasn't enough. Perhaps that was why he had never allowed himself to look at a woman with permanence in mind. It was true that Azadeh had made his mother's life hell, but hate and fear had only been catalysts. Kitty's free spirit had slowly died in the desert heat, and from the many restrictions imposed on Muslim wives. If she'd stayed in Omari, her love would have died, too.

Alfred interrupted his thoughts, hanging up the phone as he said, "Mellie said that Ms. Davis did not come to the stables today."

Jamal frowned, feeling the tension return full force. "Perhaps she was too busy." Perhaps she had never intended to ride. No, that didn't sound like Reba, Jamal thought. In some ways she was wonderfully predictable. Once she'd given her word she would stick to it like glue. And she certainly wasn't reluctant to speak her mind, whether it angered him or not. Perhaps, though, he had scared her away, after the way he had lost control in the study.

If his head hadn't felt like cotton wool he could have come up with a hundred logical reasons why Reba hadn't made it to his ranch. Instead, his imagination ran away with him— could it have been a flat tire on a lonely stretch of road between the ranch and Scottsdale? A crazy patient, or even an accident? He reached for the phone, then stopped, suddenly realizing that he didn't know her number or her address. He started to punch Information when he saw Alfred draw his brown address book from the briefcase.

"Sometimes your perception scares me," Jamal muttered, then pressed the numbers Alfred read to him.

"Perception, my foot." Alfred slid the book back into the case. "Even a blind man could have read your thoughts."

Which was a warning that he was so damn tired his emotions were too close to the surface. Impatiently, Jamal counted the rings, wondering what he would do if she didn't answer the phone. Call Rafe? Call the hospital? Call—

"Yes?"

He hadn't realized how much he had needed to hear her voice, that husky, sometimes astringent and always so wonderfully sane voice. With his world slowly spinning beyond his control, he needed the sanity most of all. Even the one breathless word was enough to diffuse the restless energy that had kept him going since yesterday afternoon. "You didn't ride this morning."

At the unexpected sound of his deep voice, Reba sat down on the side of her bed, glancing at the TV where she'd watched Jamal on the evening news only moments ago. He'd been so surrounded by security men she'd barely caught a glimpse of him. Now pleasure ran through her all the way down to her bare toes. Pushing her wet hair from her face, she said, "I overslept. I was an hour late for work."

In the background she could hear the high-pitched whine of jet engines. Obviously, he was at the airport, but which one? New York? Or had he flown on to Washington? "Where are you calling from?"

"The airport."

"Very funny. Which one?"

"Here."

"But how? I just—" She caught herself before she blurted out that she had watched the news, no, had watched him. Then she started again, more cautiously this time. "You certainly made the trip in record time. You must be exhausted."

His mouth twisted in a wry smile as he tugged at his tie. He was an expert at reading between the lines. Not that it would have taken an expert to interpret her reactions. As long as she had believed him thousands of miles away, she had felt safe enough to lower her guard. She also had watched the news, not to keep up with world events, but because of him. Why else would she try to hide the fact? And now, knowing that he was but a few miles way, she was crawling back into her shell.

"A little," he admitted cautiously. He was getting to know how her mind worked. If he told her that he was utterly exhausted, she would use it as a reason not to see him. And he needed to see her. He hadn't rushed back only to hear her voice, which he could have done from New York,

Omari or anywhere else in the world. No, he had wanted to see her, to touch her, to be with her. It sounded crazy, dangerous. And wonderfully sane. "Have you eaten yet?"

After the bout of self-pity she'd indulged in upon her return to the apartment, she was in no mood for company. And the mere thought of food made her stomach turn. All she wanted to do was pull the covers over her head and forget about this awful day. But there was such weariness in his voice, a roughness that tugged at her heart. She shook her head, realized that he couldn't see her and said, "No." On impulse she added, "I was just about to heat up some leftovers Maria packed for me. Are you interested?" Then she realized that she'd just offered leftovers to a prince and groaned. "Have you ever eaten leftovers in your life?"

He grinned widely, the first carefree smile since he'd left Arizona. His thoughts flew back to a small ranch house in East Texas and the pot of black-eyed peas his grandmother had restocked every morning. "I've eaten my share. I'll pick you up in twenty minutes. We'll have dinner at my house. Not because I don't want to eat leftovers, but because I have to make a few phone calls later on." It wasn't a lie; he did need to check on Muhrad, and his father was expecting a full report. But it also wasn't the complete truth either. Tired or not, he still wanted her. With Mellie, Alfred and Hassir as chaperons, his home would be less intimate than an apartment.

What did a woman wear for dinner with a prince?

After hanging up the phone, Reba had raced into the bathroom and dried her hair in record time, only to waste precious minutes staring at the clothes she owned.

She had nothing to wear!

Her walk-in closet was filled with everything from evening gowns to riding gear, but not one garment seemed appropriate. He had already seen the white dress. The blue silk jumpsuit was a little too clinging and sexy. In the end she settled for a pair of black satiny pyjama-style pants and a loose, white silk blouse, a wide, beaded turquoise belt and mid-heeled sandals. Simple, understated elegance and not sexy at all.

When the knock came, she was fastening the buckle of her second shoe. With a passing look in the mirror, she raced downstairs and threw open the door.

He looked tired and drawn. The light was behind him, glinting in his hair, but his face was all deep lines and shadows. His eyes were a dull mud brown and his mouth was tightly compressed. She wanted to hug him, soothe away the tension and tell him how good it was to see him. Caution made her keep her distance. "You didn't sleep at all."

"I dozed on the plane." Jamal walked inside, closed the door and leaned against it. She had left her hair loose, pushed behind one ear, revealing the long elegant line of her neck. A clean, lemony scent drifted toward him, spicy and fresh. He breathed in deeply and some of the weariness seemed to flow out of him. "I like your outfit," he said, running his eyes over her. "It's very sexy."

Reba shot him a rueful grin. "That wasn't my intention."

Cocking one dark brow, he studied the white silk shirt, blousing above her small waist and caressing the gentle swell of her hips, then followed the long line of her legs. Somehow, she appeared more fragile today. "Very elegant," he modified obligingly, eyes glinting. "And sensual enough to make me want to carry you upstairs."

"Stop it." Reba groaned, heat bubbling like champagne in her veins. He had taken off his jacket, removed his tie and opened the top buttons of his shirt, but he still wore dark suit pants, soft leather dress shoes and gold halfmoon cufflinks in his sleeves. For all his teasing, he'd been too weary to change, she thought. Impulsively, she laid a hand on his arm. "I watched the news. It looked so grim. They said the man who died was young."

Somehow her touch seemed to draw the words right out of him. Not about the destruction of the building, another increase in security, lodging complaints at the U.N. with some of the countries known to support the HIB. But the one fact that should have taken precedence over everything, and that had been merely labelled "unfortunate." A man had died. A young man. "Faisal was only twenty-three years old. He left an eighteen-year-old wife and a six-month-old son."

Reba was moved by the frustration and the bitterness she heard in his voice. "I'm so sorry for his poor wife."

"His wife and child will be taken care off." Jamal grimaced. "I'm not sure I did them a favor settling a pension on them, though." Seeing Reba's puzzled look, he explained. "The pension will be administered by the head of the family. If her father-in-law is poor, he may not want to lose the income and may refuse other offers of marriage for her."

"But that's cruel," Reba protested. "Can't you arrange it so that she'll have at least some say over how it will be spent?"

Jamal nodded, smiling slightly at her reaction. "I could, but I doubt that it would change anything. Even if she received the money outright, she would still be expected to hand it over to her family."

Reba shook her head in disagreement. "One option gives the woman a choice and control if she really desires it, the other makes her totally dependent on someone else. Right now, it may not seem to make a difference either way. But you've said yourself that traditions are changing, so why condemn her to live in the past instead of the future?"

Jamal looked at her quizzically, wondering at her agitation. "If it means so much to you, I'll do it your way," he agreed softly. The smile she gave him made him cover her hand with his. He would have pulled her into his arms, if she hadn't stiffened slightly. So, she was still wary of him, he thought wryly. "Are you ready to go?"

"Just about. I have to get my purse and keys." Withdrawing her hand, she stepped back and walked to the coat closet. As she opened the door, she looked over her shoulder and teased. "Is one allowed to keep princes waiting?"

He smiled in response and some of the arrogance returned. "Just this once. Because I gave you such short notice."

"How generous," Reba quipped, reaching for her purse on the top shelf. It felt good that the tension eased.

As she stretched with the smooth unhurried movements of a cat, he felt his body stir. He wanted to make love with her, slowly, gently, feeling her strong, slender body merge with his. He wanted to bury himself in her warmth and forget about Faisal and Muhrad. The intensity of his feelings rooted him to the floor.

His glance slid past her to the white walls where watercolors of desert landscapes hung. He recognized the smooth lines and soft shades from the paintings he'd seen at the ranch house; they must have been her mother's work. Apart from the kitchen to his right there seemed to be only one large room downstairs, furnished with big, comfortable mauve and muted turquoise couches and chairs, glass tables and light wood bookshelves. The color scheme was repeated in the kitchen with its bleached oak cabinets and mauve and turquoise tiles.

"I like your apartment," he said, watching her transfer her keys and billfold from one purse to another.

"Thank you." She looked up, pleasure lightening her eyes. "I bought it after I started working at the Rana Clinic." She'd paid for it with the proceeds from the sale of Sir Lance. "Before the accident I lived on the ranch and worked part-time at the hospital in Broken Promise. But it's too long a drive from the ranch to the Clinic to commute."

"And you needed to get away."

"Yes." She closed her purse with a snap and gave him a level look. "Since we are speaking openly..."

"You always meet trouble head-on." Amused, Jamal leaned against the door.

Reba bristled. "Are you saying I've no finesse?"

He raised his hand, palm up, in a gesture of peace. "I prefer directness to evasions. By all means let's be open." He dropped his hand, slid it back into his pocket and continued, "Yesterday afternoon shouldn't have happened. Not in the manner it did, anyway." He smiled ruefully. "We could begin to apologize all over again. I guess this time it would be my turn."

She shook her head, torn between frustration and exasperation. "I wish you hadn't said that. I feel much safer when I'm annoyed with you."

Chuckling, he pushed himself away from the door, crossed the space between them with long smooth strides and raised his hands to her face. "All right. I'm not going to apologize for something that is going to happen again." Softly, gently, he kissed her lips. "Does that make you feel safer?"

His eyes were not secretive or glinting now, but a clear burning flame of longing and need. "I—" She managed to turn her head away and said, "I won't be another notch on your bedpost, Jamal."

He brushed her cheek lightly with the back of his hand. "Are we back on that subject again? You seem to be obsessed with my affairs. I wonder why that is?"

Reba managed a casual shrug and moved past him to the door. It was a question she didn't want to answer, especially not out loud.

"What a marvelous view you have from up here." Reba leaned against the three-foot wall of the veranda and looked out over the hills. Dusk was settling, casting long shadows over the valley. Here and there lights began to twinkle like a Milky Way of distant silent stars. A slight breeze teased her hair and the air smelled sweet and fresh. She sighed. Standing here, she could almost forget that afternoon's ugly scene with Mr. Buckman.

"I'd almost given up looking for a suitable place for the stud when my mother heard of this one." Jamal filled two goblets with wine, returned the bottle to the silver cooler, then slowly walked over to her. "It suits me. There's plenty of land for the horses to roam."

"Roam free? Isn't that a little risky?" she asked, turning around. The hacienda-style house had been built on a hill, its U-shape open toward the valley below. With its heavy carved oak doors and wrought-iron grilles covering the windows it looked solid and comfortable rather than ostentatious. The living room she had passed through on her way outside was larger than her entire apartment, and was furnished with leather, wood and glass. Compared to the Randalls' overdecorated rooms, Jamal's home seemed rather austere. And comfortable.

Jamal handed her a glass of Chardonnay and leaned by her side, giving her a sharp, searching look. Some of her usual sparkle seemed to be missing. There was a droop to her mouth when she thought herself unobserved. "Well, not completely free" he answered her. "There are fences and herdsmen, but yes, I allow them to run during the day. Most of the horses are desert bred and never saw stables until I bought them." He leaned across the wall and pointed to a cluster of mesquite bushes. "There's one group on their way home now."

Following his hand, Reba spotted them, small and dainty looking from up here, running with their tails flowing and their beautiful heads proudly raised. The sight blew Dan Buckman right from her mind and she smiled naturally. "They're a beautiful sight running free like that."

This time her smile was so spontaneous and free that he knew he hadn't imagined the shadows. He didn't have to be clairvoyant to guess at the cause of the trouble, either. "You had a meeting with the builder today. What happened?"

How could he have possibly remembered that? Reba wondered, tasting the wine. He had more than enough on his mind and there was no need to burden him with her troubles. Compared to what he'd dealt with during the past twenty-four hours, the loss of her office seemed so small. She shrugged, trying to look and sound casual. "He upped the price. I didn't want to pay it." She took another sip to wash down the bitterness, then added lightly, "So tomorrow I'll start looking again."

"Did he give you a written quote or did he merely mention a price over the phone?" Anger curled in his stomach and his fingers tightened around the slim crystal stem.

"Everything is in writing. I made certain of it. But that's not worth the paper it's written on," she said, unable to keep the bitterness from showing. "There are always loopholes."

Jamal remembered how she had looked Saturday night, excited, happy, with stars in her eyes. Now he wanted to take her into his arms, hold her and kiss away the pain. But today his control was almost nonexistent. This time, he might not allow her to run from him. "Let me have a look at it."

She shook her head, watching the herdsman below come into view. "It wouldn't do any good. Oh, I don't want to talk about it anymore. I'll find another place." Turning, she faced the courtyard where flowers lined the walkways and surrounded a fountain with water spilling over its rim. "It's so peaceful up here," she said, watching through the glass doors as the housekeeper, a slim elderly woman with a Texas accent, placed another setting on the dining room table.

"I could buy the building for you."

Reba smiled wryly. He was talking about buying a building at the drop of a hat, while she had scrimped and saved for years and still couldn't meet the builder's price. "I doubt that Dan Buckman would want to sell. He's already leased five of the six suites. The place is a gold mine.''

''That should please my accountants. Personally, I couldn't care less. And after I'm through with him, he will ask me to buy.'' The grim purpose in his voice wiped the smile from her face.

''I thought you were joking.'' But his eyes showed her that he was dead serious. She suddenly realized that Jamal had the power to destroy Dan Buckman with a single order. Her mouth went dry, wishing she hadn't mentioned the builder's name. ''Jamal, the man has the right to choose his tenants. It's his building.''

''Discrimination is against the law,'' Jamal pointed out harshly. ''Or did he harass you?''

''Neither,'' Reba denied firmly, describing the changes that had upped the price. Dan Buckman wasn't worth the time they were wasting discussing him. She would feel guilty for the rest of her life if Jamal punished him. Buckman wasn't worth one sleepless night, much less a lifetime of guilt. ''I really did change my mind.''

Because Jamal didn't look convinced, she laid her hand on his arm for emphasis. ''Thank you for caring.'' Her brows rose. ''Not for offering to buy the building, though.'' When he started to protest, she shook her head firmly and added, ''If I had wanted the office at any cost I would have gone to Rafe for a loan.''

''Buckman doesn't deserve to get off so lightly,'' he growled.

Reba grimaced. Like her brother, Jamal had a strong protective streak.

Jamal shook his head impatiently. ''Sometimes, Reba, you amaze me. Don't you have any capacity for hate?''

''Oh, I do. I hope that the major will be buried in a maximum security prison for the rest of his life,'' Reba said heatedly. Then she shrugged and continued in a calmer voice, "But why should I waste strong feelings on a man like Buckman?"

Jamal stiffened imperceptibly, silently cursing his brother once again. Staring at her pure profile, he wondered what her reaction would be if she found out the truth. He knew she wouldn't blame him for Muhrad's deeds. Reba was one of the most fair-minded people he knew. Still, he felt a growing uneasiness when he tried to predict her reaction if she found out that he was shielding his brother from the consequences of his actions.

Jamal tossed back his wine, trying to wash away the bitter taste. There was no reason why she should ever find out the truth, he told himself. There was no reason to feel guilty! Hell, even Rafe understood the political and personal necessity for the cover-up and he had been the major's victim.

"Is it really that simple for you to forgive and forget insults?" he asked tightly.

"No. Not always," Reba admitted honestly, twirling the stem of the goblet between her fingers. "When my *ex*-fiancé took one look at me after the accident and ran, I was so hurt and angry I wanted to scratch his eyes out." She grimaced. "Lucky for him, and me, my arm was in a cast."

He could deal with hurt and anger, Jamal thought, relieved. The only thing he wouldn't be able to handle was her hate. Then the rest of her words sank in and his eyes narrowed. "Fiancé?"

She grinned at him, sudden mischief dancing in her eyes. "A louse named Toby."

"I see." The sudden surge of jealousy made his voice hard and clipped. "Did you love him?"

"Of course. At least I thought I did. At the time we were both part of the national equestrian team. We shared the same goals. We were constantly together, training, traveling, competing. Perhaps that's why we became engaged. Then the accident happened." She took another sip. "I wasn't a pretty sight right afterward, all black and blue and bruised. Toby was horrified and ran.'' When Jamal swore beneath his breath, she shook her head. "He didn't intend to be cruel. There are people who simply cannot face the ugly side of life.''

"The damn coward left you to pick up the pieces of your life when you needed him most,'' Jamal said, his voice rough with anger and disgust. Setting down his glass on the wall, he drew her into his arms. No wonder she was afraid to trust and afraid to feel. Tilting up her face, he kissed her with a tenderness that brought tears to her eyes.

She blinked them away and reached for him, feeling a tremor run through his strong body. He, too, needed holding, she thought. She embraced him fiercely, deepening the kiss, trying to heal him as he was healing her.

Chapter 7

The morning was bright, fresh and cool. No breeze stirred the leaves of the bushes lining the road from the main house to the stables. No cloud marred the deep azure of the sky. Smiling, Reba clung to the grab bar of the open Jeep, her face tilted into the wind.

When Jamal took her home after dinner last night she'd felt better than she had in a long while. Bright, clear mornings shouldn't be romantic. Five o'clock alarms should make even an early riser feel grumpy, especially after less than six hours of sleep. Yesterday's events should have made her feel depressed, discouraged and angry. Instead, the morning was pure magic.

And the man driving the Jeep was the reason. This morning, booted and spurred, with the tired lines erased by sleep, he was once again the arrogant, powerful lord of all he surveyed. But Reba saw subtle differences. His hard face was more relaxed and the glints in his eyes warmer, as if last night had cracked the icy barriers he usually surrounded himself with. She wasn't quite certain how to deal with the

change. It was easier to keep to her side of the fence when
he kept to his, she thought, watching the wind ruffle his
tawny hair.

The stables with their red-tiled roofs, arched windows and
brass-studded gates were a mixture of Old World charm and
modern efficiency. Although it was barely six o'clock, the
activity at the stud farm was brisk. Young grooms in West-
ern-style work jeans, cowboy shirts and hats worked side by
side with older men in flowing Arab robes, cleaning stables
and tack, grooming and exercising horses in the white-
fenced training field.

When Jamal drove the Jeep into the yard, all activities
seemed to stop. Men bowed, touched their foreheads in the
traditional Arab greeting, salaamed, then returned to their
jobs. No one seemed surprised by Jamal's early arrival,
Reba noticed. "Do you always ride at six?"

Jamal parked the Jeep in the shade of the building, cut
the engine and looked at her. The short drive from the house
had tousled her hair. Her skin was glowing and her eyes were
a warm gold. Like the morning, she was fresh and radiant,
so different from the painted women of the jet set, who
rarely rose before noon. Lifting his hand, he pushed back a
few strands of black silk the wind had blown into her face.
"Yes," he said with a wicked grin. "And, in Basjad, even
earlier. By ten o'clock it's so hot there, you can fry eggs on
the asphalt."

"And at night it's supposed to be so cold that the egg
whites freeze. I've heard that story before," Reba scoffed.

"I once tried it and the eggs do jell. There was a dip in the
concrete outside my brother's apartments that had the shape
of a frying pan." He brushed back his hair with a rueful
grin. "Muhrad, I remember, was furious when he stepped
into the mess." His brother had called him a spoiled, ob-
noxious American brat, a phrase that had been a sign of reluctant affection as well as insult. During the early years
Muhrad had been pleased to see him when he'd returned

from his six months abroad, although the good times had rarely survived the first month of his stay.

Reba chuckled. "How old were you?"

"Six. Maybe seven." He hadn't thought of the prank in years, much less talked about it. He'd learned very early in life to guard his words. Even his parents had not been above using his confidences to their advantage in their tug of love. What was it about Reba that made him want to share even such inconsequential things as his childhood pranks?

He was a man who planned for the future, but who lived in the present and who rarely dwelt on the past. Yet lately, he seemed to have been doing just that. Perhaps the reason was that there was no certain future beyond his father's visit, while the past had a kind of comforting stability. Jamal shifted restlessly.

"It must have been difficult for you to leave your brother for six months every year." How much happier her own childhood had been, Reba thought. Money had always been a little tight, especially before her mother's paintings had begun to sell. But they had been rich in the important things, things money couldn't buy, like laughter, security, love.

Jamal shook his head. "We didn't have the close relationship you and Rafe share. There's an eight-year gap between Muhrad and me."

"Eight years, different customs and different faiths." Reba watched a groom lead Ol' Ann from the first building, but didn't make a move to get out of the Jeep. Jamal so rarely talked about himself she was reluctant to interrupt his mellow mood. With each day her need to know more about him grew.

"They are also my customs," Jamal corrected her gently.

"You love Omari."

"Yes. It's as much a part of me as this country," he said simply. "When I was a child I imagined that I lived in a time warp. For six months I'd play with rockets and watch episodes of 'Star Trek' being filmed. The rest of the year I rode camels and horses and slept beneath the stars.''

Reba smiled. ''That sounds like every child's dream. Did you live with the Bedouins the whole time you were there?''

''As much as possible. The desert has always drawn me. It is so timeless, a vast untouched emptiness that captures a man's soul.''

Reba felt a chill feather down her spine at the soft sound of his voice. Bright, clear mornings also had another side to them. They ripped fantasies to shreds, making a person face reality. Jamal might consider himself half American, and perhaps intellectually that was true, but Omari was his home, his first love. It wasn't his position or his obligations that tied him to the East, but his heart. And any woman foolish enough to fall in love with him would have to accept that she would have to share him. She would always come second place in his affections. He would leave her again and again, the way he had walked out of her brother's study and the way he would leave again in two days' time. Without a backward glance. She didn't want to love a man who could never be hers. ''It's getting late,'' she said, reaching for the door handle.

Jamal saw her eyes cloud and the warmth fade from her smile. She was crawling back into her shell again but he wasn't quite ready yet to allow her to withdraw. Softly, he rubbed his thumb over her unpainted mouth. ''You are stunningly beautiful, even so early in the morning.''

Reba felt his touch all the way to her toes. She tried to ignore the waves of pleasure, tried to find the strength to move her head away. But her body seemed to have a mind of its own. Even her voice sounded breathless and husky. ''Why are you doing this, Jamal?''

''Because it gives me pleasure.'' He slid his hand along her jaw and down the long slender column of her throat where her pulse beat erratically. The vision of Reba waking up in his arms, her golden eyes still drowsy with sleep, her lips swollen from his kisses, made his hand tighten with need.

Two more days.

He had promised himself not to take her until after his father's visit, but it was getting more and more difficult with each day to keep his hands off her. He wanted to turn the Jeep around, to carry her to his bed and spend the day losing himself in her.

Then he felt her stiffen and dropped his hand with a crooked smile. "I think you must be the only woman who doesn't like to be told that she's beautiful," he said huskily.

Reba shrugged. "Looks are only skin deep and temporary at best."

Something close to anger flashed in Jamal's eyes, but his voice was light when he said, "Not all men are stupid."

At this moment she wished that she was beautiful enough to draw Jamal back to Arizona after his father's visit. She wanted to be so beautiful that he'd forget about the Leonie Walterses of this world. Dreamer. "Jamal, I came here to ride, not to be seduced," she said wryly.

He laughed and gave her a long hot look from beneath half-lowered lashes. Then he vaulted out of the Jeep. Walking around to her side, he said, "How much time do you have?"

She checked her watch. "An hour. The clinic's a good twenty-minute drive from here. Besides, sixty minutes in the saddle is about all I think I can handle at this point. Once I get more confident I'd like to take longer than an hour, though. When do your men start in the morning?" Work at Rafe's ranch started at six, but these men seemed to have been up for hours.

"At dawn, after prayers. And no, I'm not a slave driver," he added, seeing a reproachful look come into her eyes.

She grimaced. "You always put words into my mouth." He wasn't unkind; Hassir and Alfred, she had noticed, were devoted to him. But he did demand instant obedience and efficiency.

Jamal opened the door and held out his hand, leaving her no choice but to accept it. "Perhaps because you're not saying the right ones," he said softly. "You can't hold me off forever, Reba. Sometime soon you'll have to make up your mind."

She was angry with herself that the mere touch of his hand or his smile could so easily make her want to accept what he offered. Two nights in his arms, two nights of hot, consuming passion and tenderness. She had no doubt that she would find everything she'd ever dreamed of in his bed. But the dreams she wanted were the kind that lasted and grew. She wouldn't, couldn't take him seriously.

She slid from the Jeep and said lightly, "Jamal, you're used to taking what you want. And for some reason you've settled on me this time. I'm not fool enough to deny that you stir something in me. But the moment I take you seriously you'll be on a plane to I don't know where."

Five days ago that might have been true. Even three days ago, he would have denied that he felt more for her than a passing interest. But last night had shown him that there was something deeper, something more powerful between them. "I might decide to take you with me. We could fly around the world together," he said lightly, brushing his lips over her hand.

Furious, Reba snatched her hand away and wiped it on her jeans. "Do you ever pause to think that I may not want to go? That I am perfectly content with my life here?" Out of the corner of her eye she spotted a slender Arab with snow-white hair and skin like dark leather leading a black stallion toward them and lowered her voice. "Thanks for the offer and the warning, Your Highness, but I'm not interested." With long angry strides she crossed the yard to Ol' Ann's side. Thanking the groom holding the mare, she ran a hand over the smooth neck.

"I'm not going to join his harem," she muttered to herself fiercely. She might not be an heiress or a socialite, but she had her pride. Take her with him indeed! And what was she going to do while they flew around the world? Twiddle her thumbs? She couldn't imagine herself as a lady of leisure, perfumed and with long, painted nails. Perfumes gave her headaches and she'd chew her nails to the quick wondering every morning if this was the day he would hand her a plane ticket home.

Gripping the saddle horn, Reba put her boot in the stirrup and mounted almost as smoothly as she had in the old days. Only when she settled into the saddle did she realize that she had just mounted without hesitation or fear. Stunned, she sat there for a moment, anger fading, a slow smile curling her lips. Taking the reins from the groom, she said very softly, "I did it."

"Very impressive." Jamal curled his fingers around his belt to keep from snatching her off the horse and kissing her glowing face. He couldn't have distracted her better even if he'd planned to make her mad. The trick was to keep Reba's mind off her fears. As long as she was annoyed with him, she'd forget to be scared. "Now take her around the yard." He deliberately made it an order, then almost laughed out loud when her chin came up and she nudged the mare into a walk.

Grinning, Jamal turned to take the stallion's reins from Saiid, his groom, when he saw Annie toss her head and sidestep nervously. Within moments Reba had the mare under control. Frowning, Jamal turned back to Saiid. "Tomorrow morning I want you to ride the stubbornness out of that mare before Miss Davis gets here," he said, running a calming hand over his horse's arched neck.

"Me, master?" Saiid's dark leathery face showed a mixture of insult and dismay. "Would not Khalid be a better choice?"

Khalid was Sultan's groom. Ever since the white stallion had arrived at the stables, the two men had become rivals. A groom's standing was determined by the horses he took care of. The better the horses, the higher the standing. In the eyes of Jamal's men, Annie was no prize. "Khalid will ride her the following day," Jamal said firmly.

Saiid bowed, but his dark eyes flashed. "I will do so before the first prayer."

He was going to have a rebellion in his stables, Jamal thought, swinging into the saddle—another reason to get Reba off that horse. He had already picked out a good mare for her. Desert Dawn was gentle enough to suit Reba's needs at the moment and had enough spirit to make riding a joy. By the time he returned from Washington she should be ready for the change. He drew a sharp breath. No matter how often he told himself that his life was on hold, that he shouldn't plan beyond the weekend, he seemed unable to do so where Reba was concerned.

Reba watched Jamal from across the yard. He mounted with clean precise movements, a fluid grace and a smooth power that stunned the senses. Seeing him ride Sultan that first night had been pure magic. Now, as Jamal calmed this eager black Arabian she sensed a bond between rider and horse that seemed far stronger than the one he'd shared with the white stallion.

Jamal turned his horse, Khamsin, and led the way past the Jeep. "I thought we'd ride down the hill. Your mare's still skittish from the move and there's too much activity in the field." Beneath the stone arch that marked the entrance to the stud, he pulled in and waited for her to catch up with him. Hassir and a second guard, both clad in jeans and checked shirts, mounted and began following at a distance. Jamal's mouth tightened, then accepted the orders his father had issued last night with a shrug. Two more days. Or a lifetime. Then the grim line eased somewhat. Yussuf had finally agreed to extend his stay in the States to have a medical checkup.

"Why aren't you riding Sultan?" Reba eyed the prancing stallion tossing his head impatiently. Beneath the gleaming black satin coat, muscles quivered with power asking to be released. In build he was finer boned and not quite as tall as Sultan.

"Sultan gets too impatient after a few minutes," Jamal said evasively. No matter how often he told himself that Sultan had merely been a pawn in Muhrad's game, the knowledge always shadowed the joy he felt riding him. Leaning forward he patted the stallion's arched neck. "His name is Khamsin. I bought him as a foal. He's not quite as fast as Sultan but his manners are better."

"I thought Sultan was a perfect gentleman," Reba teased, recalling their words across the fence.

"And so he is. Just a little more impatient and not quite used to me. I've only had him for four months." His voice was soft and filled with regret when he said, "I must have scared the hell out of you."

Reba shook her head firmly. "When I watched you ride Sultan something happened to me. I could almost taste the wind and power, and for the first time in years I wanted to feel the freedom again for myself." It was also at that moment she had fallen in love with Jamal. She realized it now. Whatever happened in the future, even if she never saw him after today, a part of her would always belong to him.

Abruptly she turned her head away, staring at a row of staff houses with small neatly kept yards. Colorful blankets were airing on clotheslines and curtains fluttered in open windows.

Jamal followed her eyes and frowned. "The grooms had air-conditioning when they first moved in. I don't know if it still works. They never turn it on."

Reba shot him an amused look. "I swear you put questions in my mouth just to annoy me," she said lightly, watching two barefoot children race beneath the blankets. Spotting the riders, they stopped playing and waved. "I was looking at the bedding instead. Their blankets are not the store-bought variety. Do the wives weave them here?"

"Probably." Jamal waved at the children, noticing that Reba did the same quite freely.

"You mean you don't pay them enough to buy blankets?" Reba teased.

He flashed her a lazy grin. "My staff is paid quite well. But you'll have to ask Alfred for specifics."

Ahead, the road narrowed into a track leading downhill, still wide enough for two horses to move side by side. Desert brush lined the path. It pleased Reba that even this close to the compound Jamal had not cleared the land. Then apprehension replaced pleasure as she viewed the drop. What if Annie decided to break into a trot on the downhill slope? Could she handle that?

She looked over her shoulder and spotted Hassir and the second rider following a short distance behind. Her mouth tightened with impatience at her own cowardice. She was not going to disgrace herself in front of Jamal and his guards. Slowly, she guided Annie down the hill. "Do your men like it here? It must be quite a culture shock for them."

"Yes. But more so for the women. The men don't care where they work as long as they have their horses," Jamal said, watching the stiffness in her back ease. Lightly, he increased their slow pace to see if she would follow.

She did so without protest, but her eyes narrowed, warning him not to push too fast and too hard. "What do you mean?"

He cocked one brow arrogantly, then continued distracting her. "There's a special relationship between a Bedouin and his Arabians. Not only because they depend upon each other for survival. The horses are part of their faith. The Prophet left very detailed instructions about their care and breeding. The Bedouins are a deeply religious people and follow the teachings of the Koran as closely as possible."

Reba nodded. "I've read that all purebred Arabians are traced back to five of Muhammad's mares. I think the story goes that after days without water, the Prophet released six mares close to a lake, then called them back before they could drink. The five that obediently turned away from the water, he bred. I always thought that was a little unfair."

"Survival isn't always easy," Jamal said grimly. "Arabians are bred for loyalty more than anything else. When a horse and its rider become separated out in the desert it means almost certain death for them both. If they stick together, they have at least a chance to find a water hole or meet another caravan."

The stallion snorted softly, pulling at the bit, impatience rippling beneath his gleaming black coat. Leaning forward, Jamal murmured soft soothing Arabic words into the stallion's ears until he settled down. "Khamsin was born during a sandstorm and was named after it. He is like the wind."

And so are you, Reba thought. Restless, blowing here and there, moving constantly. Living the life of a nomad, Jamal would value loyalty above everything else. "Is it difficult for you to be Christian in such a strict Muslim country?"

"No." Jamal raised his brows in the same arrogant way he had ordered her away from the fence less than a week ago. Few would dare challenge his authority. "In Islam there are no ministers or priests, only Imams who lead people in prayer. It is not so much a religion, but a way of life. As long as I respect the laws there is no problem."

Not unless he wanted to rule.

His power and arrogance made her mouth go dry. Inexplicably she also felt a prick of tears. Sometimes it was easy to ignore that he was more than her brother's friend, more than a man she was falling in love with. He adjusted to his

surroundings like a chameleon, a result of his unusual up-
bringing, she guessed. But this morning she felt the differences between them more acutely than ever before. Perhaps
it was the fact that she was seeing him in bright daylight for
the first time, not by candlelight or dusk. "Isn't it rather
unusual that your father allowed you to be baptized? So
often in mixed marriages the families argue about a new-
born's faith."

Jamal shrugged. "There were reasons. My father's wife
Azadeh is a very jealous woman. She always saw my mother
as a threat. I think he agreed to it to keep her content." The
action had probably saved his life, Jamal thought soberly.
Azadeh had not seen a small infidel as a rival to her son,
then.

Reba's thoughts flew back to her grandmother's words
and a chill ran down her spine. Perhaps Kitty's fears had not
been an exaggeration and Jamal's life had been threatened
even as a child.

Then the stallion pranced, growing impatient with their
slow pace. Warily, Reba eased Ol' Ann toward the side of
the path. "Why don't you give Khamsin his head?" She
tried to pronounce it the same way Jamal had. When the
word came out in a croak, she grimaced.

He chuckled, pleased at her attempt. "Try it again," he
encouraged her. This time he said the word slowly, distinctly. "Khamsin."

She made another sound deep in her throat, groaned and
started again, laughter bubbling when he winced. On her
third attempt, Jamal smiled ruefully. "That's close enough.
I don't want you to choke."

Reba stopped trying not to laugh. Holding on to the saddle horn she let the laughter bubble like clear water from a
spring. Then she realized that she was sitting on top of Ol'
Ann, laughing without fear, and her laughter ended
abruptly. She took a deep breath and looked at Jamal.
"Thank you. You're good for me."

"For stabling your horse?" Jamal asked wryly. Then he froze, caught by a look on her face he had never seen before. There was a hunger for adventure in her eyes. His sleeping beauty was finally waking up, showing a need for challenge and for risk. This was how she must have looked before her accident, fearless, glowing, a little reckless. He wanted to reach out and lift her in front of him, loosen the reins and give her the wind.

"No. For showing me freedom." She wrinkled her nose. "I know what you were doing back there, making me angry and distracting me so I wouldn't be afraid. Sometimes, you're a very kind man."

He had been called many things, but kind had not been one of them. He was generous with his checkbook, but money meant little to him. He took care of his people. That was his duty.

But kindness?

He shifted in the saddle uncomfortably, wondering if she still would call him kind if she knew the truth. "Little dreamer," he said a bit roughly. "You see kindness everywhere. In that stubborn old mare, in a nasty bull named Nero. You even defend Toby, the louse."

His head tilted arrogantly. He did not want the same tepid feelings from her with which she favored the bull and horse. And he sure as hell didn't want to be put on the same level as her former fiancé. "The reason I want to get you off that nag is so I won't have a rebellion among my grooms over who will care for her."

Reba's face froze. Their differences were already a sore point with her. To have him point out that he considered Annie beneath him, that even his *grooms* thought so, stung her pride. So Annie had no pedigree that went back hundreds of years. *She* herself could trace her family back more than a century. Her voice was stiff and brittle when she said, "I'm sorry Annie's causing problems. I'll ask Rafe to pick her up as soon as possible." Flicking the reins, she kicked her heels into the mare's flanks, too hurt to be scared, too angry to care. Startled, Ol' Ann broke into a trot, lengthened her stride and began running downhill.

Swearing, Jamal gave Khamsin his head. The stallion shot forward in a powerful leap, tossing his head before thundering down the path. Behind him he heard Hassir yell as he drove his own horse into a gallop. Jamal waved him back. Crouched low over the horse's neck, he urged Khamsin on with clicks of his tongue until they raced low to the ground.

Dust and pebbles flew. As Reba rounded the first curve, Jamal was only a few lengths behind, his eyes glued to her back, hoping, praying that she wasn't going to stiffen with fear. She was holding her own so far. Rationally, he knew that the mare was too lazy to run for long, that Khamsin would probably catch her before anything could happen. But for days he'd been haunted by the vision of the mare taking the bit between her teeth, or, worse, stopping abruptly, throwing Reba right off her back. His mouth settled into a grim line. He was going to send the nag back to Rafe. And he was going to shake Reba for scaring the hell out of him.

When he was within twenty yards of them, the mare slowed down. Jamal leaned over Khamsin's neck, caught Annie's bridle in a steel grip, and brought her to a stop. Then he glared at Reba. Her face was flushed, her eyes huge, and her hands were trembling. He made an effort to control his temper. "Are you all right?"

Reba's hands were still tight on the reins, but a smile tugged at her lips. The moment she had dug in her heels she'd realized she had overreacted. Jamal might not think of himself as a kind man, but he was. And he was never deliberately cruel, at least not with her. But once Annie had started to run, Reba hadn't wanted to stop her. After the first few terrifying seconds she had tasted freedom. Her grip went limp as emotions swamped her, her smile growing more brilliant.

She nodded. "I'm fine."

Startled, Jamal's eyes widened, then narrowed to mere slits, desire flaming, basic, vibrant, hot. He got off his horse, still gripping the mare's bridle. His voice was very low, very distinct, as he said, "Get off that damn mare."

Hesitating, Reba stared down at him. His skin was sheened with sweat, his sun-streaked hair clinging damply to his forehead. His face was a taut mask of anger, desire and need. Her mouth felt suddenly dry and her pulse drummed like thunder in her ears. He was the most magnificent man she'd ever seen. As beautiful as the cool bright morning. More dangerous than the red cliffs surrounding them. And as vital to her as the land and the sun.

She swung out of the saddle, her need as strong as his, facing him on level ground. Their bodies met, their arms chained. Without hesitation, Reba lifted her head as his mouth came down, meeting him halfway.

His lips were hard with remembered fear and anger, and desire too long repressed. He wanted to punish her for the scare she'd put him through. His hand tangled in her hair, preventing retreat. He kissed her harshly, powerfully, his tongue thrusting into her softness, expecting her to fight.

She didn't.

Her arms tightening around his waist, she returned the kiss just as fiercely as he gave it, with honesty and passion shivering through her. Restlessly, her hand moved up his shirt, then slid beneath the collar to his damp skin. As her fingertips raked through the curls she felt his hand close possessively over her breast.

She couldn't help the groan that escaped her when he teased her nipple until it was hard. Teeth raking lightly down her neck, he first fanned the heat, then soothed it with his tongue. She tasted of sweat and sun, her spicy lemon scent mingling with the horse's smell. Natural, primitive. He wanted to make love with her, here in the desert where differences faded and princes became men, where nothing stood between them, where they could be what nature had intended. A man and a woman, drawn together by desire and need.

But regrets would come later—for both of them.

Reluctantly, Jamal raised his head, stroking her flushed face. "We have to turn back if you don't want to be late," he murmured, for a moment feasting his eyes on her swollen lips. Then he turned away and whistled to Khamsin, chewing on the fresh growth of a yucca plant.

"You're right. It's getting late," Reba said with a swift look at her watch. She took a step back, wondering what had happened to the heady sense of victory only a moment ago. All she felt now was a sense of loss, of emptiness. She blinked back the sudden tears welling up. Picking up the reins, she swung into the saddle and headed back to reality.

Working girls could dream of princes, but Cinderella stories happened only in fairy tales.

Chapter 8

Praying Monk Medical Building. Now leasing office space. Prime Scottsdale location with view of Camelback Mountain. Marble foyer, high ceilings . . .

Reba stopped skimming the classified section and reread the advertisement two more times, carefully, weighing each word, wondering if it was worth looking at the building.

All ads *sounded* great. Over the past few months, though, she had become quite adept at screening out the hype. A "mountain view" often was no more than a glimpse from one window or after a climb to the roof. The high ceilings appealed to her, but often they were used to create an illusion of light and space when rooms were small. And she seemed to have developed a strong dislike for marble floors lately. Stretching, she arched against the ladder-back chair, then reached for the felt-tipped pen and circled the ad in red. At least, it was a place to start looking again. She had nothing better to do over the weekend.

Jamal was leaving for Washington tomorrow morning.

Annoyed, she threw down the pen, pushed back the chair and jumped to her feet. She'd never had any difficulty filling her weekends before. Staring at the calendar next to the phone, her eyes settled on the circled date of September fifteenth. Her estimated taxes were due on Tuesday; she still had to bring her books up to date and calculate how much she owed the IRS this time. Her apartment needed cleaning and she had a pile of laundry waiting for her. All she'd found in her drawer this evening had been this pair of cutoffs and a T-shirt that should have become a dust rag a year ago. In fact, she should start washing tonight, she decided, walking into the kitchen.

Then she yawned heartily. It was only eight-thirty, but she was too tired to stay up another two hours. What she needed was a cup of tea, a shower and about ten hours of sleep. Getting up at five every morning was taking its toll.

She opened a cabinet and reached for a mug. Jamal didn't seem to mind the early-morning hours. He even appeared to thrive at that time of day. For a man supposedly on vacation he put in long hours of work. Today, as she had been leaving the stud farm, a helicopter had brought three gray-suited men. Security experts, Jamal had explained. Yesterday he had spent all day and most of the evening with his architects. Her recommendation about changing the location of the rehab department in the hospital in Omari seemed to have solved a number of problems.

With the tip of one finger, she pushed her hair behind one ear. She was glad that her small suggestion had proved useful. With every day she seemed to slide deeper into his debt. She was a giver, not a taker, and the role she found herself in made her uncomfortable. But what could she offer a man who had so much? Frowning, she walked across the aisle to look for the tin of tea.

Jamal was leaving for Washington tomorrow and it could be months before he returned to Arizona.

Fear curled in her stomach when she thought of the continuing demonstrations. As so often during the past few days, her thoughts flew back to the funeral for Jimmy Dobson, the hostage who had died during the hijacking. Despite tight security the major had turned the ceremony into a riot, killing another man, injuring others. Even surrounded by bodyguards Jamal was vulnerable.

Enough! Reba told herself sternly. She reached for the tea tin, opened the lid and grimaced. The jar was empty. And so were her shelves. There were only two boxes of crackers, a can of beans and an open package of spaghetti. She had forgotten to go shopping this week. It was another chore to fill her weekend with. Sighing, she opened her refrigerator, reached for a bottle of seltzer and poured herself a glass.

She would miss him no matter how busy she kept herself, Reba thought, pulling down the frayed ends of her cutoffs. Jamal made the world seem brighter and more exciting. He was turning her life upside down, making her want to jump instead of taking her steps one at a time. Sometimes it was difficult to believe that only a week had passed since they'd met.

This morning she'd actually ridden one of his horses, a beautiful little mare named Desert Dawn. She was progressing faster than she'd ever believed possible. Would Jamal be there when she felt confident enough to ride the white stallion? Dear Lord, she hoped so.

How could she have allowed herself to become so...so dependent on him? He had seen her at her weakest more than once. Instead of taking advantage of those times, he had coaxed, prodded and pushed her back to strength. When she was with him, she felt...cherished.

She shook her head. Cherish was a very old-fashioned word for the modern woman she considered herself to be. She tried to tell herself that he would show the same patience with anyone else, that he had even warned her of his ulterior motives. But somehow she couldn't believe that he felt no more for her than for all the other women in his life.

Why then did he draw back every time emotions flared?

She was dreaming once again. Damn it, she would have to work harder to get him out of her mind. She reached for the phone as if it was a lifeline and called Rachel.

"Yes?" Rachel answered on the fourth ring, sounding slightly out of breath.

"Did you just come in?"

"Hmm. I was on my way out of the Clinic when Emergency paged me. Another car wreck. Thank God, the baby was strapped properly into an infant seat and suffered only a few cuts and bruises." She sighed, frustration roughening her voice. "Unfortunately, the mother wasn't strapped in and suffered a head injury. Harry is still in surgery with her." She paused, then asked, "What are you doing home so early?"

"Ramon canceled." The six-year-old paraplegic was one of Rachel's patients. "He said he saw you this afternoon. He sounded badly congested over the phone."

"Yes. He's had bronchitis for a week. And sitting in that small, cramped house all day doesn't help. What he needs is a place in the sun." She sighed again. "Do you think we'll ever get enough money together for a children's camp in the mountains?"

"Maybe we should start a fund drive," Reba suggested slowly. That would take care of the rest of her spare time.

"But why are we talking on the phone? Let's dream over a cup of coffee. I'll be right over. Just give me time to change." Rachel hung up before Reba could tell her that she was out of coffee and that she had dreamed already more than a rational, practical, modern woman should.

Annoyed, Reba opened the refrigerator with enough force to upset the milk carton poised on the edge of the shelf. She managed to catch it before it hit the tiles, but milk splattered everywhere. Cursing under her breath, she put down the carton, dampened several paper towels and squatted to wipe up the spill when she heard Rachel's knock. "The door's open. I hope you have some coffee in the house. All I have is a box of crackers."

"I'll take you out for coffee," an amused voice said from behind her.

"Oh." Still kneeling, she looked up at him. He was dressed in immaculate tan slacks, a white shirt and highly polished shoes. She shuddered when she thought of her own appearance. "I thought it was my friend Rachel. What are you doing here?"

He'd asked himself the same question on his way over here. There were a million and one things to clear up before he left for Washington at 4:00 a.m. They had said their goodbyes this morning. He should have left it at that. But all day he'd found himself staring into space, reliving the passion and the power that had run through him when he'd kissed her yesterday.

Holding out a roll of paper secured with a rubber band, he said, "I brought you a copy of the blueprints for the rehab department in the Basjadi hospital. I thought you'd like to see them."

It was the only explanation he'd been able to think of. He'd never searched for excuses to visit a woman before and the fact that he felt he needed one now didn't sit well with him. What was it about Reba that could make him feel so powerful one moment and so uncertain the next? Was it because he had something to hide?

"That was kind of you." Flustered, Reba looked from the blueprints to the spilled milk and back again, as if she couldn't make up her mind what to do first.

The signs of nervousness soothed his bruised pride a little and he grinned. "Go clean that up first."

"Yes, master," she said tartly. She wished he hadn't come. Truthfully, she was glad he was there. She hastily wiped up the spill, threw the paper towels into the trash, returned the milk carton to the refrigerator and washed her hands.

While he was waiting, Jamal had walked to the table and read the circled ad. It didn't sound too bad, he thought. He'd bought and sold enough real estate to read between the lines and could see the possibilities as well as the probable faults. "Are you going to take a look at it?"

Reba walked over to him, running her hand through her hair. "I have to start again somewhere."

"You probably have to climb to the roof to see the mountains," Jamal warned. There were smudges under her eyes and her face looked drawn. The low cut of her T-shirt revealed hollows above her collarbones, making her seem more fragile. He frowned. She was working too hard.

Shrugging, Reba reached for the blueprints and removed the rubber band. "I know. And the rooms will most likely be too small," she said. Pushing a silvery leafed bromelia aside, she spread out the plan on the butcher-block table, using a black pottery bowl to hold down one edge of the large sheet. She wanted to ask him if and when he planned to return to the valley, but she was afraid to. Afraid that he wouldn't come back and afraid that he would.

Jamal stared down at her. With her head bent and her nape exposed, she looked so vulnerable. The thought that she might come up against another Buckman while he was gone worried him. And the more obligations she added to her already heavy schedule, the less time she would have for him when he came back. Seeing her for one hour in the morning simply wasn't enough. Not anymore. There was a thirst gnawing at him night and day, a thirst that grew every time he saw her, touched her, kissed her. "Then why waste your time? Go riding instead," he said roughly.

Startled, Reba looked up. The concern reflected in his eyes went straight to her heart, warming her, fanning the small flame of hope that kept burning no matter how often she tried to put it out. "I don't plan to make riding my career again. Living out of a suitcase for months at a time was great fun when I was a kid.'' She smiled ruefully. ''When you dream of exploring and conquering the world you don't notice lumps in your bed or leaky faucets. But somehow dreams change. I'd still love to travel. I'd still like to compete again, if only locally. But I'm not willing to sacrifice everything I've worked for for another shot at the gold.''

Jamal's eyes became intent. ''Somehow I had the impression that you didn't like traveling.''

Reba shot him a surprised look. ''What gave you that idea? I loved it. There are so many beautiful places in the world. I'm lucky that I had the chance to see some of them.'' Then understanding dawned. Shaking her head, she said, ''I didn't reject your offer because I didn't want to leave Arizona, but because I had different plans. Under different circumstances a year overseas might have been fun.''

In a brief lapse of sanity, she discarded her pride and wished that she had agreed to go to Omari. Perhaps if she could be with him for a year, she could live the rest of her life without him. Pride and independence were vital to her, but so was this man. If she had to sacrifice one to have the other . . . Swiftly, she forced her eyes back to the blueprints.

The hospital complex was shaped like an X with a large center tower. The wings, Reba noticed, seemed to be the patients' wards, while the central area apparently housed various facilities.

Pushing back a wooden chair, he looked over Reba's shoulders. ''This is a plan of the fourth floor.'' Up close her faint lemon scent filled his senses. Their arms brushed as he pointed out the elevators and the male and female wards. Jamal suddenly realized that he wanted her approval and her appreciation. ''Originally rehab was situated in opposing wings. Now it occupies about seven thousand square feet in the tower, with a view of the sea.''

His deep voice was a soft lure as he pointed out the large gym area and the offices, both sharing a glass wall facing the gulf. Light and space. Reba felt excitement growing with each new feature he pointed out.

The whirlpool area was large enough to accommodate a Hubbard tank, a butterfly-shaped whirlpool in which a patient's body could be totally submerged, equipment she'd wanted for years. In one room the floor would be padded to treat children alone or in a group. Another great feature was an indoor pool whose bottom could be raised to various heights. The last two ideas he had copied from a university hospital in Germany he'd visited last year, Jamal explained. There was even a large storage room for rarely used equipment.

Reba turned her head to look at Jamal with glowing eyes. "This is every therapist's dream. I'm treating a six-year-old paraplegic who would love the pool. Ramon used to swim like a fish." Then her eyes clouded over. "For the poor, such facilities are always out of reach. Only the wealthy will be able to afford this luxury."

For several moments Jamal said nothing. Did she know how much her approval meant to him? "We have free education and medical care in Omari," he finally explained softly.

"You do? How marvelous! You can't imagine the frustration we often feel because our patients are discharged too soon." How she'd love to work under these conditions. "When will the building be finished?"

"September next year." Jamal put a hand on her shoulder and gently turned her around. "The job is still open," he said with a casualness that went no deeper than the hard mask of his face.

Perhaps for the first time in his life he understood why Yussuf had married Kitty. Like his father, he wanted a woman who he knew was probably wrong for him, to whom he could bring only unhappiness; but he wanted her anyway. "I'm not asking for an answer now. Just think about it."

There was such hunger in his hazel eyes, such need, she would have promised him a lifetime if he'd asked for it. "I—"

Before she could finish the sentence, he covered her mouth with his own. He didn't want to know what her answer was. At the moment he needed to believe that there was a future beyond tomorrow, no matter what happened during Yussuf's visit.

Her lips responded instantly, soft and moist. His arms went around her waist, drawing her closer, fusing her softness to his hardness, kissing her with harsh need until her hands slid nervelessly to her side and her head tilted back. If he had carried her to the bedroom and made love with her then, he knew she wouldn't have resisted him.

Abruptly, he drew back. He didn't want to take advantage of her while she was off balance or wring a promise about the future from her in the heat of passion. Whatever her decision, he did not want her to regret it later on. In Omari it would be easier to hide their relationship from the press. Still, it would be a life of subterfuge he was asking of her.

And before she made a decision, he owed her the truth.

Gently, he released her, viewing her dazed look with satisfaction. She was his now, he thought. But for how long? Would she turn away from him once she knew everything? "Go change," he murmured, "We need to talk. But not here, I think," he added with a taut smile, stepping aside.

It was then Reba remembered Rachel. "I have to make a call first," she said, moving toward the phone just as it began to ring.

"It's me," Rachel said when Reba answered it. "Lupita just called. Ramon's temperature is sky-high. I'm driving over to take a look at him."

Reba glanced at the clock on the microwave, frowning when she saw that it was close to nine. Lupita, Ramon's mother, worked the night shift at a fast food chain, leaving her husband José to take care of their son. Most evenings she left the house by eight. "José Ramirez is often drunk around this time of night," she warned. "If Lupita isn't home, he may not allow you past the door."

"She didn't go to work today. I just hope I don't have to admit Ramon to the hospital again."

"So do I. Be careful," Reba warned uneasily, running her hand through her hair. From past experience she knew just how unpredictable José Ramirez could be when he was drunk. Once he had ordered her from the house and left her stranded without her purse and keys. Glancing at Jamal, she hesitated briefly, then offered, "Perhaps I should come with you."

"Don't worry. If José gives me any problems, I'm going to call the police," Rachel said firmly. "I'll ring you when I get there."

With a troubled look, Reba hung up the phone, then dialed Ramon's number. Lupita assured her that her husband had been so worried about his son, he hadn't touched a drop of alcohol tonight. Somewhat reassured, Reba hung up the phone and turned back to Jamal. "Do you mind if we stay here until Rachel calls?"

Jamal shook his head, a frown on his face. "Does this sort of thing happen frequently?" he asked tightly, feeling a chill run down his back.

"That Rachel makes house calls?" Reba asked, deliberately misinterpreting his question. "No. She saw Ramon in her office this afternoon, but since then his condition has become worse."

"That's not what I meant." Jamal vaguely recalled Reba's friend as a petite, slender woman with curly brown hair. Hardly a match for any man, much less an alcoholic with a history of violence. "Wouldn't it be safer to have the boy brought to the Emergency Room?"

From Jamal's point of view it was a perfectly sensible suggestion. Reba nodded, smiling tightly. "There's just one problem. The Ramirezes already have a mountain of unpaid medical bills. They can't afford the hospital fees unless it's an absolute emergency."

Jamal slid his hands in his pockets, balling them into fists. The thought of Reba exposing herself to violence made him want to shake some sense into her. "How often has the father been drunk while you were there?" he asked harshly, his temper straining at control.

"I take reasonable precautions," Reba explained evasively, "especially since that incident. Lupita is always there when I treat Ramon. José usually doesn't start drinking until after his wife has left for work."

Reasonable precautions! Jamal had used the phrase too often to feel reassured. "Are you mad to take such risks?" he demanded harshly. "Don't you understand what could happen to you?"

"What would you have me do? Deny a six-year-old boy treatment because his father tries to drown his sorrow?"

Jamal gripped her slender shoulders. "Of course not. But this is no job for a woman," he insisted, his voice rough.

"Unfortunately, most male therapists I know are either potbellied or have back trouble from handling all those patients we *poor* females are too weak to treat." A gleam came into her eyes as she added lightly, "I don't want to brag, Jamal, but I'm in far better shape than they are."

He couldn't help a smile from curving his lips. "Your shape is definitely something to brag about," he agreed softly, running his hands from her shoulders to her waist and drawing her close.

"That's not what I meant," Reba protested huskily, feeling her flesh tingle beneath his firm, sure touch. Sudden shivers ran over her skin and her breathing became shallow and quick. She grasped his wrists as if to push his hands down, then slid over his arms to his strong broad shoulders to hug his neck. "I can take care of myself. It's you I'm worried about."

His strength was no defense against bullets and his height made him such an easy target, she thought, sudden fear chilling her. Her fingers curling into his crisp hair, she pulled his head down. "Kiss me, Jamal," she whispered, her voice a little unsteady and her lips trembling.

She heard his swift intake of breath before his head came down and his arms closed tightly around her back. "That's the first time you've asked me to touch you," Jamal groaned against her lips. Yet even as their breath mingled and their lips met, he wondered if he would ever hear the words again.

His mouth closed over hers with sudden purpose, determined to lose himself in her and take what she so freely offered. Once he had taken her, once he had assuaged his sexual frustration, he would smile about this crazy compulsion to tell her the truth.

His tongue delved deeply, tasting, tempting, seducing. As always, her kiss was passionate and generous and her body arched into him. His hands slid under her T-shirt, caressing her subtle, firm curves. Cupping her breasts, his thumbs slid beneath the scraps of lace and found her nipples, gently teasing them until they hardened with passion. Reba moaned and shivered in response, but she didn't stiffen and she didn't pull back. She held on to him tightly, as if trying to shield him from harm.

That defeated him.

He was no better than Toby, the louse, he thought, a bitter taste in his mouth. Abruptly, he raised his head, firmly placed his hands on her shoulders and held her away. "You, my sweet, need a hefty dose of self-preservation," he said with a rough edge to his voice.

He had done it again! Reba stared at him, still a little dazed and a whole lot frustrated. "And you, Your Highness, are a tease," she snapped, before the meaning of his words sank in. When it did, she shook her head in rueful exasperation. She was surrounded by overprotective idiots, always trying to save her from herself. "You are not only a conceited jerk, Your Highness," she told him softly, "but also an honorable fool." Her taunt didn't turn the frown into one of his lazy smiles as she'd intended. His mouth tightened instead.

"I want your promise that you'll find someone else to treat the boy," he demanded. "Or treat him at the clinic and send me the bill."

Her smile faded abruptly and her chin went up a notch. "If you promise not to go to Washington tomorrow," she argued. "Your risk is far greater than mine."

"The hell it is. I don't take gambles the way you do every time you treat the boy!" Jamal's hands balled into fists with the need to shake some sense into her. "And I can't hide every time someone threatens me."

"These threats are not coming from just *someone*," Reba said fiercely, her eyes flashing like polished gold. "We're talking about the HIB, an organization that even managed to penetrate the tight security at the funeral of the young man killed during the highjacking. You were there. You know what it was like!"

"I'm not likely to forget it! But you probably saw more on the news than I did," Jamal said with harsh bitterness. His eyes were hard and empty, looking straight through her, as if he was reliving the nightmare all over again. "One moment I was watching the limousines drive up. Next all hell exploded."

Just thinking about it he could feel the acrid smoke stinging his eyes and burning his nostrils. "I remember the sounds, the thunder and the screams, but I saw nothing. I was flat on my face, being crushed by Hassir's bulk, and secret service agents holding me down. By the time I was allowed up, it was all over. One agent was dead, others were injured. I," he added grimly, "had grass stains on my elbows."

"Risking your life wouldn't have kept anyone else from getting hurt," Reba reasoned, laying a soothing hand on his arm. She could feel a volcano of anger and bitterness seething beneath the thin layer of control. How he must have hated being forced to safety, having to watch and wait while others took risks, fought and protected in his stead. And how bitter he must have felt, seeing his vision of peace turn into a bloody nightmare. "You were not responsible for what happened."

"Wasn't I? Does carelessness absolve a person from responsibility?" Jamal tossed her arm aside and strode down the kitchen aisle, striving for control. Hands clenched, he turned and said grimly, "I didn't plan the hijacking. And I didn't finance it. But I pushed for an alliance with the States, knowing that my brother was afraid to give up neutrality. My only excuse is that I did not realize how cornered Muhrad felt."

Stunned, Reba swayed and grasped the ladder-back chair. "Are you saying your brother had something to do with the hijacking?" Just for a moment she hoped she had misunderstood Jamal, that her ears were playing tricks. But the grim slant of his mouth told her that she was not mistaken. "I don't understand," she whispered, staring at him with a mixture of horror and disbelief.

Jamal cursed silently. He hadn't meant to hurl the facts at her. Crossing the space, he gently pushed her into a chair. "I'm sorry. I threw this at you with all the gentleness of a charging bull," he said, looking down into her pale face. Beneath his hand he could feel fine tremors shaking her. "Do you have any liquor in the house?"

"Yes. In the wall unit in the living room. Glasses are on the shelf below." Touching his hand briefly, she added quietly, "I don't think there is a gentle way to tell bad news. This can't be easy for you, either."

"No," he agreed quietly, wishing she wasn't so calm, so reasonable. Abruptly, he walked into the living room, returning moments later with a bottle of brandy and two glasses. He rolled up the blueprints, then poured a generous amount of brandy into a glass and handed it to her. "Drink it," he ordered when she just cradled it in her hands.

"I don't feel like it right now." Her head was already spinning enough. She needed to keep a lid on her feelings and a guard on her tongue. During the past week she'd lived through more emotional upheaval than she had in the past five years. She didn't know how much more she could take before her control snapped. She didn't want to hurt him with an incautious word or add to his guilt. He was already doing a great job of blaming himself.

Pushing the glass toward him, she said quietly, "I'm shocked, but I'm not about to faint." Frowning, she went on, "Why should your brother fear the treaty? It seems to me that he had more to gain than to lose. The base will provide security and quite a few new jobs. The peace also would attract a number of firms and foreign investments. It doesn't make any sense. Unless he opposed the changes because of personal reasons."

She never ceased to surprise him, Jamal thought. "Muhrad has accused me for years of trying to usurp his position. In Omari succession is not automatically assumed by the oldest son," he explained in a flat voice. "Theoretically, my father has the right to choose between Muhrad and myself." Pulling out a chair, Jamal sat down, reached for the brandy and tossed it back. "Power means everything to Muhrad."

"While you prefer the open desert to palace walls," Reba said with calm certainty, still trying to accept that all the terror and nightmares had been caused by one man's blind jealousy. And Jamal had been as much a victim as anyone else.

Stunned, Jamal stared into the empty glass held between his hands. He had expected questions from her. He'd been prepared for doubts. But not this total belief in him. Even Alfred, who had known him for ten years and whose loyalty to him was unquestionable, had demanded explanations why he did not want to rule. He stirred uncomfortably. "I should have seen it coming, though."

Reba touched his arm. "Perhaps. But would you have believed him capable of it? I know I tend to deny flaws in the people I love."

Her understatement made Jamal shake his head. "Your blindness includes stubborn old mares and nasty-tempered bulls. You even defend Toby, the louse. And now, you've added an *honorable fool* to the list." With mocking inflection, he added, "I don't particularly care for the company I find myself in." Then his smile vanished. What Reba didn't realize was that it was her very blindness that gentled him. "But I've always known Muhrad for what he is."

Reba's thoughts flew to her brother. The few times Rafe had mentioned Muhrad, his voice had been flat, the way it always went when he disliked someone. "Rafe knows," she guessed.

"Without Rafe we would still be in the dark." Jamal poured himself another drink, then continued quietly. "He was reading a book about Arabian horses on the flight to Beirut. Seeing it, one of the terrorists bragged that his father bred horses fit for kings. Two of his stallions had recently been sold to royal studs, one to Hassan in Morocco— and the second one, Sultan, to Prince Muhrad of Omari."

Frowning, Reba gave Jamal a questioning look. "Don't you have horses in Omari?"

"Yes. But my brother hasn't ridden in years. Muhrad has no interest in horses and rarely visits nomad camps. But I never suspected anything when Muhrad gave me the stallion as a belated birthday present,'' Jamal said with quiet savagery.

Reba felt tears prick her eyes. She wanted to tell him to stop. There was no need to reopen the wounds, to relive the pain and betrayal. But perhaps the sores had festered so long, he needed to talk about them before they could heal. With her hand on his arm, she listened as he went on, ''Not until I heard about Sultan did everything fall into place. And later I discovered proof.''

Each of his bitter words cut into her like the sharp point of a knife. Now she understood his reaction whenever the rescue was mentioned. It also explained so many other things. His offer to teach her to ride—and also the way he drew back from each kiss. Had all those actions been prompted by guilt?

''Stop blaming yourself,'' Reba said fiercely. ''Your father signed the treaty, so the final decision was his.'' The press called Yussuf a survivor, shrewd, wily, sometimes cruel. ''Or does your father also hold you responsible for your brother's actions?''

''My father doesn't know the truth, or, if he does, he's playing a waiting game.'' Swiftly, Jamal explained the precarious state of Yussuf's health. ''He has finally agreed to see a doctor. On Monday he's checking into the Houston Medical Center.''

Reba's eyes flew to the blueprints on the table. ''That's why you've been rushing construction.'' Her heart contracted painfully. A weaker man might have crumpled under the burden he had carried for months. And she had added to it with her thoughtless words. ''I'm sorry I accused you of not caring for your father.'' She looked at him with anxious eyes. ''Can you shield him until his health has improved?''

Jamal ran a hand through his hair and said wearily, ''A week ago, I would have sworn that only a handful of people knew. But every day I find the knowledge spreading. I honestly don't know.''

He was always so decisive, so certain, his grim resignation tugged at her heart. ''What will happen to your brother if your father does find out?'' Yussuf's swift, harsh desert justice had shocked the world four months ago when he'd had three terrorists executed in the market square. Would he punish his son in the same way?

''Exile.'' Jamal raked his fingers through his hair again. ''To put Muhrad on trial would stir too many waves in the Middle East and the States.''

''Then you would become the next emir of Omari.''

Jamal pushed back his chair and rose to his feet. ''I hope it won't come to that,'' he snapped, pacing the kitchen floor. ''Muhrad's son, Hussein, would be a much better choice. But at fifteen he's too young to take control. If my father dies, Muhrad will try to reclaim his right. Hussein would not be able to stand up to his father.''

Reba shivered and rubbed the goose bumps on her arms. ''It wouldn't be very easy for you, either,'' she said quietly. Because somewhere beneath the anger and the sense of betrayal she knew he cared for Muhrad.

Jamal shrugged. ''My father once said that what made him different from the man in the street was not his wealth. The man in the street, he pointed out, was free to give away his heart, his body and his soul. An emir belonged to his people.''

It wasn't fair, Reba thought, her eyes filling with tears. Jamal was being torn apart by his duty to Omari, his love for his father and his brother's guilt. How long until he would turn bitter and hard? ''And what about your wishes?'' she asked hoarsely. ''Don't you have a right to happiness?''

''Would I be happy denying responsibility?'' Jamal stopped in front of Reba. Looking down, he saw her shake her head, the movement sending a single tear down her cheek. He had never seen her cry before, not even on the night she'd lost a piece of her dream. Yet she was crying for him.

"Softie," he taunted a little roughly, catching the tear with the tip of his finger. "My father once tried to snatch at happiness. I often wonder if one year was worth all the misery that came from it." He slid his hands into his pockets, shrugged and said softly. *"Inshallah."*

Before he could give in to temptation and repeat his father's mistake, he walked to the door. With his hand on the knob, he looked over his shoulder. "Perhaps I should warn you. I sent Ol' Ann back to the ranch this morning."

"You did what?" Reba jumped to her feet, anger drying her tears. "You arrogant—" The devil's glints were back in his eyes, taunting her. Abruptly, she bit her lip. "That wasn't very nice," she said more calmly, refusing to let him goad her into anger.

His teeth flashed white against his tan. "I definitely prefer *conceited jerk* to *honorable fool*."

At that moment the phone rang. Reba went to answer it. Jamal listened to the brief exchange and waited until Reba had hung up before asking, "Everything all right?" When she nodded, he opened the door. "And find someone else to treat the boy."

Chapter 9

A storm was brewing in the hills.

Dark clouds seemed to come out of nowhere, racing across the late-afternoon sky, mingling with the lengthening shadows and the yellow and orange hues cast by the setting sun. The hot, dry air seemed to crackle with static. Reining in her horse, Reba could almost smell the sulfur fumes. As she wiped her forehead, she saw the first streak of lightning flash in the hills and shivered. She hated storms.

"It is coming this way. We have to go faster, Ms. Davis," Saiid urged in his accented English, leaning forward to calm the prancing black stallion with a touch and soft words. Raising his deeply tanned face toward the sky, he sniffed the air. "Little rain, but plenty of thunder and lightning."

"An electrical storm. How can you tell?" Swallowing, Reba dug in her heels. The silver-gray mare responded instantly.

"With my nose." Touching his beak, Saiid grinned, revealing several gold teeth. "Bedouins can smell water many kilometers away."

Since Jamal's departure, Saiid had been riding with her every day, entertaining her with stories of nomad life. Usually his outrageous exaggerations made her laugh. Today, her smile was tight. "You're not going to pull that one on me again. Bedouins don't sniff out wells. Especially not these days. Your wife told me that you have big water trucks following the caravans through the desert."

Saiid shook his white head and said in a doleful voice, "My poor wife does not remember the old times, the times before the water trucks. And in the high desert there are still many places without roads. You ask my master when he comes back."

That, Reba thought, had the ring of truth. Whenever Saiid mentioned Jamal his voice held a mixture of devotion and respect. "I will," she promised, wondering if she'd ever get the chance. Nine days had passed since he left.

Thunder rumbled in the distance, sending a wave of fear down Reba's back. Gritting her teeth, she tried to distract herself and allowed her thoughts to stray. Since Yussuf's state visit a week ago, Jamal seemed to have dropped off the edge of the world. He wasn't with his father in Houston. Kitty Barron had visited her former husband at the hospital for a few days, but the press had not mentioned Jamal. There had been no phone calls and no messages from him on her answering machine. Silence sometimes did speak as loudly as words, she thought bitterly.

Watching Saiid come up on her right, Reba wondered if the old Bedouin knew his master's whereabouts, but she didn't ask—partly because she felt she had no right to question Jamal's men, and also because she didn't want to know where he was—or with whom. During their week together she'd been so caught up in valiant princes and sinister villains she had started to believe in fairy tales. And it had to stop.

She'd spent last weekend doing chores and watching TV. By Monday morning her apartment had been spotless, her laundry washed; even her taxes were done a day early. Since then she'd tried to regain a hold on reality. Today she had combed Scottsdale for hours, searching for another suitable office location. She couldn't put her life on hold indefinitely.

Reba winced as lightning sparked again. The sky grew darker with each passing minute and thunder was rolling closer. The first flash of panic hit her. "Do you think we'll make it?" she shouted above the pounding of the hooves. Speed still made her uneasy, but now her fear of storms was driving her on. She loosened the reins and crouched low over the mare's neck. Desert Dawn didn't need any urging. Stretching, she raced up the track, her silvery-gray mane flowing over Reba's hands.

"We have five minutes. Maybe less," Saiid estimated, riding as close to Reba as safety allowed, checking Khamsin's more powerful stride until both horses raced neck to neck.

Then the first drops hit Reba's heated skin. By the time they neared the stables, the storm was almost overhead, brilliant flashes and sharp cracks chasing each other with ever-increasing intensity. Saiid's nose wasn't infallible; the rain came down in sheets. Both Reba and the groom were drenched within seconds. Saiid's loose desert robes clung like wet rags. Reba's yellow cotton blouse stuck to her skin and the reins in her hands had become as slippery as soap. And each flash, each thunderclap chipped away at her self-control.

It wasn't going to happen again, she told herself mechanically as they raced past the staff houses and turned toward the stables. She was not going to be locked in a stall again. Another minute and she would be safe. Despite her thoughts, her mouth was dry and her breath came out in gasps.

Suddenly a group of horses raced past them into the yard, Sultan in the lead, his teeth bared and his ears laid back. The horses slipped and slithered on the slick clay soil, which absorbed water like a dry sponge, adding to the confusion and heightening the sense of urgency.

Beneath Reba, Desert Dawn strained and bucked, trying to join the herd. For an instant Reba was tempted to fling herself out of the saddle and run. But at the moment her only safety lay in staying in the saddle and getting out of the storm. With all her remaining strength, she pulled the mare's head down, her legs wrapping tightly around the horse's barrel. Then she heard a familiar voice rise above the noise, shouting orders in Arabic.

Jamal was back!

Just the sound, so strong and controlled, smoothed the jagged edge of her panic. She cast Saiid a swift, reproachful look. "Why didn't you tell me?"

"I did not know. The master is like the wind. One moment he is here, the next he is gone," Saiid shouted back. As the last of the herd thundered by, he followed, controlling the stallion's panic with the ease of a man who had spent his life in the saddle. "Stay close to the fence," he warned.

With a taut nod Reba followed him into the yard, trying to stay clear of the confusion fueled by each flash of lightning and thunderbolt. Grooms, slipping on wet clay, were lunging for halters and lead ropes, trying to pull horses out of the storm into the shelter of the buildings. Jamal was gripping Sultan's halter, trying to keep the frightened horse from breaking free.

For a moment Reba forgot her own fears, watching him pitch his strength against the bucking stallion, two powerful bodies fighting for control. Lightning struck nearby, followed by a deafening clap, which shook the ground. A second of stunned silence followed. Then all hell broke loose.

Sultan squealed, lashed out and reared. Jamal slipped, lost his hold, barely escaping the slashing hooves. Free, the stallion bolted and raced straight toward the fence, biting cruelly into Desert Dawn's rump before breaking through the rail. The mare neighed shrilly and slammed straight into Khamsin. Reba's world became a nightmare of rearing horses, slashing hooves and high-pitched screams.

Time seemed to be in slow motion, as it had on that other afternoon. Instincts taking over, Reba fought to stay in the saddle, watching the world around her go mad. Saiid was unseated, but managed to roll to safety beneath the rail. Seconds later Reba was also tossed into the air. She hit the mud, rolling and twisting, trying to get to the fence, but Khamsin was between her and safety. The black stallion was rearing, his eyes rolling in fear, teeth bared and hooves slashing the air. Reba screamed in pure terror.

Jamal was running to her. He saw Saiid scramble to his feet and drag Reba by the shoulders from beneath the slashing hooves to safety. Racing toward the fence, Jamal put his hand on the top rail and vaulted over it.

Then he was kneeling on the grass next to Reba. She was lying on her back, her face turned to one side, wet, muddy hair covering her face. Gently, he pushed the tangled mane from her neck and searched for her pulse. For a moment all he heard was the beat of his own racing heart. He held his breath, expelled the air and calmed himself so that he could concentrate on feeling her pulse. A lifetime seemed to pass before he picked up the steady beat. Relief hit him with stunning force.

"Is she all right?" Saiid knelt on the grass opposite Jamal, wiping his mud-streaked face.

"Her pulse is steady and strong. Thank you for pulling her to safety." He glanced at the groom. "What about you?"

"Fine." Saiid got to his feet as if to prove his words. "I'm sorry, master. I should have told Miss Davis to stay out of the yard. Do you want me to call a doctor?"

Jamal shook his head. "There's no need to blame yourself, Saiid." Jamal ran his hands over Reba's mud-coated limbs, checking for injuries. Finding none, he raised his head. "I'll take her to the hospital. Have Rashid bring the limo around."

Though lightning still flashed across the sky and thunder boomed, the rain seemed to be easing. The storm was moving on. Behind him, Jamal heard Hassir bellow orders to get the horses into the stables.

Groaning, Reba stirred, opened her eyes and tried to sit up.

"Don't move, Reba," Jamal said, enforcing his order with a hand on her shoulder, resisting the need to gather her close. "Desert Dawn threw you."

Reba's head was spinning and she sank back on the grass. Moving her limbs experimentally, she let out a sigh of relief. There was no pain, no numbness, either. Somehow she seemed to have escaped those steel-shod hooves. "I'm fine. Just give me a minute to catch my breath." Slowly her eyes focused on his anxious face, glistening with raindrops. "Saiid? I saw him fall. Is he all right?"

"He's in better shape than you." Jamal relaxed a bit. The fact that she seemed to recall the events immediately before her fall was a good sign. Some color seemed to seep back into her ashen face. With an unsteady hand he pushed her wet hair back. "Saiid pulled you under the fence."

"That was nice of him." *Nice* seemed so inadequate a word, but at the moment she couldn't think of anything else. "I saw the hooves coming down on me and fainted. I can't believe I passed out like a Victorian heroine." A look of disgust crossed her mud-streaked face and she pushed herself up determinedly.

"What do you think you're doing?" Frowning, Jamal held her back. "Rest until the limo gets here. I'm taking you to the Clinic."

"You're not." Reba's eyes narrowed in protest. "I'm fine. I don't think I even have a bruise. The mud acted like a cushion." She looked down at herself, and a faint grin tugged at her mouth. "Rita, the charge nurse, would have a fit if I walked in looking like a mud pie." She took a deep breath, then said curtly, "Let me get up, Jamal." Pushing his hand away, she tried to stand.

Grimly, Jamal pulled her to her feet with startling ease. It took a few seconds for the spinning in her head to stop. Then she looked around. Miraculously, the yard was almost empty. Sultan had been caught, Saiid was leading the still nervously dancing Khamsin toward his stall and another groom was walking Desert Dawn past the fence.

Before Jamal could guess her intention, Reba twisted free of his hold, slipped between the rails and stalked over to the mare with knees that felt like Jell-O, but with her mouth firmly set. Her stomach was churning, whether from fear or reaction she didn't know. Ignoring the queasiness, she turned to the groom. She had to get back into the saddle, before she froze again. During the past few weeks she had come too far to start all over again. "Hand me the reins," she asked the groom.

"Don't be a fool, Reba." Coming up behind her, Jamal took the reins from the groom and sent him off with a nod. Her knees still wobbled and her eyes were slightly unfocused. "You don't have to prove anything. Not tonight."

Reba gritted her teeth, fighting the dizziness. Tears pricked her eyes and she blinked them away. "Give me the reins," she demanded curtly, holding out a trembling hand. "If you don't, I drive straight out to the ranch."

Jamal swore beneath his breath. Bending, he helped Reba into the saddle. "Two times around the yard," he said harshly. The set of his jaw promised her that if she ignored his order he'd haul her out of the saddle. "The ground is very slick, so take it easy." Reluctantly, he handed her the reins, then stepped out of the way.

As she rode off, Jamal saw her color fade again, a grayish white against the black of her hair. She rode stiffly and twice she shook her head as if to clear it.

Jamal watched her with his hands clenched and his body coiled, ready to run and catch her the moment she faltered. But she fought her weakness with such determination and stubbornness, Jamal felt pride well up and a deep, aching tenderness.

He had tried to put her from his mind, he thought, watching her start on her second round. But even after nine days of absence and a trip to Omari, the need for her was still there, constant, gnawing, aching. Memories of her had followed him everywhere. In Washington he'd caught himself wondering if she was watching the news. In Omari, while visiting the hospital construction site, he'd asked himself if she'd enjoy the view of the sea and the warm salt air coming from the gulf. Driving through Basjad he gazed at the superhighways and skyscrapers and thought of the unpaved streets and mud-brick office structures his mother had faced so many years before.

He sighed. On the outside the changes in Omari were dramatic. Behind the walls, however, life continued much as it had done for centuries. Women still were treated as second-class citizens; they even still wore veils.

But watching her ride toward him now, caked with mud and holding on by sheer will alone, he realized that he'd been fighting a loosing battle with his conscience. When she stopped in front of him, she was swaying in the saddle. Cursing under his breath, Jamal pulled her into his arms.

Looking up at him, Reba smiled shakily. "I'm sorry, Jamal, but . . . I think . . . I'm going to—"

She fainted before she could hear Jamal's very blunt comments about stubborn women in general and Reba in particular.

"There's nothing wrong with you, *chiquita,* that a shower, a stiff drink and some rest won't cure," Harry Mendoza told Reba an hour later at the Rana Clinic. He'd just finished making his rounds when Reba was brought in.

With a rueful smile Reba jumped off the examining table. "I didn't want to come here in the first place. Only I wasn't given any choice." Arguing with Jamal when his mind was set was like kicking a brick wall, she'd discovered.

"It was the sensible thing to do," Harry said firmly. Then a grin spread over his handsome features. "The gossip this will cause! You are going to be in for some tough days."

"I'll never hear the end of it." Wrapping the flaps of the hospital gown around her, Reba groaned. "Rita almost had a heart attack when she saw us come in, dripping mud all over her clean floor."

"That's right. I should make you clean up the mess, too." Rita Taylor, R.N., pushed the turquoise curtain aside and bustled into the cubicle, handing Reba a pair of white pants, a blue blouse and a plastic garbage bag. "This is all I found in your closet. I didn't see any shoes."

With a grateful smile, Reba reached for her clothes. One look at her mud-caked boots and she decided to go barefoot instead. Tongue in cheek, she offered, "If you find me a broom and a mop—"

"Housekeeping will take care of it." Rita shook her short steel-gray curls. "I'd rather get rid of those packing hulks out there," she said tartly. Rita divided the human species into two groups, those who needed her help and those who didn't. "They're still dripping mud everywhere. Luckily, we aren't busy at the moment." A little smile tugged at her stern lips. "You did look a fright! I'll find you a brush so you can comb some of that stuff out of your hair." Tugging at Harry's white coat, she drew him outside.

The moment the curtain dropped behind them, Reba slipped into her clothes. The fact that she had fainted, not once, but twice, still rankled. Then she tried to look at the bright side of it. Even now, the thought of getting back into the saddle held no fear. Buttoning her blouse, she smiled in relief.

Jamal was still pacing outside the Emergency Room, a trail of dried dirt crunching beneath his boots. Hassir was leaning against the wall, his eyes darting from his master to the double doors and to the staff watching them curiously. Both he and Jamal started forward when Reba and Harry walked out.

When he recognized the man he'd thought of as the gigolo at the Labor Day party, Jamal's eyes narrowed fractionally. Taking the plastic bag from Reba, he tossed it to Hassir, then reached for her hand. With a look at the name tag, he asked, "Dr. Mendoza?"

"Reba's fine. What she needs is a lazy weekend."

Reba gave Jamal an I-told-you-so grin, then turned to Harry. "Thanks. I'm sorry I kept you late."

Harry chuckled. "*De nada, chiquita.* I wouldn't have missed this for the world. Oh, by the way, there's an office space that might suit you opening up on the first floor in my building."

The position in Basjad that Jamal had offered her had caused her more than a few uneasy moments. She still didn't know what to do about it. On the other hand, Harry's office building had always appealed to her. And she knew that the lease would be within her budget. "When?" she asked, refusing to meet Jamal's eyes.

Jamal tensed, wondering if she had decided against working in Omari. Smoothly, he said, "Surely that can wait."

Harry looked from one taut face to the other thoughtfully. "I'll find out the particulars for you," he offered, turning back to the Emergency Room.

"Let's get out of here," Jamal muttered, and he scooped Reba up in his arms and made for the sliding doors.

Reba noticed the curious glances of two ambulance drivers and the receptionist and groaned silently. Pushing against Jamal's shoulder, she muttered, "Put me down. There's going to be enough gossip already."

"Then don't add to it," Jamal advised curtly, carrying her through the doors.

Outside, only a faint increase in humidity lingered after the storm. The pavement was dry and the evening sky was clear. Rashid must have spent the time cleaning the inside of the car, Reba thought, as she sank into the back seat. There was not a speck of dirt anywhere and the blanket she'd been wrapped in before lay neatly folded on the seat.

"Where to, master?" Rashid asked, holding the door open.

"Home." Jamal knocked dried dirt off his boots and joined Reba. "We'll pick up clean clothes for you later."

Reba opened her mouth to ask Jamal to drop her off at her apartment, then reconsidered when she remembered that she needed her car. Wearily, she watched Hassir and Rashid slide into the front seats and listened to the front doors click shut. The restless energy that her driven her until now seemed to flow out of her and she leaned her head back against the seat. As the motor purred to life, she said, "Thank you. But there's no need to trouble yourself. My car's still at the stables. I can drive myself home."

His lips tightened in exasperation. Did she always have to be so damned independent? "You're not driving anywhere. You are going to rest. Doctor's orders."

"I can do that the moment I get home. You've had quite a welcome, Jamal. I'm sure you have a number of things to see to."

"You definitely have a knack for understatements," Jamal remarked dryly, studying her taut profile. "Reba, I didn't fly more than ten thousand miles to see you only to spend the evening alone."

For a moment Reba was too stunned to speak. Happiness flooded through her. Then she recalled the days she'd spent waiting for a phone call. And the nights she'd lain awake worrying, and her temper flared. "Do you know how incredibly arrogant you sound? I am not a piece of property you can walk away from without a backward glance and expect to be there when you come back." With an uneasy glance at the front, she stopped, wondering how much sound filtered through the glass partition.

"The glass is bulletproof, reasonably soundproof and impossible to see through from the front." Jamal wished he could read her mind as easily as her face. Whatever she felt for him, he was determined to bring it out into the open. He was tired of making all the moves, of having her melt in his arms one moment and reject him the next. His lips pressed together angrily. "I didn't call you, because I tried to put you from my mind. God knows, I don't need any more complications in my life. And you definitely are a complication."

"And this grudging admission should make me happy?" Reba asked sharply. But somehow it did. Reba felt a smile tug at the corners of her mouth.

With a groan Jamal pulled her against him, cupping her face with his hand. "I must be losing my mind, but I did miss that sharp tongue of yours." This was what he needed, to touch her, to challenge her, to forget the world beyond this valley, if only for moments at a time. He hadn't realized just how much he felt for her until he'd seen her fall. "Tell me you're glad to see me."

Reba caught her breath, trying to see past his face into his heart. She wanted to believe that he felt something real for her, that he needed her as much as she needed him. She had missed him, more than she wanted to admit to herself or to Jamal. "Of course I am," she admitted cautiously. "Life was positively dull without you. No mud, no bossing around, no—"

"Witch." Laughing, Jamal stilled her teasing lips with his mouth. Folding her tightly against him, he kissed her deeply until the laughter stopped, until her body began to tremble and her arms held him as tightly as he was holding her.

"Now let's try this again," he said, raising his head, his deep voice sliding over her like rough silk. "I missed you."

How could she still doubt that he wanted her? Desire blazed in his eyes and his face was hard with need. For now, for today and perhaps for tomorrow, he belonged to her. "I missed you more," she said softly, circling the passionate outline of his mouth with her fingertip. "Riding wasn't nearly as much fun without you."

He nipped her finger, his eyes glinting wickedly. "I hope tonight will make up for it," he whispered, before taking her lips in a powerful kiss.

Reba's hand moved to his shoulders, sliding up the strong column of his neck and resting on his cheek. He responded by pulling her closer. Reba arched into him, wanting more of him.

A shiver running through her, she wished that this moment could last, but knew that it would end. Dear Lord, she thought, would she be strong enough to pick up the pieces of her life when Jamal left?

Jamal felt her tense and abruptly raised his head, swearing beneath his breath. He should have realized that the fall had left her more shaken that she wanted to admit. Whatever needed to be brought out into the open would have to wait until after she'd had some rest.

Leaning back against the side of the car, he shifted her until she lay with her head on his shoulder and her legs curled up on the seat. "Try to sleep. Everything else can wait until you're stronger."

"Oh, I'm fine. I'm no more off balance now than at any other time you are around," Reba said wryly, watching the car pass by Smitty's, one of her favorite places to shop. Was she mad to leave solid ground and take the leap knowing she might fall, and fall hard? She swallowed. She was tired of playing it safe; she had proved that this afternoon. If she crawled back into her shell now, she'd regret it for the rest of her life. "How is your father?"

"Like a bear with a sore head." Jamal smiled into her hair. "They took away his cigarettes, put him on a low-sugar, low-cholesterol diet, and they search his servants for concealed food every time before they are allowed into his rooms. Yesterday when I visited him, he threw a pillow at my head and told me not to show my face again. But he's well. Better than I dared to hope."

"I'm glad," Reba said softly. "How much longer does he have to stay?"

"A week. Ten days at the most." Jamal felt Reba stir, sensing her question before she could put it into words. He shrugged. "I have no idea how much he knows about Muhrad." After all his fears, Washington had been an anticlimax. There had been nothing, no wrong move, no suspicious word, not one damn hint. Since then, even the HIB was quiet. Sometimes it felt like the calm before a storm. "Perhaps he's biding his time until after his return to Basjad."

Reba felt frustration and anger rippling through him, a silent rage demanding to be released. Her arm went around him in a gesture of comfort. "I'm sorry I brought it up."

Jamal shook his head. Nothing could ease his frustration and anger, but it was a relief not to have to hide it all the time. "I should be the one to apologize. I didn't want you to become a part of the deception."

How much longer could he stand the strain? Reba wondered. How much longer could he compromise his honor and integrity? There could be no winners in this power game, no matter what the outcome. Everyone would loose. Muhrad, Yussuf and especially Jamal. She swallowed the sudden lump in her throat. "I'm glad I know the truth," she said softly, "I can deal with deceptions and lies, as long as they don't stand between us."

Ten days.

She would have him for ten days, Reba thought. But ten days was more than she'd hoped for. At that moment the

limousine turned, slowing down as it approached the tall
wrought-iron gates. Reba decided she would have no regrets about the brief time remaining for them.

After reading the same sentence four times without taking in a word of it, Jamal tossed the *Financial News* on his
desk and pushed back his chair. How much longer should
he let her sleep? he wondered, pacing the room. More than
two hours had passed since Reba had fallen asleep in the
Jacuzzi. She had barely stirred when he wrapped her in one
of his robes and carried her to bed. Each time he had
checked on her since, she had been in the same position he'd
left her in, curled up on her side with her beautiful hair
spread out like a fan.

The last time he had touched the strands, they had been
dry and smooth as silk. He frowned. Each time it was harder
to pull away. He wanted to lie down beside Reba and simply hold her. He would be content with that. Just holding
her. He was lucky to have the chance; things could have
turned out differently this afternoon.

Pacing back to the desk, he picked up this week's *Etoile,*
a French newsmagazine, flipped through it, stopping to stare
at a photo of himself on his boat at Cap d'Antibes six weeks
ago, with Marina Picard, the French foreign minister's
daughter, draped all over him. It seemed like a million years
ago.

Reba would hate being labeled his latest affair. He wanted
to spare her the sly looks, the sneers and the whispers. The
Clinic would be full of gossip. But all his money and all his
power could not shield her from it.

Only marriage could do that.

He paced back to the window. How could he marry her
when his life was poised on the edge? How could he uproot
her by asking her to come with him to Omari? For all he
knew she had decided against even spending one year in

Basjad. Even frequent trips home could never compensate her for the loss of all she loved.

And then there was Azadeh, who had made his mother's life hell.

A small smile suddenly made his lips twitch. Then again, how could he doubt that Reba would be able to handle Azadeh? Reba would probably add the woman to her list of nags, bulls and honorable fools. Life in the palace would never be the same.

Abruptly, he turned and left the study. At the moment he couldn't promise Reba a future. And he didn't have the strength to send her back to the past. But he could love her while the twilight lasted.

Half-awake, Reba stirred when she heard the door open and close. Her eyes roamed the dark, unfamiliar room, staying for a moment on the wall of glass facing the bed where dark hills rolled away in silent splendor. Then she became aware of Jamal.

"Where am I?" she asked, her voice husky with sleep.

"In my bed."

"How did I get here? The last thing I remember—" Reba groaned. Startled, she sat up. A swift look down her body confirmed what her skin had already told her. The color rose to her cheeks; she was wrapped from head to toe in only a soft, white terry-cloth robe. Jamal must have lifted her out of the water, clothed her in the robe and carried her to his room. "How long ago was that?" she asked, self-consciously pushing her hair back from her face.

"About two hours ago." Jamal flicked on the recessed lights, dimmed them and walked to the bed. "How do you feel?"

She had wasted two whole hours! "Why did you let me sleep so long?" she asked, sliding from the bed, watching him cross the wide expanse of carpet toward her in his graceful, powerful stride.

"Because you needed it."

His bare feet sank into the thick plush, making no sound. The taut half smile now curving his lips made her catch her breath and heat spread through her veins. Lord, he was beautiful! she thought, letting her eyes slide over his broad shoulders, his sculpted chest with its sprinkling of dark curls, following the narrow dark line down to the low-riding jeans. Sleek arrogant power. Hungry to feel the subtle strength and heat, she reached out to him. How good it felt not to have to hide her feelings anymore, to be able to touch him freely and to move straight into his arms. "Love me, Jamal," she asked softly. Tonight, this first time together, she ached for some tenderness. Tonight, she needed the illusion that he returned her love.

"Try and stop me," Jamal groaned, splaying his fingers along her jaw. For weeks he had waited and teased himself with loving her. For weeks he had fought the sharp desire and his conscience until his body was a furnace of need and frustration. Now that she was here within his arms, the sharp edge softened. He didn't want to rush her. Or himself, he suddenly realized. This first time he wanted to linger, to discover all the secrets she'd kept hidden for so long. He wanted her to remember tonight as something special, a slow, gentle dream.

Thus determined, he gently traced her face with his fingertips. Then his arm went around her waist, molding her slender body against him. His fingers combed through her hair, fragrant, vibrant, black silk. "I like your hair loose," he murmured, tracing her high cheekbones with the tip of his tongue. "I've dreamed of the feel and scent of it. You've haunted my days and nights ever since we met."

She closed her eyes briefly, glad that she hadn't been the only one to feel the magic. Opening them, her hand touched his face, drawing his mouth back to her. "You looked unreal that first evening, like an illusion created by twilight. Until you faced me across the fence."

Lightly, she traced the line of his jaw, slightly raspy beneath her touch. "You were so arrogant, as if you owned the world. But like any other mortal you were hot and sweaty and your shirt stuck to your skin. Even then, I wanted to touch you." Her lips met his with sudden urgency, as if she still couldn't quite believe that this was real, that she was here in his arms.

They didn't speak after that.

Their lips touched and opened; tongues met and intertwined. Breath mingled with breath. Tenderness slowly changed to tremors, warmth to passion.

His skin was dark against her tan. His nipples were sensitive, hardening at her touch, and the skin covering his flat hard stomach quivered as she raked her nails over it. Encouraged, she ran her palms freely over him.

A groan escaped him, his control fraying. He caught her wrist, stilling her hand. Lifting her in his arms, he hungrily took her mouth again.

Moonlight shining through a wall of glass danced on the brass frame of his bed and formed a pool of light on the white carpet. Beyond, the hills rolled away in silent splendor.

He placed her within the pool of light and slowly slid the robe from her shoulders, revealing all he had tried to ignore when he carried her from the Jacuzzi. He caught his breath sharply at the strength and grace of her long legs, gently rounded hips and firm breasts. She was perfection from her head to her toes, as stunningly beautiful as Aphrodite rising from the foaming sea and as sensual as the houri of his Arab soul.

They reached for each other. Passion flared with the touch of their bodies. Trembling, Reba's hands went to his jeans and opened the snap, removing the last barrier.

With a single fluid movement Jamal carried her to the king-size brass bed, placing her on the silky sheets, and joined her. In the soft darkness they discovered each other with their hands and their lips.

Her breasts fitted into his hands as if they had been made for him—firm, yet soft and sensitive to his touch and his tongue. He lingered there, feeling her body tighten with each stroke and each taste, until she moaned softly. The skin of her stomach was as soft as satin, though the muscles beneath were firm, tensing beneath his touch as her hips arched into him.

"Jamal!" Her husky voice was both protest and invitation. The few times she had allowed her fantasies to stray she had imagined them coming together in a clash of impatience, desire and heat. Never had she imagined such sweetness, such patience, such tenderness. As if she were infinitely precious to him. She felt wanted, needed. Cherished. That was enough, wasn't it? It had to be, she told herself, because he could never give her anything else. Her body strained toward him, opening to him.

Slowly he joined her, filled her, feeling her tight sheath pulsate and her heat seep into him. He filled her more with each stroke, fanning the fire slowly until it began to burn like a bright flame. He could smell the fresh lemony scent of her mingling with the musky smell of passion, felt her grow wild beneath him, matching his own hunger and need. Desire expanded and soared until their fences shattered into a million pieces, leaving only a man and woman, joined together in love.

Afterward, Jamal held her sweat-dampened body in his arms, looking out the window with unfocused eyes. He couldn't speak. He couldn't move. He was stunned by the incredible release of emotions. What they had just shared had been more than tenderness, more than desire, hunger and need. More than he'd ever experienced before—and more than he would ever feel again with another woman. For him it had been a revelation.

He was in love.

He had lain here countless times, drawn by the infinity of the sky, planning his next trip, his next deal. Until now, he'd never questioned his restlessness, but had taken it as part of his Bedouin heritage. He was a modern nomad who used planes and cars instead of camels and horses, trading oil instead of blankets, livestock and rugs. And when he'd thought of marriage, he had planned to choose another nomad, one with a background similar to his.

Instead, he had fallen in love with a woman with roots so deep in this arid land she could never be truly happy anywhere else. A woman as unsuitable for him as his mother had been for his father.

And yet the only woman who felt right in his arms.

Reba stirred slightly and opened her eyes, watching the moon shine through the window, wondering if she was floating on a cloud. She was lying with her head on Jamal's shoulder, her hand resting above his heart. He had made love to her like a man searching for something elusive. Had he found it? she wondered. Had she been woman enough to fill his needs?

"I've fantasized about making love with you here before. But my imagination fell far short of reality," Jamal answered her silent question, gently brushing her tangled hair back from her face. He wanted to look at her, in this, perhaps the most important, moment of his life. Her eyes were half-closed and still dazed with pleasure and there was a slight smile on her lips. "No regrets?"

She still felt too stunned to move. But as her eyes began to focus, she spotted stars winking at her as if they knew a secret she had yet to discover. Her lips curved and the pressure of her hand increased over his heart. "I'm still floating. You're a wizard, a dream maker, Jamal. I didn't know making love could be so beautiful. How could I regret it?"

Jamal traced her lips with his fingers. Her answer should have pleased him. And a few hours ago it had been all he wanted to hear. At least that was what he'd told himself at the time. Now, he realized he wanted more. His arm closed around her tightly, his hand buried in the wild tangle of her damp hair. Desire stirred, hardening his body and clouding his mind.

Rolling over, he filled her with firm hard thrusts and felt her body begin moving with his. He urged her on with driving, insistent strokes, taking her on the wild ride he had promised her.

Later, when she could think again, she warned herself that no matter how intense his feelings at the moment, they wouldn't last and couldn't last, because he didn't belong to her or to himself. One morning she would wake up alone again. But tonight he was hers. She fell asleep with her arms wrapped tightly around him.

Listening to her breathing deepen, Jamal wondered what his parents would think of Reba. Kitty would be happy. She'd wanted him to marry an American woman for years. Predictably, his father would be furious. He shrugged. The tug of love, between his parents and between his worlds, had always been there. He had learned to live with it long ago, just as he had accepted that dream makers were realists.

But as he looked out into the night with Reba's body curled into him, with her breath moistly flowing over his skin, he wanted to dream like any other man. Of a future with Reba. Of Reba sharing his life, of Reba having his children, of growing old with her.

They were dreams as fragile as the moonbeams now dancing over them.

Chapter 10

Unlike those in the rest of the house, the furnishings in Jamal's sitting room embodied a mixture of styles, old and new, Western and Eastern. There were modern couches, light and comfortable; rosewood tables, intricately carved and inlaid; tasseled leather hassocks; prayer rugs and cases filled with old books and paperbacks. This room, Reba thought, walking over to the concert piano, was a true reflection of the man she loved.

"Who are all these people?" she asked, idly studying the photos displayed on the gleaming surface of the piano. "I recognize your mother and your father."

"Point out the photos that interest you and I'll tell you who is who," Jamal said lazily, leaning back against the couch, swirling the cognac in the snifter. He enjoyed watching her move around the room with her unhurried grace. Like him, she wore a *dishdashah,* a loose-fitting white garment covering her from neck to toe. As she moved, the soft cotton dragged over the white carpet, molding itself to her body with each step. Just watching her, he felt his desire stirring once again.

Reba lifted a silver frame showing two beautiful young women with huge dark eyes and dusky faces, wearing European clothes.

"Those are Muhrad's two wives, Miriam on the left and Lana on the right." Jamal raised the snifter to his mouth, controlling the heat slowly coursing through his veins. Her interest in his family was a good chance to draw her closer into his life.

Reba heard the warm affection in his voice. Carefully, she replaced the frame, trying to hide the swift surge of dislike his brother's name always caused. "The concept of a harem seems such an anachronism in this day and age," she said, trying to keep her voice casual.

"For an Arab, no more so than the American communes of the sixties." Over the rim of his glass Jamal threw her a narrow-eyed glance, wondering if he'd imagined a certain tightness in her voice. "Today, a harem is mostly filled with female relatives and young children, not concubines. Both Miriam and Lana have a Western education, but they preferred marriage."

"Did they have a choice?" Reba asked dryly.

"They didn't object and seem perfectly content. A Muslim woman is more practical about marriage than women in the West. She views it as her only way to gain respect, social standing and security. Miriam studied music in London and has done much to promote young artists in Omari." He pointed at the sculpture of a horse in full gallop, so beautifully detailed it almost seemed alive. "That was carved by one of Miriam's protégés. Lana was a business major at the Sorbonne." Amusement crept into his voice. "Don't ask me how she ever managed to get her degree. At the moment her sole purpose in life seems to be to fill as much closet space as possible with haute couture clothes."

A grin crossed Reba's face. "She sounds more typical." Then her glance returned to Kitty's photograph and she shook her head. "I still don't understand how your mother thought she could live in a harem."

He'd often asked himself the same question. Now, for the first time he understood. "Kitty is impulsive and emotional, more guided by instincts and feelings than common sense. She loved my father, and to her, love meant marriage. Also, she didn't live in the harem. During the months she spent in Omari, she shared my father's apartments."

In some ways he wasn't so different from his mother, after all, Jamal thought, drinking his brandy. For the first time in his life he wanted a permanent relationship. He wanted to slow down, take things easy and delegate more, so he would have more time to spend with Reba. He had visions of lazy evenings like tonight. And if he was away it would be nice to call her at the end of the day or simply think of her before he went to sleep at the other side of the world. He grimaced. Such relationships rarely worked.

"Despite all their differences, your parents managed to remain friends," Reba said thoughtfully. "The news mentioned that your mother went to Houston."

"They still meet occasionally." Jamal stared down into his glass and added slowly, "I remember the early years after they separated, when Kitty would be depressed for weeks afterward. I promised myself then, not to repeat my father's mistake. A marriage between East and West rarely works."

At his warning Reba's heart twisted painfully. No regrets, she told herself sternly. "You're talking about extremes," she pointed out with calm logic. "Perhaps if your father hadn't been married already, they might have had a chance. Why didn't your father divorce Azadeh instead?"

Jamal shook his head. "Kitty hated the heat, wearing the veil, even the music. And Yussuf's marriage to Azadeh was a political necessity. He was barely twenty when my grandfather was murdered by a member of the Al Assam, the second-largest tribe in Omari. My father fought them for years. He finally stopped the blood feud by marrying the daughter of their sheikh.''

Leaning back against the piano, Reba said softly, ''I can't help but feel sorry for Azadeh. To have to marry under such conditions is bad enough. But to lose her husband's affection so completely must have hurt and humiliated her.''

One of Jamal's dark brows shot up and he smiled at her crookedly. ''So. You would feel sorry for the wicked witch of the East? That's what I used to call her as a child,'' he added lightly, placing the empty glass on the table. Getting to his feet, he walked up behind her and wrapped his arms around her waist. He was tired of watching her from a distance.

Without hesitation, Reba leaned against him and pointed at the portrait of a young man with angular features and dark wavy hair.

''That's Hussein, Muhrad's son.'' He noticed a small tightening of her lips when he mentioned his brother's name. Slowly, Jamal went on. ''The photo was taken only a few weeks ago, before he returned to school in Montreux.'' Firmly, he turned Reba around, cupping her chin. ''Is Muhrad the reason why you've decided not to work in Omari?''

''I haven't decided either way.'' Reba chose her words carefully. ''It seems such a long way off. So much can happen in a year.'' Your father could find out the truth and you would have to give up your nomad life and settle down behind the palace walls. Perhaps even marry for political reasons, like your father did. The thought made her fingers curl into the soft cotton covering his chest. ''And yes, your brother is part of the reason,'' she added.

Abruptly, Jamal released her. Walking to the patio door, he looked out into the garden where a Jacuzzi spilled water into a brightly lit pool. "Is it hate or fear that makes you hesitate?" he asked harshly.

Reba stared at his straight back with troubled eyes. He looked so distant suddenly, so lonely, his broad shoulders braced beneath the thin cotton of his Arab dress. Slowly, she followed him and laid her hand on his arm. "Both, I guess. Not—" Jamal cut her off.

"Contrary to your opinion, Reba, I am not a fool." He stiffened, brushed off her hand and turned around, his face impassive. His voice was neutral as he spoke. "I protect what is mine. My brother need not trouble you."

Oh, the fragile ego of macho men! Frustrated, Reba felt her temper rise. "In the first place, I'm not yours to take care of and protect, Jamal. Also, the job should not be contingent on our personal relationship."

Jamal's brows lifted arrogantly. It was rare for someone to question him and his motives. "I disagree on the first point, but I go along with the second. That's not all, though, is it?"

Shaking her head, Reba stared down at her twisted hands. "No matter how hard I try, I cannot help but . . . but resent your brother. Not only for what he did to the passengers and their families, but also for what he's doing to you." She splayed a hand on his chest. "If you want an answer tonight, I would have to say no."

Jamal looked down at her hand, so slender and delicate, and from there to her vulnerable, sensitive face. Her softness was deceptive. He knew she had a strength capable of dealing with whatever life handed her, of facing setbacks without allowing herself to become bitter and hard. Was that why he loved her?

He hadn't wanted to fall in love. Love made a person vulnerable and dependent, weaknesses he couldn't afford, especially not now. Why couldn't he have met her months ago, before fate had decided to turn his life upside down?

He wished he could take her away somewhere, where they could be an ordinary couple in ordinary times. A mountain cabin somewhere in the Swiss Alps, perhaps, without servants, bodyguards, telephones and helicopters. He shrugged. He couldn't change who and what he was. Still, the cabin sounded nice, he thought, making a mental note to have Alfred look into it. "It can wait a few more days," he said slowly, reluctantly.

Reba felt as if she was letting him down, and his understanding only made her feel worse. Illogically, she wished he had been more persistent. Perhaps that was why her anger flared when he continued on a sharper note.

"Talking about work reminds me of something else. Did you find someone to treat the child?"

Reba snatched her hand away. "I only treated Ramon once since you left," she said, trying to stay calm.

Jamal's eyes narrowed and his lips compressed. "In other words, you haven't even started to look."

"That's right. And I'm not going to." Reba's chin came up in challenge. Damn it, he had no right to tell her what to do! She couldn't allow him to interfere in her life to such an extent. "Perhaps it's just as well that this issue is coming up now. My professional life is my own, Jamal. Where my patients' welfare is concerned, I make the decisions, whether it's here or in Omari."

"We're not talking about your patients' welfare, but about your own!" he ground out, starting to pace the room. "And don't speak of reasonable precautions to me," he cut her off when she opened her mouth to argue, "I know exactly what that means!"

"I'm sure you do," she said, her eyes glowing dangerously. "You don't want me to worry. Now I'm telling you the same."

He was through with logic, Jamal decided, striding back to her and gripping her shoulders. All that mattered was her safety and he *would* protect her. "I want your promise that you'll find a solution or I'll take the necessary steps to keep you safe," he demanded between gritted teeth.

Reba stared at him, her face taut with anger. "The day I find one of your men following me is the last day you'll see me," she promised him furiously, trying to twist away.

He held her firmly, staring down at her for long seconds while he tried to control his temper. "Threats don't work with me, Reba. You should know this by now," he finally said, his voice cool, firm and distant. "If you value your independence and pride more than our relationship, then I haven't lost much, have I?" Abruptly, he left her, opening the door and walking out into the warm night.

"Oh, hell!" Reba muttered, running a shaky hand through her hair, her eyes following him to the edge of the pool. She hadn't meant to hurt him. She hadn't known that he cared enough to be hurt! Her heart thudding, she went after him and wrapped her arms around his waist. "I'm sorry, Jamal," she whispered huskily, leaning her face against his back. "I will talk to Social Service on Monday and see what can be done."

Jamal slowly willed his tension to ease. He didn't renew his offer to pay for the boy's treatment. To him the sum meant nothing and her safety everything. But pride and independence were important to her, more so now and with him, he suspected, because of the differences between them. Turning, he reached for her and framed her face with his rough hands. "You've got a nasty temper, my sweet."

Reba's lips curved. She started to mutter something about calling a kettle black when his mouth came down and shut her up. Lifting her in his arms he stepped to the edge of the pool.

"You definitely need cooling off," Jamal told her with a glint in his eyes, his arms tightening around her suddenly squirming form.

"You wouldn't dare." Seeing the purpose in his eyes, Reba wrapped her arms tightly around his neck, laughing up at him, excitement pushing the argument to the back of her mind. "I'll take you with me!"

"Of course." With his mouth on hers he stepped over the edge into the warm water, sinking to the bottom in a tangle of legs.

"You're crazy," Reba sputtered when she surfaced, taking deep gulps of air.

"Yes. About you." Jamal trod water easily.

"You didn't even know if I could swim." Reba wrapped the clinging material around her waist to free her legs.

"For once I'd behave like a gentleman and rescue the lady in distress." Jamal splashed water into her face, then lunged for her.

Reba's eyes narrowed, excitement bubbling up. She waited until he surfaced less than a foot away from her, then blinded him with a big splash. Before he could recover, she swam to the shallow end, stripped off her garment and tossed it away. Turning, she watched Jamal pull the *dishdashah* over his head in the middle of the pool before he sliced through the water with long powerful strokes.

Laughing, Reba waited until he'd almost caught up with her. The moment he came within touching distance, she dived as sleekly as a mermaid, swimming to the side of the pool. As she pushed herself up, his hands fastened around her waist, pulling her back into his arms. His hands slid up her wet skin, cupping her breasts while capturing her mouth in a hot burning kiss.

A stab of fierce pleasure ran through Reba and her arms went around his back, her fingers raking his skin until a shudder went through him. Then Jamal pushed himself off with his feet, taking her with him to the wide shallow steps. He made love to her there until the water sizzled, until the thin wall of resistance crumbled. Until she came apart in his arms.

Early-morning sunshine rose over the hills, flooding the room with light. Blinking, Reba raised her arm to shield her eyes and rolled over. Today was Sunday, she thought drowsily, and she didn't have to go to work. She could spend the whole day with Jamal. Squinting, she turned over and reached for him.

The spot was empty, the sheets cool. Frowning, she sat up in bed, afraid for a moment that she had dreamed it all. Her eyes went from the rumpled sheets to the dented pillow next to hers. Hugging her legs, she expelled a soft sigh of relief. Last night hadn't been a dream.

"Do you always pop up like a jack-in-the-box when you wake up?" Jamal stood in the doorway to his dressing room, rolling up the sleeves of a cream-colored shirt. Brown denims hugged his narrow hips and he wore gleaming riding boots.

"No. I thought— I guess it's the strange bed." It was ridiculous to feel self-conscious, Reba thought. After last night, there wasn't an inch of her body Jamal didn't know, but she pulled the satin sheet a little tighter around herself. Perhaps seeing him dressed while she was still naked beneath the covers made her feel vulnerable. "Where are you going?"

Jamal closed the door behind him, came into the room and stopped at the side of the bed. "The office. I have some phone calls to make." She looked just as he had always imagined she would first thing in the morning. There was a glow on her face; her eyes were still heavy with sleep and dark with passion, but they grew brighter with each second. His gaze lingered on her mouth, still swollen and full, then moved to her hair. Bending over, he buried his hands in the wild tangle and tilted her head up. "Go back to sleep," he said, kissing her softly.

"You shouldn't have to work. It's Sunday and barely six o'clock," Reba protested, tasting the freshness of his mouth. The mattress sank beneath his weight as he lowered himself and pushed her back on the pillows.

"Sunday is a working day in Omari, and in Basjad it'
already 4:00 p.m." Leaning over her, he breathed in he
scent, his hands sliding over her soft warm skin. "I won't be
long. Two hours at the most. We'll still have time to rid
before it gets too hot."

Reba looked up at him. He'd taken a shower and his fac
was full of vitality, without any trace of the wild night they
had just spent together. What had she expected? Reba asked
herself ruefully. For him it was no novelty to wake up wit
a woman in his bed.

She sighed. She had promised herself not to dwell on the
negative, to live one day at a time. Firmly she stifled he
uneasiness and said brightly, "Then I may as well go bacl
home and change."

Frowning, Jamal stood up. "Tell Hassir what you nee
and he'll get it for you."

Her lips flattened. She did not want to wear clothes tha
had probably been left by her predecessors. "It would be s
much simpler if I drove home."

Reaching for his watch on the nightstand, Jamal fas
tened it around his wrist, trying to control the swift flash o
anger. "My mother keeps some things here," he said evenly
"Kitty is about two inches shorter than you, but you ar
about the same size."

Reba bit her lips, feeling ashamed, but also relieved. Sh
would have to stop suspecting his every word and gestur
and learn to trust him more, she told herself sternly. Noth
ing killed a relationship faster than suspicion. "Thank you."
She pushed herself up on one elbow. "But since you'll b
working for the next two hours I may as well get my ow
clothes. Also, Rachel and Harry will be worried if I don'
come back."

Jamal's eyes narrowed. Did she already regret last night
Was that why she wanted to leave? "Harry knows where yo
are," he pointed out coolly. He knew she didn't trust him
that she was afraid to allow herself to feel too deeply. H

wanted to reassure her and tell her that she had nothing to fear. If he told her that he loved her, that it was different with her, she wouldn't believe him. How could she? Trust would have to come gradually, a day at a time. "And so, I guess, does the rest of the hospital."

Reba shrugged. "I've dealt with gossip before." His protectiveness made her reach for his hand and press it to her cheek. "When I broke my engagement to Toby Randall so soon after my accident, the papers had a field day." She saw anger flare in his eyes and kissed his rough palm soothingly. "Let me worry about my reputation."

"If you don't mind, I'll worry about it, too." He tilted her face up and stilled her protest with a firm kiss. Her lips responded instantly, warm and eager, an invitation hard to resist. Before he succumbed to temptation and joined her in the bed, he pulled back. There was a harsh edge in his voice when he said, "I can't stop the talk at the hospital. But I'll do what I can to keep your name out of the papers." Walking to the door, he added, "Hassir will drive you. Be back in two hours."

"Yes, master," Reba said in mock deference.

"Keep it up." Grinning, Jamal closed the door behind him.

It had taken her three hours.

She hadn't drawn out the time deliberately, Reba told herself as she waited for the wrought-iron gates to open. First she had wasted time arguing with Hassir. She preferred her own car, just as she preferred her own clothes. They kept her in touch with reality, reminding her of who she was. And the drive to her apartment had taken more than twenty minutes each way.

Smiling now at the dusky-skinned guard, she drove through the gate. As she went up the steep hill, the suitcase slid against the car's back door. She'd packed enough clothes for any eventuality—swimsuit, slacks and evening wear. She could hardly run around in her riding gear for the rest of the day.

She found Jamal sitting behind a big glass-topped desk which was littered with stacks of papers and a silver coffee tray.

At her entrance, he looked up and leaned back in his chair. "Did your watch stop?" he asked with a glint in his eyes.

Her apology died on her lips. "No," she said calmly, stepping into the middle of the big room. "It just took me longer than I thought. I told Hassir that I'd probably be late. Didn't he give you my message?"

Nodding, Jamal pushed back his chair and strode across the thick white carpet to her side. During the three hours she'd been gone he'd accomplished hardly any work. Cupping her chin, he asked, "Why the hell did you drive yourself?"

"Because knowing that Hassir is waiting makes me nervous. Also, both the limo and Hassir are rather conspicuous. And I like to be in control." But mostly I need to keep my independence, she added silently.

Jamal ran his thumb over her mouth. "I was worried about you. What if you had a flat tire or an accident on that lonely stretch of road?"

Her lips responded instantly and her heart warmed at his concern. But a small part of her mind resisted the seduction. "I've driven half of my life without an accident. And I know how to change a tire."

He wondered if she'd ever get used to bodyguards. He'd been surrounded by them all his life and there were still times when their presence irked him. "I hope you're better at changing automobile tires than fixing bicycle pedals," he muttered before taking her lips in a fierce kiss that melted her resistance and left her clinging weakly to him. Threading his fingers through her hair, he viewed her face with satisfaction. "I want you to move in with me."

Slowly, Reba withdrew her arms from around his neck and took a step back. "Jamal, that isn't a very practical solution. I can't just close up my apartment and live with you."

"Why not?" Jamal challenged her with narrowed eyes. "I can't move into yours, not unless we pitch a tent outside your place." He saw her lips twitch and pressed his advantage. "I want you, Reba, and not just in my bed. As busy as we both are, we won't have much time to spend together if you live half an hour away."

Reba's heart leaped at his words and she bit her lip in indecision. The temptation to live with him, to share his life, if only for a little while, was so great she wanted to throw caution to the wind. Then she thought of all the impractical changes a move would involve and shook her head. "It seems silly to close my apartment, to change my mailing address and telephone number for the short time you'll be here. Let's just enjoy the hours we can share. There should be no regrets from either of us when you leave."

Abruptly, Jamal turned away and walked to the window overlooking the valley. Could any woman be in love and remain so reasonable at the same time? Didn't she resent the hours away from him? Damn it, he'd paced the floor since she left, wondering if she would come back or if he would have to chase her clear across town. Raking his hand through his hair, he wondered if, for the first time in his life, he'd misread the signs. He was too much a diplomat to confront her openly. Instead, he offered her an alternative. Carefully he said, "Then at least keep some clothes here."

Reba's lips curved. "I packed a suitcase this morning."

Briefly, he closed his eyes in relief. Turning, he said, "There's something else I wanted to discuss with you." Walking to his desk, he picked up a stack of papers. "I'm not going to press you for an answer about the job. But the equipment has to be ordered soon. Also, will you hire the rest of the therapists? Place ads in the journals and whatever else is necessary?'' When she nodded, he added, ''And I need help with these.''

Curiously, Reba walked to his side and took the sheets he was holding out to her. Reading, she realized that they were order forms for hospital equipment—beds, mattresses, nightstands. Halfway down the page she came across sixty stretchers. She frowned. ''I don't like this brand of equipment,'' she said firmly. ''The price is outrageous. What you pay for are little gadgets like different brakes, bars that collapse instead of fold and ball-bearing wheels that break down constantly. And the frame is oversize and barely fits into regular elevators. The company is also very slow to send replacement parts.''

Jamal hid the gleam of satisfaction beneath lowered lashes. ''What other equipment don't you like?''

Reba skimmed the rest of the page. Shaking her head, she said, ''I don't know much about any of the other items, but I can find out for you.''

Jamal leaned against the glass top and crossed his legs. ''Under one condition only,'' he said softly. ''I'll hire you as a consultant.''

''No. I don't want to get paid for it. I'll help you in my spare time. If that isn't enough you'll have to hire someone else.''

''The Clinic would be pleased to lend you to me,'' Jamal challenged her. ''I'd rather not go through Tim Horner, though.''

Reba glared at him. ''That's blackmail.''

He ran his finger lightly down her neck, sliding beneath the collar of her crisp white shirt. ''No, Reba, that's good business sense. I know you'll do a more thorough job than a stranger.'' He could feel her pulse skip and leap beneath his touch, saw her eyes darken. He bent his head. ''And there are other benefits. I want you with me as much as possible.''

Reba felt a stab of panic. "You're pulling solid ground from beneath my feet." Her fingers clenched.

When she started to shake her head, he framed her face with hard determined hands. "Then hold on to me. I won't let you fall." And somehow he would keep the promise, he swore to himself. With her face still caught in his hands he kissed her. His mouth demanded a response.

For a few breathless moments she resisted. She could feel the hint of anger and frustration, and the determination in his kiss. Then desire flared beyond her control. If it had been possible she would have pulled back, would have ended it here and now; but already solid ground seemed too far away.

Her arms went around his corded neck, holding on to him. As the kiss deepened she ran her fingers through his hair, drawing his head closer, and sighing his name. In response he crushed her to him until not even a breath fit between them.

Passion consumed them, fast, furious, spinning out of control. This time it was Reba who tugged at his clothes, removing the barriers between them, needing the contact of flesh against burning flesh. Her need fanned Jamal's. With a groan he tumbled her onto the carpet, reaching for buttons, buckles and zippers.

Last night had been gentle, teasing, passionate, but it hadn't been like this—wild impatience growing into frenzy, a challenge of two strong wills. Reba did not want to be swept away on a magic carpet, or to be tossed like a leaf into the air. She snatched at control and power, rolling him over onto his back.

Hungrily, her mouth slid over him, from his lips, down his throat to his chest, nipping, then soothing, raking her nails through the curls, following the narrowing hairline all the way to his jeans. His flat stomach hardened as she pulled at the snap—pulling, tugging, stripping.

"Reba." With the last shreds of control Jamal reached for her, drew her mouth back to his, trying to slow down the pace. Then she lowered herself to him, capturing him body and soul, arching as the pleasure filled her. Faster and faster she drove them on. With a groan Jamal snatched her to him, rolling her beneath him in a wild tangle of limbs. Then he took her to fulfillment in a bright surge of power to a wild release.

Even after their bodies had cooled down and their breathing had returned to normal, he held on to her. With a rueful smile, he glanced at his desk, wondering how he would ever be able to work here again without memories teasing him. "Are you all right?"

"Yes." Her voice sounded dazed, even to her own ears, as she tried to come to terms with her wild behavior. "What about you?"

"Fine. But I think we've done enough exercise for one morning. You were supposed to have a lazy weekend."

"I am," she said, pushing herself up on one elbow to look at him. He looked younger, more relaxed than she had ever seen him, she thought, trailing her fingers over his face. "So many people feed off your strength," she said quietly, circling his mouth. "But who takes care of you?"

His eyes were a velvety dark brown as they stared back at her. "Are you applying for the job?" he asked softly.

"Temporarily." With a tender smile she brushed his unruly hair back. Her office could wait for another few weeks. "Long enough, I hope, to teach the dream maker all about dreams."

When the newspapers called Jamal's life-style crazy they hadn't exaggerated one bit, Reba thought ten days later, driving past the spot where she'd met him that first evening. He used his helicopter and plane as she did her car, flying in and out of the compound for trips to Los Angeles, Denver and Houston. Except for a two-day trip to Washington, he always returned at night, sometimes exhausted, sometimes filled with restless energy. There were times when he was waiting for her and others when he came back after she'd fallen asleep.

They shared every night. Despite her earlier objections, she had all but moved into his house. But at least during the day they went their different ways. The arrangement should have suited her, Reba thought, watching a Harris hawk dive from the sky. She was hanging on to her independence. Even her pride was mostly intact. She frowned. What had been enough ten days ago wasn't enough now. Not anymore.

She blamed the new job for her discontent.

How could she keep her days and nights separate when she spent her lunch hours talking to the Purchasing Department, asking physicians and nurses about their preferences in equipment, poring over consumer ratings and checking with friends?

Yet she loved every minute of it.

In talking to Jamal's grooms' wives she'd learned facts about life in Omari that she couldn't have gained from books. Her lips curved. Even Jamal hadn't known that there was a perpetual shortage of soap at the hospitals in Basjad, and that the powdered milk used was little more than colored water.

Her riding was improving with each passing day. Speed no longer scared her. Whether it was her determination to keep up with Jamal or her distaste at being left behind in a cloud of dust, she didn't know. She followed him up and down hills. She matched him whether in a walk or a gallop. She even leaped over small crevices.

But she balked at jumps.

Every time she approached an obstacle, she froze. And though she'd fed and walked Sultan many times, she knew she wasn't ready yet to get on his back. Sometimes, she wondered if she'd ever have enough courage to take the final step.

The wrought-iron gates were barely visible now in the fading light. As she neared them, Reba took her foot off the accelerator and glanced up the hill. Jamal had stayed at home today. The temptation to stop and talk to him, if only for a few minutes before she treated Ramon, was hard to resist. Her hands gripped the wheel and her foot pressed on the accelerator, sending the car downhill. A few minutes wouldn't be enough.

And, if she was honest with herself, she also wanted to avoid another confrontation about Ramon. She had talked to the social worker and to various other organizations, but money was tight everywhere and the bureaucracy moved slowly.

At the bottom of the hill she turned on the lights. Tomorrow Yussuf was returning to Omari. She was dreading Jamal's departure. She couldn't bear to lose him, not now. She kept telling herself that he wasn't hers to lose, that their arrangement was temporary. Jamal's obligation lay far beyond this valley. He was a wizard at bridging distances with telephones, computers and fax machines, but sooner or later he would leave.

And when he did, their affair would end.

A physical relationship such as theirs could not be kept alive through machines. She wondered if he would break things off before he left or if he would ease out of the relationship slowly, allowing distance to dull the pain.

No regrets, she told herself firmly, peering into the darkening sky. She had known that things between them couldn't last. She watched the beam of her headlights reflect off a yellow warning sign: Narrow Bridge Ahead. Twilight was fading fast. For them there was no bridge large enough to span their worlds. Cinderella and her prince. She managed to smile a little.

Ten minutes later, Reba slowed down and turned into the rutted track leading to Ramon's house. She was running late tonight, she thought with an anxious glance at her watch. As the wheels sank into the ruts, the Jeep dipped and swayed. Dust stirred, dancing in the beam of the headlights. Mesquite bushes lined the road and Reba caught a glimpse of one of José's cows. Finally the small adobe house with its tin roof and brightly lit windows came into view. Slowing down, Reba frowned. Lupita's car was gone.

Slowly, she turned off the engine, reluctant to go inside. She was too tired to face another confrontation with José, but Ramon had missed another treatment last week because of his lingering cold. With a sigh of resignation she slid from the car, hesitating. She'd better be prepared in case José threw her out again.

Knocking on the screen door, she could hear the blaring sound of the TV. When no one answered, she knocked again, louder this time. Finally, she opened the door and walked inside, her eyes warily sweeping across the clean but sparsely furnished room. The place was stifling hot and liquor fumes filled the air.

José was sitting on the black plastic couch, his head with its dark curly hair clasped in his hands. His sweat-stained T-shirt strained over the paunch he had developed over the past few months. He looked up, and his bloodshot eyes narrowed. "Where did you come from?" His voice was slurred. "I told you not to come back."

Reba's eyes darted to the empty bottle. Her lips thinned and anger flared. She tried to stifle it, but her voice was tight when she said, "Ramon needs his treatment, José."

José lurched to his feet, swayed and fell back down with a thud. "Get out of here. No more doctors," he snarled. "You take every damn cent I have. And for what? Ramon still can't walk."

And unless a miracle happened, he never would. Reba's heart wrenched with pity. José was too poor to pay the medical bills not covered by Lupita's insurance, and his

pride wouldn't allow him to accept charity. Neither Reba
nor Rachel was sending him bills, but the medication alone
cost a small fortune every month. The liquor bills didn't
help, either. "Let me make you a cup of coffee," Reba said
crisply, with a worried look at the closed door to Ramon's
room.

Glaring at her with bitterness, José lurched to his feet.
"Don't need coffee," he muttered, swaying toward her.
"I'm going for a drive."

To get a new bottle, Reba thought. "You're in no condition to drive anywhere, José. At least have some coffee before you leave," she coaxed, blocking the doorway.

He was too drunk to be reasoned with. With one strong
shove he pushed Reba against the wall, knocking the breath
out of her. Behind her a picture dropped from the wall. Before she could stop him, he'd charged through the door.
Stunned, Reba watched the screen swing back behind him.
Seconds later she heard an engine roar to life and tires spin
on the dry ground. Running to the door, all Reba saw was
red taillights swiftly disappearing in the dust.

"Papa! Reba!" Ramon's cries broke the sudden silence
that had settled over the house. Reba rushed to the bedroom door, wondering if she should call the police.

"Did Papa leave?" Ramon asked from the hospital bed
at the far side of the room. Tears were running down his thin
pale face and his frail shoulders were shaking.

"He'll be back." Reba gave the boy a comforting hug,
then she made for the phone.

"Reba was right about that company's stretchers. Over
the past few days several people have warned me against
them." Alfred closed the folder in front of him, resting his
head on the back of the chair.

"I never had any doubts." Jamal rubbed his neck where
a headache was beginning to throb. She was thorough and

meticulous and had spent far more time on the project than he'd intended. "Yesterday she talked to Saiid's wife, questioning her about the hospitals in Basjad and found out that the Bedouins tend to carry off and hoard bars of soap. I didn't know that there was a chronic shortage of soap at the hospitals."

"Why should you? The administrators wouldn't come to you with such little complaints," Alfred pointed out.

Jamal shifted impatiently. "Reba suggested that they order those little bars hotels use instead." He frowned. "Personally, I hate them."

Alfred grinned. "They tend to slip out of your hand. But the council will love it. It could save millions over the years."

Jamal's brows rose. "That much? Perhaps we should plan on a soap factory next. What do you know about making soap?"

"Only that it stinks—literally. I hope that's one job you plan to delegate to someone else."

Jamal's eyes lit with amusement. "You can always take a vacation during that time." He looked at the clock on his desk. It was already past nine. She should have been back by now.

"I had hoped that Reba would give up some of her private patients. That was one of the main reasons why I asked for her help." He drained his coffee cup. Setting it down, he added, "At least she hasn't taken on any new ones. Do me a favor, Alfred, and convince her that she needs a business phone in her car. I worry about her being out this late at night."

Alfred made a valiant effort to remain serious. Fighting back a smile, he said, "I never thought I'd see you so tied up in knots over a woman. I've bought all your presents in the past. This is one time I refuse to get involved." Alfred's smile faded. Rubbing his chin, he added quietly, "Why don't you just tell her how you feel? I find that a direct approach always works best with her."

"I've thought of it." Jamal smiled grimly. "I seem to have thought of little else. But until Muhrad's fate is decided, my hands are tied."

Alfred snorted. "That might be months down the road. Your father will live to be a hundred, long enough for Hussein to grow up and take his place, if need be. What are you going to do in the meantime? You can't reschedule your meetings indefinitely. The French foreign minister wasn't very polite when I canceled your appointment. You have promised to speak at the OPEC conference in two weeks and you can't get out of that. What's going to happen when you leave?"

Jamal shook his head. "I don't know." The question had haunted him for days. Until now he had played a waiting game, giving Reba a chance to adjust to his life-style. He had promised himself to draw her into his world slowly, to allow time for her trust to grow. Though his own patience often amazed him, the outside world didn't wait for anyone. Time was running out. And he was growing impatient. He was no more certain of her feelings now than he had been ten days ago.

Abruptly, he pushed back his chair, got to his feet and walked to the window. Today, his father had been released from the hospital with a relatively clean bill of health. At this moment Jamal was about as free as he would ever be. He could promise Reba frequent trips back to Arizona. And practically unlimited wealth, which she would probably use to turn Omari into a welfare state. He could offer her his love.

Was that enough to compensate for what he was asking of her? And, more important, did she care enough to accept him?

Jamal was shaken from his musings when the phone rang.

There was a taut look on Alfred's narrow face when he held the receiver out to Jamal. "It's Rafe. There's been an accident."

Chapter 11

Jamal's face was gray and rigid as he snatched the phone. "Is she all right?" he asked Rafe.

"I don't know. It only happened a few minutes ago." Rafe's voice was hoarse. "Her car went through a guard-rail and down a hill. They haven't been able to get to her yet. They found her purse, though. Sheriff Hawkins is an old Army friend. He called me the moment he was certain that it was her car. Jamal, she may be perfectly all right."

"Where? Where did it happen?" Jamal demanded, watching Alfred speak into the intercom.

"About ten minutes south on your road. Where the bridge spans the valley. I'm leaving now."

"Let me send the chopper." He tried not to think of the steep slope dropping into the valley.

"I'll drive. It won't take any longer," Rafe said flatly, hanging up.

Jamal ran out to his car and claimed the driver's seat while Alfred slid in on the passenger side. Hassir got into a second car to follow them. Jamal raced down the drive through the open gates with the other car following right on his bumper. Hitting the road, he tried to clear his mind, as he always did during a race.

The accident sight was a mass of flashing lights and uniforms—police, fire fighters and paramedics. Jamal cut through the crowd gathered near one end of the bridge and made straight for the sheriff, who was standing at the broken rail.

Sheriff Hawkins was a lean man of medium height with a hard, weathered face. He was directing the rescue efforts through a megaphone, with a voice that carried far down the slope. As Jamal cut through the police line, the sheriff's eyes narrowed. He opened his mouth to order the tall blond stranger back, but even before recognition dawned he noticed the aura of command, the hard purpose. And the fear.

"My men only put out the fire a few minutes ago," Hawkins said after a brief greeting, pointing down a drop of thirty feet where smoke still curled from the charred remains of what had once been a car. "It's still too hot to get close enough for us to check if anyone's inside the wreck."

Jamal forced himself to look down. Cacti and outcrops of rock dotted the steep slope. The car had come to a stop halfway down and was wrapped around a large boulder. He swallowed against the hard lump in his throat. He'd looked upon death many times. Always before there had been a certain acceptance of what couldn't be changed, a grim sense of reality. This time, looking at the smoking wreckage, he refused to believe. Like her purse, she could have been thrown clear. He wanted to tear the twisted metal apart with his bare hands until he had proof that Reba wasn't inside. He would *feel* it if she were dead, wouldn't he?

"Do you want the men to fan out and search, Master?" Hassir asked hoarsely. His bulldog face was deeply grooved and his ham-size hands clenched with the need for action.

Jamal nodded. His throat felt too tight to talk. Abruptly, he turned his head away from the sight, concentrating on a battered old pickup wheezing up the road, parking beyond the flares. The door flew open the moment the truck stopped.

A woman jumped down from the cab.

Jamal sucked in his breath sharply. Above the heads of the spectators, he caught a glimpse of long, dark hair and a flash of blue—the color of the shirt Reba had worn when she left this morning.

For one instant Jamal stood rooted to the ground. Then he shouldered his way past the sheriff, past the police line and through the crowd, his unblinking stare firmly fixed on Reba's face, afraid that she'd vanish the moment he blinked. He wouldn't fully believe his eyes until he held her, touched her and heard her voice.

It was her voice that reached him first, breathless and choked, floating ahead of her. "Oh, Jamal, I had no idea— I'm so sorry!" She flew into his arms.

Absorbing the impact, his arms closed around her, hard, crushing, bruising her. For long moments he just held her, letting the warmth of her life drive out the deathly chill. She was alive. Well. Unharmed. "How?" he muttered against her hair. "The sheriff seems so damn certain that it's your car down there. They found your purse. I thought—" He lowered his head and kissed her harshly, punishing her for the hell she'd put him through.

Jamal's men closed around them at a distance, shielding them from curious stares.

Reba threw her arms around his neck. She could feel him shaking and, despite the hard pressure of his mouth, his lips were trembling. Her arms tightened and she kissed him fiercely, then touched his face as the words tumbled out of her. "I'm sorry. I left my keys in the ignition and my purse on the car seat when I went into the house. José was drunk when he left. He took my car, only I didn't know it at the time. I called the police but they were looking for his pickup, not my Jeep. I kept hoping he'd come back. I couldn't leave

Ramon alone in the house. I had to wait for his mother before I could go. One of her customers told her that there was an accident on the bridge. I was afraid— Is José all right?''

Jamal's hands gripped her shoulders, bruising them. His voice was filled with bitterness as he raged. "Why the hell didn't you call me? I was only ten minutes away from you.''

Reba winced as his fingers dug into her already tender shoulder, but she didn't complain. She'd thought more than once about phoning him, then had decided to wait. "Ramon was already upset enough. I didn't want to frighten him further. Where is José?''

"I don't know. They're searching for him now," he said grimly. She was so damn independent. Did she need anyone? With an effort he managed to control his fury, but the bitterness remained. "I don't go around scaring children.''

"No, you're very good with them," Reba said soothingly. "But Ramon is shy around strangers.''

"Damn it, Reba, you scared the hell out of me. And Rafe is on his way over here believing—''

"No, he knows I'm all right. Matt caught him just as he was leaving. He's coming anyway. I phoned you, too, but you had already left. I'm sorry, Jamal.''

With quiet bitterness, Jamal noticed that she'd called her brother first. Not him. He could tell himself that it was a logical move, because she knew Rafe would be contacted in case of an emergency. But with her, at this moment, logic was the furthest thing from his mind. He wanted to have the right to be on top of that list. He needed to be the one she turned to for help. "You could have been hurt.''

Abruptly, Reba's eyes filled with tears. Digging her fingers into his arms, she asked hoarsely, "Is that my car down there?'' Before he could answer, she pushed against his hold, needing to see the wreck for herself.

"There's no need to look at it," Jamal said, holding her firmly, wanting to spare her the charred sight.

Reba's back stiffened. "I watched on television as you stood on that crumbled pile of masonry outside the Omari mission. That was your duty. This one is mine," she insisted curtly. "The accident is partly my responsibility. After all, I left the key in the ignition."

"No. He could have taken his own truck instead," Jamal pointed out quietly. But he released her, albeit reluctantly.

Reba walked to the rail. Below, men with searchlights moved around the wreck. The black twisted heap of metal could have been anyone's car. Nearby a stretcher lay on the ground. Tightly, she gripped Jamal's hand. At that moment someone called up the hill, "There's no one in the wreck."

The sheriff raised his megaphone. "Fan out and search the hill."

Relief flooded through her. There was hope yet. Leaning against Jamal, she said quietly, "José isn't a bad man. The past year has been tough on him, emotionally and financially. Seeing his son confined to a wheelchair hasn't been easy for him to accept. Disasters like that often tear families apart."

Watching three lights slowly creep up the hill, she went on, "Sometimes a little distance helps us accept. Unfortunately, children like Ramon have nowhere to go. Rachel, Harry and I found a spot up near Sedona that would be perfect for a camp to give children a few weeks in the sun, and families time to heal." A small smile curved her lips. "Last week Rachel spoke at a meeting of the local Association for the Disabled. At least they were interested enough to look into it."

She definitely needed a keeper, Jamal thought, listening to her. That smoking heap of metal down there was her car, and here she was defending the man who had wrecked it. No, not defending, he thought, but attempting to remedy a system that had no room for the Ramons and Josés of this world. He tried to imagine his mother in a similar situation and failed. Kitty could act out a scene, but in real life she would have burst into tears. She certainly wouldn't have thought of ways to help. His arms tightened around Reba's waist.

Coming to her side, Alfred touched her shoulder. "I'm glad to see you in one piece."

Reba smiled at him shakily. Reaction was setting in. Her knees felt as wobbly as pudding and her teeth began to chatter.

Jamal swore silently, cursing himself for not realizing how shaken she was. "Have the men help in the search," he ordered, knowing that Reba would refuse to leave until she knew José's fate.

At that moment shouts came uphill— "We found 'im," followed seconds later by, "He's alive."

Reba ran forward, placing her hands on the rail, watching as the men crowded around a saguaro cactus halfway between the road and the wreck.

Long, anxious minutes later they brought José up on a stretcher and placed him in the ambulance. Jamal watched Reba as she talked to the paramedics. He knew the exact moment she decided to ride in the ambulance with José. When she turned to him, he gripped her elbow firmly. "You're coming home with me. I'm not letting you out of my sight again," he muttered, lifting her in his arms.

"I can't just leave," Reba protested, struggling.

"Reba, you're shaking again," Jamal said firmly walking her to his car.

"All I need is a cup of tea, and I can get that at the hospital," Reba said weakly.

His arms tightened around her. Turning to Alfred, he said, "Rafe should be here any moment. You'll take care of things?"

Alfred nodded. "Don't I always?"

Closing her eyes, Reba buried her face in the crook of Jamal's neck. It felt good to be told what to do.

Just this once.

An hour later, Reba sat curled up on the couch in Jamal's sitting room. After a long warm shower and a hot cup of tea, she no longer felt shaky or weak. A little tired perhaps, but that was to be expected.

She stiffened slightly as the door opened, relaxing when she saw Jamal enter the room. "Is there any news?" she asked him.

"They're still running tests on José. All Alfred could find out was that he's in serious but stable condition. A concussion, a fractured femur and some cracked ribs." Jamal sat down on the couch beside Reba and gazed at her intently. "You should get some sleep."

"I'm not tired," Reba insisted, smoothing down the white satin of her robe. "I thought I'd wait until Rafe gets here."

"Rafe's having a beer with Hawkins and won't arrive for another thirty minutes. He's spending the night here, so there's no need to wait up for him." Jamal stroked her cheek with the back of his hand. He wanted to hold her and love her until the nightmare had faded. He forced himself to keep his touch light, and his voice as well. "I want you to take tomorrow off. Is there anyone you need to call?"

Reba pushed herself up on one elbow, shaking her head. "I'm not sick. Friday's always a bad day. There's a department-head meeting and—"

Leaning forward, he stilled her protest with a light kiss. For an instant heat flared and his mouth lingered. Then he raised his head. "You don't have a car," he pointed out, a determined gleam in his eyes.

She would have to rent a car and call her insurance company tomorrow morning, Reba thought. "There's Rafe's truck. He can pick it up later during the day." Her eyes bright with challenge, she added airily, "And don't worry about me getting home. Rachel and Harry live in the same complex. Either will give me a ride."

"Is that a threat?" Jamal asked with a glint in his eyes, then taunted softly. "There's the gate. How are you planning to get past it?"

She grinned wickedly. "With a smile."

Chuckling, Jamal pushed her back into the pillows, his lips hovering within an inch of hers. "If you kiss me, I'll drive you to work."

Her arms went around him, hugging him tight. "Just one kiss?" she asked huskily, brushing her lips across his mouth in a teasing caress. Dear Lord, she loved him so much she was aching with it.

"For a start," he groaned, covering her body with his.

"Your sister needs a keeper," Jamal said to Rafe some time later out on the patio. For the past few minutes he'd been reassuring his friend and filling in for him the missing pieces of the night's events.

Rafe leaned back in the patio chair, eyeing Jamal with a narrow look. "She's always managed her life pretty well."

Jamal pulled the tab off a beer and handed it to Rafe. Glancing in the direction of his bedroom, he reached for another can, opened it and walked to the wall. "I'm going to marry her."

Rafe raised the can to his mouth, took a deep swallow, then drawled, "Are you telling me of your decision, asking my permission or seeking my advice?"

Jamal's teeth flashed white in the darkness. "Now I know where she gets her sharp tongue."

Rafe studied the label of his can as if he'd never seen one before. "This is a rather sudden decision."

Jamal looked at him calmly. "If you're asking me in a roundabout way if tonight's events have anything to do with it, the answer is no." Then he shook his head in exasperation. "Few would ever call me a fool to my face. Except Reba and you. That must be another family trait."

"Not a fool, but human," Rafe corrected him quietly.

Jamal looked into the valley below. The lights seemed to have moved closer during the past few weeks. There was still a distance, always would be a distance, but the feeling of isolation had disappeared. He had planned to draw Reba into his world and instead found that she was drawing him into hers and teaching him to dream. Turning back to the courtyard, Jamal said quietly, "I'd planned to ask her tonight."

"Does your father approve?"

Jamal made an impatient movement with his hand. "In matters of state I've always deferred to him. My private life is my own."

"Your marriage could become a matter of state." Rafe shifted uneasily, crossing his booted legs. "We seem to have had this conversation before."

"Things have changed since." Jamal raised his beer and drank deeply. "Yussuf's cardiac condition is not as bad as I'd feared. With care, the doctors say, he may live to a ripe old age. And with every day the likelihood of a confrontation between my father and Muhrad becomes less." He shrugged off the uneasiness that thought always brought. "In any case, there's still Hussein. In five years, my nephew will be old enough to assume control if necessary."

Jamal rubbed the back of his neck wearily. "I've considered it over and over again. My parents are the best example that a marriage between East and West doesn't work. I would never ask Reba to marry me, if I didn't believe that I am free to do so. There will be times when I'll be tied down in Omari for weeks and months. But we'll have plenty of opportunities to come back here. To be absolutely fair and honorable I should wait." Then he shrugged and his chin set determinedly. "I find that honor and fairness can be compromised."

"Yes," Rafe agreed quietly. "And some men manage to live with the knowledge comfortably for the rest of their lives. You're not one of them." With slow deliberation, he set the beer can on the table and got to his feet. "Seems to me you have two choices, Jamal. You can either wait five years or solve the problem now." With a quiet good-night, he walked toward the house.

Jamal stared after Rafe until he disappeared. His hand slowly squeezed the can until it was nothing more than a twisted piece of metal in his hand. There was no honorable or fair solution. He'd tried to find one for months. His options stank. He could tell his father the truth and jeopardize his health. If he made a move against Muhrad, more lives would be lost. No matter which way he turned, he would hurt people he loved and people he'd sworn to protect.

His sense of honor demanded that he face his brother. Fairness demanded that he see him punished. How could he ask Reba to marry him when his own brother had almost killed hers? How could he ask her to sit at the same table with Muhrad? Someday she might even have to kneel to him!

Never!

Furious, he threw the can against the wall. It bounced back with a clatter, rolling on the concrete like the ball in a roulette wheel. Was he going to sit back and allow fate to decide his life? It was time to confront his problems and shape his dreams.

When Jamal entered the dark bedroom sometime later, he found Reba standing at the window, clad in her short robe. Closing the door, he came up behind her. "Why didn't you join us?" he asked quietly, wrapping his arms around her waist.

She turned her face into the crook of his neck, smelling the beer on his breath. "I only woke up a few minutes ago."

"Nightmares?" he probed, pressing a kiss to the soft skin at her temple. He guessed that she was also worried about the cost of a new car in addition to the Ramirez family's problems. His mouth set into a hard line. She used her independence like a shield. She still didn't trust him enough to allow him to take care of those problems for her. Didn't she realize that her pride was precious to him? Hadn't he made one concession after another in order to show her that? "Sometimes it helps to talk about them."

With Harry, Rachel or Rafe she could have groaned about picking up another loan. They would have understood how she felt, sympathized and gone shopping for a car with her. But with Jamal she was always careful to avoid discussions about money. It was a matter of pride. Shrugging, she nestled closer to him. "It's nothing I can't handle."

Patience, already strained, ripped inside him. He spun her around in his arms and took her chin in a hard grip. His voice was rough with restraint. "Maybe *I* want to share your problems. Maybe *I* want to handle them. I'm tired of being told that your problems are none of my business."

Surprise widened her eyes. "Have you ever filled out forms for an insurance claim? Or applied for a car loan?"

His brows raised arrogantly. "No. I also don't wash my own clothes, cook for myself or repair my cars. An insurance form isn't the issue."

Because she could never think clearly when he touched her, she twisted out of his grasp. Sliding her hands into the pockets of her robe, she tilted her head up. "No, it isn't. But I wonder what is." There was a slight edge to her voice, but she kept it calm, reasonable, patient.

"Why didn't you call me?" It was as good a place for him to start as any other. She stood with her back to the window, a blur in her short white robe. He didn't turn on the light. Perhaps it was better to fight this out in the darkness.

"I told you—"

His anger hit the surface. "You told me nothing! I was ten minutes away from you and you didn't call for help. Instead of taking your car, he could have killed you."

Her fingers clenched into fists and her heart leaped into her throat. He cared, more than she'd ever hoped for. She had felt it in the way he had held her at the accident site. Even now, beneath his anger she could sense the fear. Perhaps he even loved her a little. Softly, she said, "From the moment he left the house I was perfectly safe. You couldn't have done any more than the police did."

The need to protect was as natural to him as taking charge. Whether it was his friends, his country or his woman, he took care. "The hell I couldn't. I have more security staff than Hawkins has deputies, and they're a hell of lot better trained." He tried to get hold of his anger, but failed. "Damn it, you knew he was drunk and you walked into the house anyway."

"You went to New York knowing there would be more violence."

A guttural curse escaped his lips. "I was so stifled by bodyguards and police, I could barely breathe. You went alone into that house. Damn it, you promised me you would find someone else. I trusted you."

She bit her lips, knowing she was guilty of taking the risk. "I'm trying to get financial help for them. But that takes time. I can't stop treatment until that happens. I hadn't seen Ramon in two weeks."

"Then another day wouldn't have made a difference." He turned away from her, pacing to the wall and back again. "From the moment you leave here in the morning until you come back at night I don't know where you are. It's driving me up the wall."

"I'm at the Clinic, mostly," Reba said reasonably. "And I don't ask where you're going."

"That's right. You never ask. But I always make sure that you know where I'm going, even when I plan to be back," he shot at her, bitterness rolling like thunder in his voice.

Reba's mouth tightened angrily. "It isn't the same. You tell me about airports, cities, destinations. I never know whom you meet, where you stay or what you do."

"I don't tell you because I keep waiting for you to ask. But you never do. You hide behind your pride and independence because you're so damn afraid of being hurt again." Jamal drew a harsh breath, then added more quietly, "Sometimes I wonder if you will ever have the courage to jump across that fence."

She stared at him, her eyes slowly filling with tears. He had promised her once that he would catch her if she fell, but she'd been too scared to trust him, too scared to believe that he wanted more from her than beauty and passion. Her voice low, she tried to explain. "Every time you leave here, I am afraid. Afraid that something will happen to you. And—" She drew a shaky breath, tears shimmering in her eyes as she tossed pride aside and admitted quietly, "And afraid that you won't come back to me. Every time you leave, every time you're late, I'm sick with fear."

Jamal sucked in his breath sharply, knowing what it had cost her to say those words. With a groan he gripped her shoulders, and pressed on, because caring, even love wasn't enough. "Do you trust me enough to believe that I would never want anyone else? That I wouldn't have walked out on you, even if today you had been injured, even scarred?"

She desperately needed to believe that he loved her, that his feelings were not a twilight's illusion but strong, solid reality. But how could she still doubt when his hands were biting into her shoulders and his voice was harsh with feelings? Her need was so great there was no room for doubts. Not anymore.

Joy, brilliant as the morning sun, rushed through her and she swayed toward him. At the last moment she hesitated, placing her hands on his chest. Tonight had shaken him badly. Would he regret the promises in the clear light of day? It wasn't lack of trust, but love for him that made her remind him, "No regrets. We agreed on that."

Control shattered. The veneer of civilization disappeared. Male dominance, the primitive need to conquer burst forth. He lifted her into his arms. "To hell with words," he growled, carrying her to the bed. Putting her down none too gently, he followed her before she could roll aside. Ruthlessly, his mouth captured hers while his hand went to her belt, tugging at the knot, pulling the robe down her arms, leaving her defenseless and open to his touch.

Reba struggled, twisting her head from side to side. He stopped her words of protest with a ruthless kiss. His hands roamed over her, seeking out the most vulnerable places, places he had discovered and explored in gentler ways. Now he used that knowledge to tear down her defenses with the force of a desert storm.

All coherent thought fled. Their bodies became a tangle of throbbing emotions, assault and defense. Fences toppled like dominoes. Pride, too, was cast aside, leaving only love. Caught in the whirlwind, Reba wrapped her arms round Jamal, holding on to him. Together they rode out the storm.

In the ensuing silence they lay side by side, their ragged breathing the only sound in the room. With his arms folded behind his head, Jamal stared at the ceiling. He despised men who used their superior physical advantage to coerce. Now he seemed to have become one of them. The fact that she had surrendered willingly in the end didn't change the fact. The realization that he was capable of forcing her filled him with disgust. "Did I hurt you?"

She lay curled next to him, facing but not touching him. "No." In the predawn light seeping into the room, she could see the movement in his throat. How he must hate himself for his loss of control, she thought, aching for him. Slowly,

she reached out, laid her hand on his chest and tried to show
him in the only way she could think of that she understood
"I love you, Jamal. I didn't—"

The words were never said.

"Enough." He rolled out of bed. He couldn't bear to hea
her finish saying that she didn't trust him. He reached for hi
clothes. Dressing, he thought that he couldn't remembe
taking them off. "Love without trust is like water in a bow
of sand," he said, fastening his belt.

For a moment he looked down at her, curled up in th
middle of the bed with her head turned away from him. Hi
hand reached out, then stopped before he could touch he
How could he ask for her trust when his whole life was
tangled web of lies and deceit? Abruptly, he turned awa
and walked to the door.

His hand curled around the doorknob, he looked over hi
shoulder. "I'm leaving for Omari this afternoon." He sa
her breathing stop and his resolve almost fled. Roughly, h
said, "You are very precious to me, Reba. I don't want t
hurt you, yet tonight I almost did." He balled his hands int
fists. How could he ask her to marry him with his life i
turmoil and his future still uncertain? Her pride and inde
pendence were such a vital part of her. He loved her to
much to see them compromised. "There are some things w
still have to discuss. But not here and not now. Later,
think, when we're both calmer. Will you meet me fc
lunch?"

What else was there to talk about? Reba wondere(
watching dawn creep over the hills with burning eyes. Th
important words, the words that truly mattered had ju
been said. Jamal was leaving. The bitter irony of it was tha
she had pushed him away. She swallowed, trying to clear he
throat. "Yes. I'll wait for you in the foyer at noon."

"I'll see you then."

Reba listened to the door open and close, pressing a fist to her mouth to keep herself from begging him to stay. With dry, burning eyes she watched the night fade and dawn rise over the hills. The time for dreams was past.

Slowly she rose and dressed in her work clothes.

Chapter 12

Jamal strode down the plushly carpeted hall of the gue
wing, his steps long and purposeful, but no longer imp
tient. The decisions he had struggled against and fought f
so long had finally been made and accepted.

When he knocked on Rafe's door, it opened almost i
stantly. Rafe was still dressed in the clothes he'd worn la
night, jeans and a black-and-white-checked shirt. A lo
past him to the bed confirmed Jamal's suspicion that
hadn't slept, either.

Putting his hands into his pockets, Jamal walked into t
room. "I'm leaving for Omari this afternoon."

No surprise showed on Rafe's harsh, proud feature
"Yeah."

Jamal cocked an eyebrow. "That's all you have to say'

Rafe shrugged. "What else is there?"

"Some men would voice concern for their sister," Jan
pointed out quietly.

Rafe glared intently at Jamal through narrowed eyes.
thought I did. Earlier."

Raking his hand through his hair, Jamal said, "So you did." Abruptly he walked to the window and looked across the courtyard to his bedroom. What was she doing now? For a moment the need to turn back, to gather her close, was so strong his nails bit into his palms. Then he turned his back. "Do me a favor and drive Reba to work. If she needs anything while I'm gone, let me know."

Rafe hesitated. "Do you plan to tell her that you're coming back?"

Firmly, Jamal shook his head and said grimly, "In this I stand alone. I've compromised my honor enough. I'm not going to tarnish it further by making promises I might not be able to keep. And without them, how can I ask her to wait?" He thought of how he'd left her. Quietly he said, "She may not care anyway."

Rafe doubted that, but he kept silent. For a man who had a great dislike of meddling, he had already interfered enough.

Jamal drove into the stable yard at first light. Around him all lay still in the silence before dawn. The grooms were still at their prayers. Only the night watchman greeted him. He entered the first building, his steps ringing out on the concrete floor, carrying him to Sultan's stall.

This morning he wanted speed and challenge. As if the stallion had been waiting just for Jamal, he stood with ears pointed and head held high. "I've ignored you for too long," Jamal said softly, running his hand over the strong arched neck.

As he groomed the stallion his thoughts flew to Reba. He would miss their early-morning rides. Every day he had watched her grow more confident as her riding skills and courage were tested and rewarded. He dragged the curry-comb over the stallion's flank. Reba no longer needed to be distracted. She mounted without hesitation and rode with ever-growing ease.

And each morning this past week, he'd held his breath when, with her mouth set, she had walked up to the white stallion with an apple in her hand. Somehow, her courage to take this final step had become a symbol of her feelings for him. If she loved him, if she trusted him, she would take the risk.

He swallowed when he thought of the way he'd left her, curled up in his bed. He'd finally broken through the wall she always kept between them, had even drawn an admission of love from her, but he felt no satisfaction at the thought. Perhaps that was why he hadn't prodded her to ride Sultan. He couldn't force her trust.

Around him the stables started coming to life. Voices and laughter broke the silence, doors opened and closed. Jamal returned the comb to its place and reached for the bridle. Sliding the bit between Sultan's teeth, he saddled the stallion and led him outside.

Cool morning air brushed his face as he rode down the track. Beneath him the stallion was eager and fresh, straining against the bit. He wasn't a horse for corrals and exercise fields; he'd been bred for power and speed. Easing the reins, Jamal gave him his head. Sultan tossed his silvery mane, whinnied, then thundered down the path.

Crouched low over his neck, Jamal drove him on. He, too, needed the wind and the freedom. For months he'd been sitting back, waiting, watching, fearing. It was past time to face Muhrad, and his father—and most of all himself.

Abruptly he veered off the path. For months he had compromised his own honor and beliefs. He had allowed himself to become involved in the deception. He had done so out of love, duty and loyalty, but by shielding Muhrad he had betrayed the trust of those he loved.

He crested the hill from which he'd spotted Reba the first time and checked the stallion's stride. Below he saw Rafe's truck racing down into the valley, taking Reba to work.

Taking Reba out of his life.

Not completely, though. They still had a business relationship. It was the one contact he was not going to break. Almost all of the equipment and supplies had been ordered. But hiring the staff would take months.

Perhaps it was just as well that he hadn't pressed her into working in Omari. That too, had been a compromise. One year would never have been enough for either of them. His hands tightened on the reins. If there was a way, an honorable way, he would come back. If there wasn't, he wanted Reba to have her dreams. He was determined on that.

Suddenly he heard thunder in the distance. Eyes narrowed against the glare of the sun, he searched the cloudless sky. Within seconds the rumble became more distinct, chopping, coming closer at great speed. He froze. Even before the helicopter became visible, Jamal knew that he didn't have to fly to Omari. His father knew the truth. With a click of his tongue he turned the stallion back and raced toward the stables.

She couldn't believe it was over, Reba thought woodenly as she slowly walked down the Clinic stairs to her department. She'd packed her clothes, her cosmetics, her toothbrush. She'd gone through all the motions of leaving, but she still couldn't believe it. She felt dazed. She'd taken the jump and had fallen, just as she'd always known she would. And not because Jamal had not been there to catch her, but because she had hesitated too long before taking the leap. Her eyes squeezed tightly, fighting the sense of loss and despair.

But that, too, would pass, wouldn't it?

She was early and the door to the department was still locked. Reba searched for her keys in the purse Alfred had returned to her last night, opened the door and turned on the lights. In retrospect, the whole evening seemed so bizarre, she thought, bending to pick up the treatment requests slipped beneath the door after hours. The wreck didn't seem real, either. If she blinked, her car would be in the parking lot and her clothes back in Jamal's closet.

She looked down at her leather bag. It was scratched and scuffed, and at the bottom was a long cut. Her eyes burned. When she blinked, the scratches didn't disappear and she could still see the lining through the tear in the leather.

After locking her bag in the filing cabinet, she took the coffeepot to the sink and filled it with water. No regrets, she told herself sternly, carrying the pot into her office. Measuring coffee into the filter, she closed the lid firmly and plugged in the cord. At her desk she began to schedule the new patients, then she checked the supplies and called the lab to have the whirlpools tested.

Cinderella's working day had begun.

She'd never really believed in fairy tales, she thought, staring blankly into space. But, oh, how she wished she had been weak enough to believe in magic and dreams. And strong enough to trust her dream maker. Had Cinderella ever doubted her prince?

For the second time that morning Jamal strode down the hallway of the guest wing. His hands had been tied for too long; he'd hated the inactivity almost as much as the deceit.

The apartment at the far end of the wing was reserved for his parents, though Kitty used it almost exclusively. As Jamal turned the corner, he spotted a great deal of activity. Servants dashed in and out of rooms, some lugging suitcases. He spied a baseball bat peeking out of one bag. Jamal stopped abruptly, staring at the gold-lettered monogram, H.B. Hussein had arrived with his father.

Jamal could think of only one reason for his nephew's presence now: Yussuf was using the son to control the father. Muhrad truly loved Hussein. Grimly, Jamal acknowledged the effectiveness of the move. He wished his nephew could have been spared the pain. But if Hussein wanted to rule one day, he would have to learn to stand up to his father and place duty before love. Sighing, Jamal entered the room.

Hussein stood at the window, a slim figure, dressed in jeans. His narrow shoulders were hunched beneath a red knit shirt. Abdul, his servant, was placing socks in a drawer. At Jamal's entrance the older man looked up, closed the drawer, bowed, then left.

For a moment, Jamal stared at Hussein with compassion. In the six weeks since their last meeting, Hussein must have grown at least an inch. Strong thigh muscles strained against the tight fit of the denims. His shoulders were still slender, though. Would they ever fill out enough to carry the burden of command? Jamal wondered.

"Salaam, Hussein," he said quietly in Arabic.

Slowly, reluctantly, Hussein turned around and his dark head tilted defiantly. With bitter pride he challenged his uncle, "I will not kneel before you." But his dark eyes were damp with tears and his bottom lip quivered.

Jamal's jaw clenched. Hussein was so young. Too young yet to hide the pain and bitterness his father's betrayal had caused. But there was pride and courage in him. Perhaps, in time... He sighed. "Did I ask you to?"

"No. Not yet. But Grandfather—"

"May live to be a hundred," Jamal said firmly.

Hussein's bottom lip stilled. He stared at his uncle searchingly. "You always said that you did not want my father's position. I believed you despite what Papa said. Yet how can you refuse now?"

"I cannot." Jamal placed his hand on Hussein's shoulder. "Not at the moment anyway. But there may be an alternative. I have to talk to Yussuf first, though, before I can discuss it with you." With a reassuring squeeze to his nephew's shoulder, Jamal left Hussein and went in search of his father.

Two bodyguards flanked the door to the sitting room. Brushing past them, Jamal entered with a brief knock. The suite was more opulently furnished than any other part of

his house. Both Yussuf and Kitty had a passion for an-
tiques, velvets and silks.

His father was alone and the doors to the bedrooms were
closed. He was stretched out on a cream-colored velvet sofa,
with his eyes closed and his head pillowed on his arms. His
thick, silver-white hair was ruffled and fell onto his lined
forehead, not neatly brushed back as it usually was.

Jamal stood in the doorway, rooted there by the sight of
him. The last time he visited Yussuf in Houston, his father
had looked ten years younger, vital, almost well. Now his
weathered face was deeply lined and there was a bluish tinge
to his lips. Jamal walked in and closed the door softly. "The
trip has tired you. Do you want me to call a doctor?"

"Salaam, Jamal." Yussuf opened his eyes and looked at
his younger son. Jamal was so tall, so direct, so intense.
"No more doctors," he said firmly in Arabic. "I wasted
enough of my time with them."

Jamal walked to the couch and kissed his father's cheek.
"I would have met you in Houston." He pulled a chair up
close to the couch.

Briefly, a smile lit the tired hazel eyes. "I know." Then his
face set firmly. "A hotel suite is no place to discuss . . . business."

Jamal rested his elbows on his knees and looked down.
"How long have you known?" he asked quietly.

Yussuf's steel-gray brows snapped together and he threw
up his hands, a big ruby flashing on his finger. "By Allah,
I am greatly cursed. Both my sons believe me a fool. Those
five terrorists couldn't have disappeared without a trace
unless they had help. That's how I picked up the foul smell."
His mouth compressed into a thin line. "I followed the
stench all the way to the palace."

Jamal's hands clenched. "Five months!" he accused
harshly. "Did you enjoy seeing Muhrad squirm? Did you
enjoy watching my fear?"

Yussuf allowed himself a brief moment of pain. Then he
pushed his weakness aside. "Omari's safety and prosperity

come first. The treaty and new business took precedence. How many companies would invest in Omari's future with an internal power struggle going on?''

Abruptly, he sat up, swung his legs to the ground and walked to the window, shoulders hunched. "As a father I've tried to understand what drove Muhrad to it. He is blinded by jealousy, fear and greed. I tried to make allowances, Jamal. I even gave him time to come to his senses and confess. Perhaps if he had—" His shoulders rose fatalistically. "As his father I can weep. As ruler of Omari, I am forced to punish my own son."

The word *punish* instead of *exile* sent a chill down Jamal's back. He jumped to his feet and strode to the window, urgently placing a hand on his father's shoulder. "Then judge him as a father as well as a ruler."

Yussuf looked at Jamal piercingly. For a moment he hesitated, then said slowly, "If that is what you wish, then exile it is." He spread his fingers and added, "It was written in the stars that the fox would raise a lion cub and that the cub would rule one day. If I exile Muhrad there is no other choice. Do you accept your kismet?"

Jamal dropped his hand. He had been prepared for his father's demands. What he hadn't known was how the cunning old fox would try to force his hand. "Father, there is Hussein."

"A fifteen-year-old boy? Muhrad would rule through him." Yussuf strode angrily across the room, his white *dishdashah* swirling around his legs. "The tribal council will never accept him."

"They will obey you," Jamal pointed out grimly.

Yussuf nodded. "As long as I live."

"Dr. Graff said—" Jamal stopped, his eyes narrowing in suspicion. His voice was rough with sudden fear when he asked, "Just what did he say? The truth!"

Yussuf brushed off the demand with a wave of his hand. "I gave up my cigarettes. I swallow my pills. Only Allah

knows the truth." Then he returned to the subject most important to him. "It is your duty. You are my son."

Jamal made a mental note to call the doctor in Houston,
then said firmly, "Hussein is Muhrad's son. It is his right."

"The right is mine to give and mine to withdraw. That is
the law of Islam," Yussuf said with cold finality.

Jamal ran a hand through his hair, taking a deep breath,
before saying quietly, "I am Christian. How can I uphold
Islamic law? For me to rule would mean a lifetime struggle.
You know as well as I do that the Al Assams would fight me
every inch of the way. Every cousin, no matter how distant,
will claim a greater right to rule, because he is a True Be-
liever. Is civil war the future you want for Omari?"

Yussuf returned to the couch and sank into its soft depths,
staring at the table's checkered pattern of light and dark
wood. Then he made his next move. "Abdul Assam has a
beautiful daughter. She has gone to an American university
and has lived in this country for several years."

"I've met her." Jamal slid his hands into his pockets,
balling them into fists. Outright objection never worked
with his father. He chose his words carefully, as if his life
depended on it. And, in a way it did, because without Reba
there would be no life. "She is very much like her aunt,
Azadeh. Is this what you want for me?"

Yussuf's glance slid to a small, enameled snuffbox on the
table, similar to the one he had bought for Kitty in Paris a
long time ago. "There are other choices. You need to marry
a daughter of Islam," he said, looking at his son with
piercing eyes. What he saw made him add, "You cannot
think of marrying this woman you've been living with."

Jamal's eyes narrowed, but he wasn't surprised; he would
have been amazed if his father hadn't known about Reba.
It was the casual dismissal in Yussuf's voice that he ob-
jected to. "Her name is Rebecca Davis—"

"I know all about her. In many ways she is more suitable
than your mother was, but she's not for you." Yussuf
reached for the snuffbox, his gnarled fingers not quite

steady as they slid delicately over the smooth surface. "When I divorced your mother, the birds stopped singing. In time they started again." Placing the box back on the table, he said firmly. "There are many birds in the East. You must choose from among them."

Jamal met his father's eyes levelly. "If—" He let the word hang in the silent room, then went on with quiet finality, "If I can find a way of securing Hussein's position, I will choose as I please."

Yussuf hesitated for a long moment, then nodded. "You have my promise. But I doubt that you will succeed. Muhrad's word alone means nothing. Not anymore."

Jamal expelled a soft sigh of relief. Once his father had given his promise he would honor it. And if there was a way to tie his brother's hands, he'd find it. Abruptly, he walked to Yussuf's side and laid a hand on his suddenly frail-seeming shoulder. "Rest. We'll talk again later."

Steel-gray eyebrows shot up. "I'm still Emir of Omari. *I* will dismiss."

Jamal's eyes softened. Whatever their differences, there was also love. "Yes, sir," he said in his best Texas drawl.

Reba leaned against the nursing station on the surgical ward, reading José's chart. The compound fracture of the femur would keep him in the hospital for several weeks. Long enough, she hoped, to dry him out. Returning the chart to the rack, she stifled a yawn, then went down the hall to his room.

At her entrance, Lupita jumped up from her chair near the window, her face pale and drawn,. Nervously, she fingered the collar of her red blouse, her dark eyes filling with tears. "I'm glad you're here. I was going to come downstairs in a little while. I know you're always busy just before lunch and I didn't want to disturb you. Thank you for not pressing charges."

Placing a hand on her thin shoulder, Reba gently pushed her back into the chair. At twenty-four, Lupita was too young to carry such a heavy burden, Reba thought. "It was as much my fault," she said, handing the woman a tissue. Giving her time to compose herself, Reba walked over to the bed.

José was still sedated, his face battered and scratched. His fractured left leg was raised and in traction. Checking it, Reba adjusted the position of a pulley, then turned to Lupita. "Did the social worker talk to you?"

Lupita nodded. "This morning. I have to bring our income tax records tomorrow. Mrs. Young said she can't promise anything until she's seen them, but we may be eligible for some assistance." She shot an apprehensive glance toward the bed. "By the time José leaves here, he'll be used to the idea."

Reba smiled reassuringly. José required more than debt relief, but it was a start. "Where's Ramon?"

"At my sister's. I thought I'd leave him with her for a little while. She has two children of her own, both a little older than Ramon. They've always played well together."

"That sounds great. He needs to be with other children. If you need anything, let me know." As she turned to go, Lupita caught her arm. "What about your car, Reba? We—" Her eyes filled again. She swallowed, then began again, "We don't have the money right now, but we'll pay you back."

"My insurance will pick up the cost," Reba reassured her. Though her car had been in excellent condition, it had a great number of miles on it. In another year, she consoled herself, she would have had to look for a new one anyway. "Don't worry about it. Try to get some rest tonight."

Returning to the desk, she met Harry, dressed in his surgical greens.

"You look like you could do with an early night, *chiquita*," he said, raising his voice above the almost continuous pagings of the loudspeaker overhead. Tracing the circles beneath her eyes, he added, "The grapevine told me about your car. If you need wheels, feel free to borrow mine. I'm on duty tonight."

"Thanks." Reba blinked her scratchy eyes. "If I can't find a ride to a car rental, I may take you up on it."

The voice over the PA called out, "Dr. Reed, 298." Harry frowned. "That's the third emergency call in five minutes. I'm going down to see what's going on." Turning back to Reba, he added, "Give me a call. I also received the information about the office today. The envelope's in the car."

Reba forced her lips to curve in a smile. She would have to start looking for an office again. At the moment she felt too drained to feel even a spark of enthusiasm. "It can wait until tomorrow," she said with a look at her watch. Eleven forty-five, she thought. What was Jamal going to say to her when they met at noon? "I have to run. I'll let you know about the car later."

As she started for the stairs, the loudspeaker suddenly blared, "Ms. Davis, 335, stat. Ms...."

Impatiently, Reba turned back to the desk. If she didn't hurry she would be late meeting Jamal. Reaching for the phone, she swiftly punched in the number to her department. "What happened?" she asked when Katie answered it.

"Nothing down here. But Prince Jamal just called. He's in the Emergency Room. His father apparently went into cardiac arrest."

Jamal paced the small employee sitting room that had been put at his disposal—eight strides, wall to wall. Hussein sat hunched over a chipped Formica table and Alfred was tipping one of the bright orange plastic chairs.

His father couldn't die, Jamal thought, rubbing a hand over his face. He was too tough. All his life he'd outfoxed and outmaneuvered his enemies. He would win this battle, too.

Yussuf had looked so much better when they shared a late breakfast by the pool. There had been no more arguments between them. Jamal had refused to discuss their differences until after his father recovered from his trip. Later, he had left him resting on his bed to have a talk with Hussein.

The door opened now and Reba walked in.

For a moment she hesitated near the door, feeling uncertain after what had happened this morning. Her eyes flew across the room, all her questions concerning Jamal's father fading at the sight of him.

Jamal's tanned face was a pale gray, almost the color of the wall he was leaning against. Pain and fear had carved lines into his features. Their eyes met. For a moment Reba saw his control slip, catching a glimpse of his pain before he brought up his guard again.

Uncertainty fled. She walked up to him, wrapped her arms around him and held him. "I'm so sorry." The words sounded so inadequate, so utterly useless. "They're taking your father upstairs to the coronary care unit now."

Jamal gripped her shoulders. There was much he wanted to say to her. But explanations and questions had to wait. Whatever the next few hours brought was beyond his control. For the moment it was enough to have her here, beside him. She couldn't remove the fear and the pain, but her presence made them easier to bear. "Thank you," he said simply.

They moved to another waiting room, on the third floor across from the CCU, larger, with comfortable furniture and filled with light. Hassir and Mubarak, Jamal's security chief, flanked the door. Guards and hospital security personnel took up positions outside the CCU.

For the rest of the afternoon, Reba would come into the room, stay a few minutes to share the vigil, then leave to treat her patients. Alfred also came and went, bringing food that no one but Hussein touched. By midafternoon the world-renowned cardiologist, Dr. Graff, who had treated the Emir in Houston, was on his way to Scottsdale. A few hours later, Yussuf's condition seemed to be improving. Cautious hope filled the room.

With the restless energy of the young, Hussein jumped to his feet. He was wearing a sweatshirt, jeans and high tops with their laces untied. "Is there a burger place around here?" His dark eyes moved from Reba to Jamal in speculation, as they had off and on all afternoon.

"About two miles down the road," Reba looked past the empty bag of chips and soda cans to Jamal in rueful communication. Junk food. Teenagers the world over seemed to thrive on it. "The coffee shop downstairs makes great hamburgers."

Hussein shrugged. "That will have to do." Though his English was fluent, he spoke with a musical French accent. Walking up to Jamal, who was leaning against the window, he held out his hand. "I need money." When Jamal took a bill out of his wallet and handed it to him, he looked at it. "Is that all?"

Reba grinned at the words. How often had she watched other teenagers walk up to their parents with the same demands and the same complaints? Princes were not so different, she thought, maybe not ordinary, but human nonetheless.

"How much does a hamburger cost?" Jamal glanced at Reba questioningly.

"Three-fifty. The coke's a dollar. I don't remember the price of the French fries—"

Jamal ruffled Hussein's dark curls. "That's plenty."

Hussein looked from his uncle to the bill, then flashed him a cocky grin. "Can I keep the change?"

For the first time all afternoon, Jamal smiled. "Get out of here." As Hussein left, Jamal ordered Hassir to follow him.

"He sounds like any other teenager," Reba said after the door had closed behind him.

"Boarding school has been good for him." Jamal's smile faded and he looked across the hall to the room where his father was fighting for his life. Hussein had argued with Yussuf for months before he finally agreed to the Swiss school. "At first he hated the discipline and the fact that he received no special treatment. Now he loves it. It's a pity he may not be able to go back."

"Why not?" Reba gave him questioning look, waiting for Jamal to decide how much he could tell her. She wanted to walk over to him and smooth the tired lines from his face. But there was a new wall between them now, after last night.

"Security reasons. He's constantly slipping out at night and getting into trouble. Until today there was little harm in it."

Reba felt a cold hand squeeze her heart. "Then your fa ther knows."

"Yes. It's out in the open." Jamal raked his hand through his hair. He tried to hold back the resentment and anger. "He knew all along. He was biding his time to make hi move."

Reba couldn't bear to keep her distance anymore. Push ing herself out of her chair, she crossed the room and placed a hand on the rolled-up sleeve of Jamal's white silk shirt. "He came to you today," she pointed out gently.

Jamal could think of several explanations of why his fa ther had flown West instead of East. But it was true that he had made the trip despite his poor health, and somehow the knowledge eased his resentment. His rough hands cupped Reba's face. Even with dark smudges beneath her eyes and her face drawn she was beautiful. "Sometimes I wish I wa an ordinary man," he said hoarsely.

She placed her hand across his lips. "No regrets," sh ordered softly.

Chapter 13

Shortly after two the following morning, Dr. Graff entered the room, a tall, spare man in his fifties with stooped shoulders, a receding hairline and a narrow compassionate face. "Your father is resting comfortably now, Prince Jamal," he said, taking in the weary group slowly getting to their feet. "He has a will of iron and doesn't give up easily." Rubbing his burning eyes, he added, "Two weeks ago he refused surgery. Now he doesn't have the choice."

"Why didn't you tell me his condition before?" Jamal's tired voice was rough with relief and accusation.

The physician ran a long finger along the inside of his wrinkled collar. "He submitted to the tests only on the condition that their results be kept confidential." Shrugging, he added, "I didn't feel comfortable with that demand, but he's not an easy man to refuse. I am a doctor first. He threatened to leave more than once."

Jamal frowned. "He dislikes hospitals."

"Most of us do." Dr. Graff smiled slightly, his cheeks creasing. "May I suggest that you get a few hours' rest. The

Emir is sleeping now. You will be called the moment there's a change." Stifling a yawn, he added, "I will do the same. We can discuss the arrangements for surgery later today."

A few minutes later the tired group walked through the silent corridors. Not until the cool night air cleared her head did Reba remember that she had no car. She stopped on the sidewalk and gripped her purse. She was debating what to do when Jamal's hand curled around her wrist. "Stay with me tonight."

Pride was an unpredictable and unmanageable emotion, Reba thought, as it surged through her at his words. She twisted her hand free. She felt like a yo-yo, tossed away one moment, pulled close the next. He was a man under great pressure and she had tried to understand his actions. All during this long day and night she'd stayed with him. But now, at three in the morning, and with less than two hours of sleep during the past forty-eight, she suddenly didn't feel reasonable or compassionate. She was confused, exhausted, drained. All she wanted to do was crawl into her bed and sleep. "I don't know what game you're playing, Jamal, but count me out. Tonight I don't have the strength."

Jamal looked at the black limousine parked a few feet away, where Rashid was patiently holding the door open and Hussein was watching them curiously. "I'm not going to argue with you in clear view of everyone," he said softly, the weariness in his voice matching her own. Not once during this long, awful day had they had more than a few minutes of privacy. All they had been able to discuss was business. "If you don't want to sleep in my bed there's always the couch."

Reba squeezed her eyes tight against the sudden pain. She bit her lip in indecision. "I don't have a toothbrush," she told him softly.

He felt a quick rush of relief. A faint smile crinkled the lines around his eyes. "I imagine I can afford another one."

He ushered her past the waiting Rashid into the car and joined her before she could catch her breath or change her mind. For tonight, her small gesture of trust was enough.

She had no change of clothes, either, Reba realized as the car drew away from the curb. Rafe had dropped off her suitcase at her apartment, where it was probably still standing next to the door. It would take only a few minutes to pick it up.

She shook her head. She wasn't going to move into Jamal's bedroom again, not without the words she needed to hear. Maybe what she wanted was far out of her reach, but she also couldn't live with less. She couldn't spend her life dreaming of a man who could never be hers. "I will need a ride to my apartment tomorrow morning," she said.

"Any time you want to leave." Jamal's gaze slid to Alfred, wearily sprawling in the seat across, questioning him silently if he had managed to buy the new Jeep, despite the upheaval. In answer, Alfred slid his hand into his pocket and jingled the keys.

Later, once they were alone in his sitting room, Jamal handed the keys to her. "I meant to give these to you at lunchtime," he said, pouring sparkling water into two glasses. He could feel her stiffen beside him and he grew irritated. There were times when he wanted to shake her, he thought, offering her the glass. With his free hand he closed her palm over the keys and said with a crooked smile, "No strings. I can't offer you those. Not now—" he added softly, letting the words hang. They were as much of a promise as he was free to give her.

Not now, and perhaps never, Reba thought. But he did love her and he did want her—more than she'd ever dared hope. Because the gift was an expression of his love, how could she refuse? Tears filling her eyes, she lifted his hand to her lips and whispered softly, "Thank you, my love."

"I adore you," he said hoarsely, kissing her tears awa
Then he turned her around, pointing her into the directio
of the bedroom. "Go to sleep. I'll join you in a little while.

A protest rose to her lips as she looked into his grim, line
face. Every man, even someone with his strength, had lir
its, and Jamal had nearly reached his. "I know it's 1:00 p.n
in Basjad, and a working day," she said gravely, dete
mined that he should get some rest. "But will it make a di
ference if you make your calls two hours from now?"

Jamal mentally ran down the list of generals, coun
members and security chiefs he needed to contact and shoc
his head. "No, a few hours won't change anything," l
agreed, and followed her into the bedroom.

They were too tired and too drained for more than a tou
and a kiss. With their arms wrapped around each other the
fell asleep almost instantly.

Hours later, Jamal dressed quietly. Tugging in his shir
tail, his eyes flew to Reba. Her thick black hair was sprea
across the sheets like heavy silk, falling forward and revea
ing the vulnerable line of her neck. Once, an hour ago, the
had made love, slowly, tenderly. For a few minutes he ha
lost himself in her softness and her strength. But the ou
side world was still there, waiting. Silently, he walked to th
door.

"The car drives like a dream. And I like the color co
bination of white and burgundy." Smiling, Reba enter
Jamal's office the following afternoon. She'd just returne
from a trip to her apartment to try out her new Jeep Che
okee and to change into riding gear. "How is your f
ther?" she asked, closing the door behind her.

Jamal was sitting behind his desk, Alfred and Husse
facing him. At her entrance all three stood up, their fac
grave. The air in the room was thick with tension, stiflin
her. Her smile fading abruptly, Reba stopped in her track
The emir had been weak but alert this morning. Had l

ondition changed? Swiftly, she crossed to the desk. "Is he orse?"

"No. He's doing better than expected." Jamal placed a eassuring hand on her shoulder. His father had been well nough to demand that Jamal leave for Omari immediately. Timing, Yussuf had insisted in a breathless whisper, as crucial now. Though reluctant to leave his father, Jamal had agreed with him.

By now Muhrad would have learned that Hussein had een removed from his boarding school and would have ecognized the significance of the move immediately. The moment Muhrad heard of his father's illness, he would try o secure his position and, because officially he was still the eir, the military would rally around him. Jamal knew that e had to get to Basjad before Muhrad closed off the airorts and the harbor, before it was too late to offer his rother an alternative.

Before brother had to face brother with weapons drawn.

Dropping his hand, he looked at Alfred. "Take the docments to the hospital and have my father sign them. here's no need to rush. We're not leaving until eight."

Jamal heard Reba draw a sharp breath. He watched Alred gather the thick vellum sheets that would serve to strip Muhrad of all his power and rights.

"Is there anything else?" Alfred asked grimly, snapping is briefcase shut.

Jamal's face was stern. For months he'd feared this moment, hoping, praying that it could be avoided. Now that it vas here, a strange calm had settled over him. He didn't vant to fight his brother, and he prayed he could still avoid loing so. He was placing all his hopes on the fact that omewhere, beneath the bitterness, jealousy and greed, Muhrad still had a grudging affection for him. That was, he uddenly realized, why he had kept the stallion instead of elling him to someone who would truly appreciate him. If

Muhrad wanted a fight, they both would lose. "No. I thin
we've covered everything."

"Do you want me to witness the signatures?" Hussei
asked, a slight tremor in his voice. His eyes were filled wit
pain and his young face showed the disillusionment of
man twice his age.

Jamal wished he could have spared his nephew. At fif
teen, the boy should be dreaming of slaying imaginar
dragons, not fighting real-life battles. And he should not b
forced to be witness to his own father's defeat. "That de
cision I leave up to you," he said, placing his hands on th
slim shoulders. They trembled slightly beneath his touch
Gently he added, "No one will expect it of you."

For a moment, Hussein hesitated, then he braced hi
shoulders. "No one but myself," he said. His bottom lip stil
quivered, but his voice was firm. Turning abruptly, h
walked to the door with his head set, his back straight an
his laces flapping.

Watching him, Reba felt her throat tighten. He wa
dressed much as he'd been last night, in a bright orange kni
shirt, jeans and high tops. Today, though, the clothe
seemed out of place. He had grown overnight from a teer
ager into a young man. She swallowed the lump in he
throat.

When Alfred had followed Hussein out the door, Reb
turned to Jamal. He stood but a few feet away, dressed i
jeans and boots, like an ordinary man, still within her reach
But what she had just witnessed took him away from he
forever.

His tawny hair fell onto his forehead. His restless impa
tience was gone. He was calm, his face grim, set, deter
mined to accept his fate. She clenched her hands, her shor
nails digging into her skin, as if she could keep the drear
trapped forever inside her fists. Then, for the last time, sh
brushed his hair from his forehead. "If you're staying be
cause of me, don't."

Jamal ran his hand beneath the open collar of his tan shirt. "Luckily, my father had the documents drawn up some time ago. Still, my presence could later be wrongly interpreted." He shook his head. "Although few people would believe me, this was the last thing I wanted."

The harsh sound of his voice tore at her heart. He was a nomad who loved wide-open spaces and needed to roam freely, from land to land. In time the palace would become his gilded cage and the green glints in his eyes would dull, his spirit hardened. The man who had shared her dreams would soon be gone forever. Princes couldn't dream.

"I know." Tears pricked her eyes. She blinked them away, determined not to break down. After he had gone, she would cry until there were no more tears left. Later, when he was alone, she would give in to her fears. But not now. Now he needed her to be strong.

She wrapped her arms around his waist and forced a smile onto her face. "Do we have time for one last ride?"

Jamal drew her closer. Her smile was a little shaky and her eyes a little misty, but he could see she was determined not to break down. Was that why he loved her more with each passing day?

"I always did admire your horses," Reba said teasingly. "They are the most beautiful creatures I've ever seen."

A gleam came into his eyes as he remembered their first meeting. His head tilted arrogantly. "I know," he taunted her, as he had that first time.

Reba flicked his lean cheek. Then, twisting away from him, she ran to the door. "You, Your Highness, are still a conceited jerk."

"Am I, now?" he asked, slowly stalking her.

Grinning, she opened the door and raced down the hall to the front door with Jamal close on her heels.

The sun burned on their faces as they left the stables a little while later and rode down the track. Jamal had ordered the guards to stay behind and for once they were

completely alone. Desert Dawn was skittish today, Reb
thought, keeping a firm hand on the reins. The big whit
stallion was making the mare nervous; she was more used t
Khamsin.

"Dr. Graff flew back to Houston this afternoon," Jama
said, as they rode side by side. "My father's scheduled th
bypass surgery for next Friday, here at the Rana Clini
Afterward, will you help take care of him?" If he reache
Basjad before Muhrad could close the airports, Jama
thought, he might make it back in time. If not— He pushe
the alternative from his mind, determined not to allo
Muhrad to spoil this last hour he could spend with Reba,
such it was to be.

"If he agrees. Your father may not want me to treat hi
when he finds out about us." Reba guided the mare awa
from a cholla cactus growing into the path.

"He knows," Jamal said calmly, wishing he could watc
his father's reaction when Reba began caring for him. Yu
suf never did like to take orders, especially not from
woman. Seeing the apprehension on Reba's face, he adde
"His bark is worse than his bite. Just smile at him. He's a
ways had an eye for beautiful women." His eyes lingered o
her face, need rising. "And you are truly beautiful."

"I'm glad you think so," Reba said softly, looking at hir
with her lips curving and her heart in her eyes.

Jamal stared at her as if he'd never seen her before. An
perhaps he hadn't, not with love and trust openly reveale
"If you dare smile at anyone else like that, my sweet, I'll ve
you from head to toe," he said, his voice rough with emc
tion.

Reba's chin went up in challenge. "Is that a promise or
threat?" she asked lightly. She added softly, "Perhaps
should warn you, Jamal, that threats don't work with me.

"I'll keep that in mind." Tearing his eyes away, he brok
into a trot, taking the lead. Then they turned off the pat
into the hills, toward a small crevice where she had froze

e first time. Today she took it in a clean jump. She now
ode calmly over the narrow ledges around which she had
uided the mare the first few times; she rode easily down the
mall dry riverbed carved into the rocks, a rocky trail
through which she had once felt compelled to walk the
are.

As Reba passed each small step she'd taken over the past
ew weeks her determination grew. Today, before they re-
urned to the stables, she would ride Sultan. For Jamal as
ell as for herself. It would be a dream come true, a dream
e had shared. Perhaps the memory of it would make him
mile sometimes.

When they reached the spot close to the road where they
ad first met, Jamal stopped and swung from the saddle. He
alked to where Reba had reined in and held out his hand.
Vithout hesitation, she slid into his waiting arms.

He looked into her upturned face, watching the sun kiss
er honey-gold skin, studying each feature, the beautiful
old eyes, the slim straight nose, her soft, trembling lips,
memorizing them. "Once I promised you that I would be
aiting for you when you finally took the leap. It's the one
romise I cannot keep." He watched her eyes shimmer with
welling tears. The salty taste in his throat roughened his
oice as he went on, "You're quite a woman, Reba. Soft
ough to cry and strong enough to dream." He kissed her
ard, then placed the stallion's reins in her slender yet ca-
able hands. "Sultan is yours."

A stunned look crossed her face and her lips trembled
ncontrollably, but no sound escaped. "Keep dreaming,
eba," he said softly, "because some dreams do come
ue."

Then he turned away, swinging into Desert Dawn's sad-
le. Digging in his heels, he rode uphill. Though she didn't
now it yet, he thought, circling a prickly pear cactus, he
ad just placed his fate into her hands for safekeeping.

Unmoving, Reba watched Jamal as he first disappeare[
behind a saguaro cactus, then came back into view, wea[
ing in and out of her sight, becoming smaller each time sh[
saw him. Her fingers gripping the reins tightly, she force[
back the tears that would blur the sight of his tawny blon[
head, the broad shoulders, the strong back. Only when h[
vanished from her sight did she turn to Sultan, snortin[
softly beside her.

She knew that within minutes Jamal would crest the hi[
where she had spotted him the first time. From there h[
would have a clear view of the road. With firm, stead[
hands she shortened the stirrups. Placing her boot into one[
she gathered the reins, gripped the saddle and swung ont[
Sultan's back.

Unused to her lighter weight, the stallion pranced ner[
vously, his ears twitching, his silver-white hide ripplin[
uneasily. He pulled at the bit, sidestepping, tossing hi[
beautiful triangular head in challenge.

"You're not going to make this easy for me, are you[
boy?" Reba muttered between clenched teeth, her leg[
clamping down hard. The leather cut into her hands as sh[
fought the stallion's head down for control. "Your maste[
told me you're a perfect gentleman, a little impatient, bu[
not mean. He would never have left you with me if he didn'[
believe I could handle you. That gives me the edge. I kno[
you don't trust me yet," she went on as the proud nec[
arched. "And as long as you keep fighting me you neve[
will."

Finally Sultan's ears pricked up and his challenge eased[
Reba released the reins a bit. Sultan turned his head, snorte[
softly, his body shivering. Leaning forward, Reba stroke[
his sweat-dampened neck. She nudged him forward into [
walk, then a canter, riding him through a small obstacl[
course of cholla cacti, yucca plants, mesquite bushes an[
saguaro. Her confidence in her own power grew with eac[
of the stallion's powerful strides, each responsive turn of hi[

beautifully coordinated body. Then her own innate reck-lessness surfaced, and her hunger for freedom. The fence was four feet high. Could she do it? Jamal had taken the jump so easily. She rode the stallion in a collected circle measuring Sultan's response to her control, testing him the same way she had tested Sir Lance before facing a brick wall.

Then she eased the reins, dug in her heels and made for the fence. The stallion responded instantly, tossing his head. Six feet to go, five—Reba collected the stallion—four, three— She gave him his head. With a surge of power they soared over the wires without hesitation or fear. There was only the heady sense of soaring, the air brushing past her face. Freedom. Tears filled her eyes and ran down her face as horse and rider landed safely on the other side of the fence.

Looking back, she saw Jamal on the top of the hill, beautiful and magnificent, his outline blurred by her tears. Waving, she blinked them away.

When she looked back, he was gone.

From the hill Jamal watched the jump with his heart in his throat, holding his breath until it was over. His heart swelled with pride and joy. The sight of her soaring over the fence on Sultan's back would be indelibly printed in his mind. Strong, confident. Free. He saw her turn, look up and wave and raised his own hand in response.

Then he turned sharply east.

"I, Muhrad ibn Yussuf Basjadhi, Prince Royal, hereby renounce all my claims and rights, present and future, to the throne of Omari, in favor of my son Hussein. . . ."

Jamal closed the folder with a snap and left it on top of his clean desk where Alfred would see it the minute he walked into the room. Legally, he thought, getting to his feet, the letter was no more than a note of intent. It would never stand up in a court of law. He hoped, though, that once Muhrad had agreed to sign it, he would not change his mind. Crossing to the bar, he poured a brandy from the crystal decanter into a balloon glass and tossed it down his throat. The sharp bite did nothing to dispel the foul taste in his mouth.

Setting down the glass, he slid his hands into his pockets and paced the room. So far, he had managed to keep any news of his father's heart attack hidden from the media, though some members of Omari's council had been informed. It was the servants' talk that worried Jamal the most. To contain gossip, especially between family members, was almost impossible.

How soon would his brother find out? Or did he already know? So far Omari's airports were still open and, the last time he had checked, the military had not been placed on alert. Everything in Omari was calm. Jamal's gaze fell to his private phone, frowning.

Muhrad had answered none of his calls.

He checked his watch, wondering why Alfred and Hussein had not returned. They had left the hospital an hour ago. Perhaps they had stopped at one of the fast food places Hussein was so fond of. Reba also had not returned to the stables yet. But Saiid was keeping an eye on her.

The intercom flashed the same moment the house phone rang. With two long strides, Jamal walked to the desk and pushed down the button of the intercom, sudden tension running through him. "Yes."

"Master," Hassir said, his voice a little breathless, "your brother, Prince Muhrad, is outside the gate."

Startled, Jamal stared at the flashing light of the phone. Muhrad had come for his son; that was the only explanation he could think of. Then another thought occurred. Without delays and stopovers the flight from Basjad to Phoenix took at least sixteen hours. His eyes narrowed. He'd almost have staked his life that Muhrad knew nothing about their father's heart attack. And, with luck, he would not find out until after he had left again. "Open the gate."

Ignoring the phone, Jamal strode down the hall, a tight smile on his face.

Muhrad enjoyed pomp and ceremony, in Omari as well as abroad. He rarely traveled without a full retinue of servants, secretaries and bodyguards. The last time he visited Paris he'd brought enough staff and family to fill fifteen limousines. Today, Jamal noticed, there were only two. His brother had left in a rush. He was scared.

As the limousines slowed to a stop, Jamal turned to Hassir. "Search his guards before they enter the house and lock them up," he ordered, watching Muhrad roll out of the first car.

At five foot eight and more than three hundred pounds, Muhrad was almost as wide as he was tall. He preferred Eastern dress. The *dishdashah* covered by a full wide robe, a *mishlah* and a headcloth, secured by double cords of gold, gave him an air of distinction.

"Salaam *aleikum,* Muhrad."

"Salaam, Jamal."

Today, they did not give each other the traditional kiss of peace. Today, they did not observe any of the formalities Muhrad was so fond of. No ceremonial coffee. No small talk. The moment they were alone in Jamal's sitting room, Muhrad was for once, as direct as his brother. "I need your help."

Jamal looked down, studying the tips of his brown Italian leather shoes. He would have preferred his office for the confrontation. "I was planning to leave for Omari in three hours," he said bluntly. "Your fate has been signed and sealed."

Muhrad braced himself on the back of the couch, his black eyes glittering like polished onyx. "So you have what you always wanted," he snarled.

Jamal's eyes looked to the couch where he'd made love with Reba only two nights ago. "Do I?" he asked wearily.

"If you refuse our father, there is only me to follow him," Muhrad challenged harshly, his pudgy hands biting into the soft velour. A big diamond on his small finger flashed with hard cold fire.

Jamal shrugged fatalistically. "I tried. Not with words, but by shielding you all these months. Yussuf knew all along. He waited for five months, watching how far you would go and how far I would allow you to push me." And perhaps, if their father had been well, he would have waited even longer. Jamal raised his head and met his brother with grim, hard resolve. "It's exile for you and prison for me. I wonder who is the real loser, Muhrad."

Muhrad's brows drew together in a straight black line, more in puzzlement than in suspicion. "By the prophet's beard, you mean it." Throwing up his hand, he muttered, "I don't think I will ever understand you."

Jamal gave him an impatient look. "It doesn't make a difference now. Father signed the documents an hour ago."

"A piece of paper means nothing. It won't be official until the council has been informed." A gleam lit Muhrad's black eyes. "There's my son. If I have to give up my rights they should go to him. How is Hussein?"

"Well and safe." Jamal hid his satisfaction beneath lowered lashes. His brother was finally considering the only satisfactory alternative, though the gleam in his eyes spoke louder than words. "Hussein is too young," he said firmly. Today, though, he had seen a promise of strength that boded well for the future. "Until he's old enough, I will be the guardian of his faith. Whether Hussein will ever rule depends on you. If you trust me." Were the ties strong enough? Was there enough affection between them for Muhrad to hand his son over to Jamal's control?

Eyes narrowed, Muhrad considered Jamal's words. Seeing the firm set of his brother's jaw, he knew Jamal would be pushed no further. Abruptly he nodded, planning beyond the next five years, beyond his father.

Hussein would be only twenty, still young and malleable. "You are amazingly foolish, Jamal, even for an American. But you are an honorable fool. You will not turn my son against me." Turning his hands palm up, he added, "I accept."

Jamal had won. Inside his pockets, his balled fists slowly relaxed. Oh, he knew that Muhrad had not given up hope completely. He might be willing to sign the documents, might even be willing to relinquish Hussein to Jamal's care, but only in the firm belief that when Jamal's guardianship ended he would be able to control his son.

He could read Muhrad's thoughts as clearly as if he'd spelled them out, Jamal thought. Would five years be enough time to remove Hussein from Muhrad's influence? Uneasiness made him pace to the window. It was the one uncertainty that remained.

Suddenly, the door opened and Hussein's accented voice floated into the room before him. "I don't know how you can stand to work at the hospital all day, Reba. It's such a depressing place. My grandfather can't wait to get out. He is going to live, isn't he?" Hussein glanced over his shoulder as he entered the room, then stopped abruptly at the sight of his father.

With a muttered curse Jamal surged forward, trying to reach Hussein before Muhrad.

Muhrad spun around sharply, his robes swirling around him, placing himself between Jamal and the door. "Stop right there, Jamal," he warned, his voice slightly breathless. His dark eyes glittering with hate, he pointed a small gun at Jamal's chest.

In the sudden silence following, the small click of the safety catch being released sounded like a shot.

Jamal shot a glance at the door where Reba was gripping Hussein's arm, trying to keep him from charging into the room. "Get him out of here," he ordered.

"Both of you, come in and close the door," Muhrad ordered sharply, his fingers gently touching the trigger.

Reba cast a frantic look over her shoulder into the hall. Where was Hassir? Or Mubarak? Usually the whole damn place was crawling with guards. Now, when they were needed desperately, there was no one in sight.

"Now!" Muhrad moved a little so that the door was within his range of vision, his eyes firmly fixed on Jamal.

Tears of desperation welled up as Reba walked into the room and kicked the door with a bang, hoping the sound would alert someone. Holding tightly on to Hussein, she looked at Jamal in anguish. During her long ride through the hills this afternoon, she had come to terms with her loss. She could live without him, knowing that he was somewhere halfway across the world, but only if she knew that he was alive and well.

Jamal concentrated on the small cylinder aimed steadily at his chest. At this distance the size of the weapon didn't matter, he thought grimly. "Let them go, Muhrad," he said, feeling pain rip through his gut. His voice was flat when he added, "I must be the world's biggest fool. It never occurred to me to have *you* searched. If you shoot, you'll never make it out of here."

The gun wavered slightly, then steadied again. "Hussein is my guarantee. No one will touch my son. How long were you planning to keep Yussuf's illness quiet? Until after you'd taken over?" Hate blazed out of control and his finger moved to the trigger. "This will solve all my problems."

"No, it won't!" With a sudden twist, Hussein tore himself free from Reba's grasp. High tops thumping and laces flapping, he ran across the room. His bottom lip trembled, and with tears in his eyes, he stepped in front of Jamal and faced his father. "Not unless you plan to kill me, too."

Muhrad's beard began to twitch and his hand to shake. Slowly, the blaze of hate died and sanity returned. He dropped his gun. For long moments, he stared from his brother to his son. Then he turned, his boots dragging across the carpet with the slow measured movement of a defeated man.

His hand on the door, he looked back at Jamal. "Today I lost my father, my brother and my son. A man without a past, present or future is a man without a soul. A man in true exile." When he looked at his son, his voice shook slightly. "When your time comes, Hussein, listen to your heart, and not to the whispers around you, as I did. Allah be with you."

For a while after Muhrad's departure, silence hung in the room. Leaning against the wall, Reba waited until her legs had stopped trembling and her eyes had cleared. There was no hate left in her heart for the man who had almost killed both her brother and the man she loved. Hate was for the strong. She felt only pity for the broken man who had just left.

She walked across the room to where Jamal stood with his arms around Hussein. She was too drained to feel anything but relief that he was safe. Touching his shoulder, she said, "I'm going home." When Jamal started to object, she shook her head. "Hussein needs you now."

For a long moment she stared into his face. Muhrad would not trouble him, ever again. Perhaps, in time, when the wounds had healed and Muhrad had come to terms with exile, the brothers could even be friends. But for herself and Jamal nothing had changed. Her twilight prince was now the prince royal, heir to the throne of Omari, and someday he would rule. "Be happy, my love," she whispered and turned away.

Jamal watched with burning eyes as she picked up her purse and walked to the door. Had he gained his freedom only to lose her anyway? he wondered, as she quietly closed the door.

Hussein stirred, raising his head. "Aren't you going after her?"

"Not now. We still leave for Omari as planned," Jamal said, looking down into Hussein's pale but set face.

"You are as mean as a she-camel and as tough as an ass's hide," Yussuf declared four weeks later. He stood in the middle of his hospital room, his head tilted arrogantly, glaring from Reba to the stationary bicycle he refused to ride. "Women should be—"

"Soft delicate flowers, bending with the wind," Reba finished calmly, biting back a grin. Each morning and afternoon they went through the same routine and, after two weeks of treatments, Yussuf was running out of new similes. "Or is it a gentle doe eating out of her master's hand?"

"You are slowly learning, woman." A gleam in his eyes, Yussuf nodded approvingly. Though he would never have admitted it, he looked forward to their sessions. They were the only interesting part of an otherwise tedious day. He was pleased with his son's choice—as pleased as he would ever be with a Westerner. "The Emir of Omari does not ride bicycles. It is beneath his dignity." He looked at Akim, his gray-haired servant, who was changing the satin sheets he insisted on even there at the hospital. "Remove the offensive object."

Reba nodded thoughtfully, her eyes meeting Akim's across the room. "Perhaps you are right, Your Highness," she agreed slowly. "A wheelchair is so much more dignified." To Yussuf, wheelchairs were even more offensive than exercise bicycles.

Like Jamal, his father hated inactivity and had to be watched constantly, because he tended to overestimate his strength. The surgery had been successful, but recovery was slow despite his iron will. It would be at least another week before he was strong enough to make the long flight back to Omari.

With Yussuf's departure, her ties to Jamal would be broken, she thought, alternately dreading and wishing for the day. The strong resemblance between Yussuf and Jamal was a daily, painful reminder of what she had lost. How long before she stopped hurting and aching?

She was going through the motions of rebuilding her life. Tomorrow she had an appointment to discuss the terms for the office space in Harry's building she had decided to lease. And the first applications in response to the ads she had placed in the professional journals were trickling in. She went through the motions, but there was no excitement and no joy.

"You are as cunning as a fox and your tongue stings like a wasp," Yussuf accused Reba, drawing her attention back to him. His gaze narrowed as he watched a slow grin spread over her face.

He never had been able to resist the smile of a beautiful woman for long. Because pride wouldn't allow his resistance to melt too swiftly, he looked past her to the door. For an instant the old man's eyes widened as he spotted Jamal, and his voice faltered momentarily. Then, with a gleam in his eye, his argument gained new strength. "Women should be—"

Jamal leaned against the doorframe, his eyes sliding over Reba hungrily, from the French braid down the blue lab coat to her white slacks and sneakers. The weeks without her had been hell. While he had dealt with the grim and complicated issues a change in power inevitably involved, he had often feared that during the final violent confrontation with Muhrad he had gained his freedom and lost Reba forever.

"Like a rose, blooming only in her master's presence," Reba repeated another one of Yussuf's sayings, a slight edge to her voice. He was more unreasonable than usual, she thought, turning her head impatiently.

Then her eyes widened and her breath caught. For moments she simply stared at Jamal, taking in the arrogant tilt of his head, the slow lazy smile, the tawny hair falling onto his forehead. He was dressed in tan slacks and a cream-colored silk shirt with his sleeves rolled up and his collar open. "Welcome back, Your Highness," she said softly.

Jamal straightened and walked into the room with the same arrogant, impatient stride she remembered so well. Watching him, her heart twisted painfully and, deep down, resentment flared. Couldn't he have given her time to heal? "Why are you here?"

Abruptly, Jamal's smile froze. Glancing at his father, he demanded sharply, "What did you tell her?"

Yussuf spread his hands. "Nothing. I do not discuss politics with women. An Eastern bird I would have handed to you in a gilded cage. With a Western bird you have to do your own hunting." Yussuf nodded at Akim, who rolled the wheelchair over. Sitting down in it, Yussuf added in Arabic, "I am pleased, Jamal. She will do very nicely—once I have trained her for you." Grinning widely, Yussuf ordered Akim to roll him down the hall.

"Thank you, Father," Jamal said, chuckling, a gleam in his eyes. "But if you don't mind I'll do the taming."

Reba watched the bodyguards follow Yussuf before turning back to Jamal. "Sometimes your father's flowery words make no sense," she said, exasperated.

"They make perfect sense to me," Jamal stated, sliding his hand into his pocket. His fingers curled around the small leather box. The stark hospital room was not the setting he'd had in mind when he planned to give her his ring, a deep yellow diamond to match the gold of her eyes. But a starving hunter did not waste an opportunity. If she accepted him, there would be many opportunities for candlelight dinners and star-studded skies. If she didn't...

"He and I made a deal," he started to explain, his eyes going to the oxygen mask above the bed. She was as important to him as the air he breathed. Without her, each day would be a painful struggle to survive. "If I could secure Hussein's position as his heir, I would be free to marry you."

For a moment happiness made her head spin. Her arm shot out, grabbing the cold steel handlebar of the exercise bicycle for support. Her eyes darted around the room. The turquoise curtains were real and so were the weights Yussuf used daily to increase his strength; the steady beep of a heart monitor was always music to her ears. This was reality. A dream come true.

Slowly her gaze returned to Jamal. "You made a deal?" she asked softly, her eyes narrowing at his arrogance. She thought of all the lonely nights, the tears and the constant pain. She remembered all the anguish she had felt thinking of him trapped behind his palace walls.

And he had made a deal!

Anger welled up and she tossed her head. "You conceited jerk! I'm not one of your Arab mares you can bargain over at a horse market. All these weeks of silence. No one knew anything. All I heard were rumors of Muhrad checking into a sanatorium in Switzerland and the speculation that Hussein might succeed him. You spend your life on the phone. What was wrong with calling me?"

His hard hands cupped her chin and his voice was rough with emotions when he said, "Even conceited jerks have their fears. What I am asking of you is not an easy life. Until Hussein comes of age, I will be tied down in Omari. If you marry me, you'll have to put up with bodyguards, reporters and sometimes a veil—"

Reba stopped the flow of words by simply placing her hand over his lips. He was telling her nothing she hadn't known for months. "Do you love me?"

With a groan he lowered his head and kissed her hungrily. "With all my Western heart and my Arab soul."

Behind them Yussuf snorted and said to Akim, "Westerners! That was the most unromantic proposal I have ever heard. I will have to take my son in hand. Soft-eyed gazelles and blooming roses sound much better, don't you agree?" He raised his voice. "And what, Jamal, is wrong with the veil?"

With a wicked smile at Reba, Jamal said, "Nothing, Father, nothing at all."

*   *   *   *   *

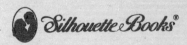

SILHOUETTE·INTIMATE·MOMENTS

NORA ROBERTS
Night Shadow

People all over the city of Urbana were asking, Who was that masked man?

Assistant district attorney Deborah O'Roarke was the first to learn his secret identity . . . and her life would never be the same.

The stories of the lives and loves of the O'Roarke sisters began in January 1991 with NIGHT SHIFT, Silhouette Intimate Moments #365. And if you want to know more about Deborah and the man behind the mask, look for NIGHT SHADOW, Silhouette Intimate Moments #373, available in March at your favorite retail outlet.

NITE-1

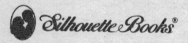

Silhouette Books®

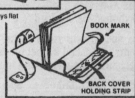

proudly presents
the long-awaited "prequel" volume of

★ LOVE AND GLORY ★

by
LINDSAY McKENNA

Dawn of Valor

In the summer of '89, Silhouette Special Edition premiered three novels celebrating America's men and women in uniform: LOVE AND GLORY, by bestselling author Lindsay McKenna. Featured were the proud Trayherns, a military family as bold and patriotic as the American flag—three siblings valiantly battling the threat of dishonor, determined to triumph . . . in love and glory.

Now, discover the roots of the Trayhern brand of courage, as parents Chase and Rachel relive their earliest heartstopping experiences of survival and indomitable love, in

Dawn of Valor, Silhouette Special Edition #649.

This February, experience the thrill of LOVE AND GLORY—from the very beginning!

DV-1